The Dog in the Outhouse

The Dog in the Outhouse

-The John Stark Marauders-

J.P. Polidoro

Copyright © 2010 by J.P. Polidoro.

ISBN: Softcover   978-1-4500-4239-0

© J.P. Polidoro 2010, Longtail Publishing, All Rights Reserved

All rights reserved. No part of this book may be reproduced or transmitted in any form or by any means, electronic or mechanical, including photocopying, recording, or by any information storage and retrieval system, without permission in writing from the copyright owner.

This is a work of fiction. Names, characters, places and incidents either are the product of the author's imagination or are used fictitiously, and any resemblance to any actual persons, living or dead, events, or locales is entirely coincidental.

This book was printed in the United States of America.

To order additional copies of this book, contact:
Xlibris Corporation
1-888-795-4274
www.Xlibris.com
Orders@Xlibris.com

63238

Dedication

A toast to

General John Stark
(1728-1822)

New Hampshire's maverick military leader

His principles, leadership skills and life as a patriot, husband, father and farmer proved exemplary, or critical, in the American Revolution and the ultimate formation of the United States of America

Prologue

History has a way of repeating itself, especially in the course of human events and the evolution of the earth and world. Geologically, the earth is millions of years old and New England, in particular, is characterized by jagged granite mountains and pristine lakes, and the Atlantic Ocean to the east, all created by the turmoil of the ancient cosmos and resultant volcanoes and glaciers of time immortal. What makes upper New England unique is the antebellum homes, the Green Mountains of Vermont and the White Mountains of New Hampshire where the Vermont range runs south to north and the New Hampshire range, northeast toward Maine. In essence, they are part of the Appalachian chain from the southern United States to the eastern portions of Canada.

The remoteness of the New Hampshire mountains is breathtaking above the capital city of Concord where the foothills begin in earnest lending themselves to 4,000-foot peaks that migrate toward the Grand Dame of them all, Mount Washington above 6,000 feet. She is the highest in New England and the only peak above 6,000 in the Northeast.

Pristine to this day, Mount Washington evolved with jagged faces, notches and ravines, like Tuckerman's and the Crawford Notch, vistas of beauty in both summer and winter. Snows remain until late spring where skiers climb all day just to have a last chance to "run the Tuckerman" as late as Memorial Day.

The indigenous peoples of New Hampshire, the Native-American Indians, inhabited the areas north. There were four federally recognized tribes: the Penobscot, Passamaquoddy, Micmac and Maliseet along with other tribes that inhabited lower New Hampshire and as far as Vermont and Maine. Those people, as Native-American "reservations," or even as individuals, scanned the land from the top of Mount Washington. The journeys to the local vistas were referred to as "vision quests."

There is no doubt that aside from the reservations and tribes of the earliest days, there were independent loners who ventured off from existing tribes. Maybe they were renegades that wanted their own tribes. Later, there were the individual British colonists who became the occasional recluse or hermit, often living off the land and perhaps trading with the Native-Americans their trappings, skins and trinkets for a piece of land or other amenities for survival. The world seemed harsh then in the northern United States.

Governor Walter Harriman, in the mid-1800's, began selling off the White Mountains as public land. He was preceded by the state of New Hampshire that did the same in 1810. By 1890, the men of the woods, loggers and eventually the railroads operated in the state.

Over 800 sawmills were operational. The workers lived in huts and cabins during the boom in the lumber industry. The 1890's were a huge period of growth for construction in New England. One does not have to look far to see the date(s) on buildings throughout New Hampshire's towns and historic cities.

The Weeks Act of 1911 allowed the "raped land" to once again be acquired by the state to preserve the forests, much as they are seen today. The White Mountain National Forest (WMNF) is over 800,000 acres today, land that was sold or bought for $13.00/ acre in the early days.

Visitors to the White Mountains each year surpass, in numbers, Yosemite and Yellowstone, a statistic hard to fathom since those prestigious parks are inundated with people all summer long. Visitors to the White Mountains are afforded access year round, for outdoor activities, lending the area to monthly "economy boosters" from vacationers.

Eventually people settle or retire to New Hampshire, either loners or families that seek the solitude and beauty of the North Country. Coos (pronounced co-os) County is one area in particular and it abuts the chain of mountains that are known as the Presidential range. The New World settlers of today are drawn to the southern and central foothills as well, focusing on the "Buena vistas" of the Lakes Region in central New Hampshire.

Festus Gravel was not the first man to do that, to infiltrate the mountainous ranges of seclusion and reclusive hibernation, co-depending on self-sufficiency in the virgin woods.

I allude to him now because time will show that history, as you know it, repeats itself. Man still seeks to be an "island," devoid of the excesses of life and sustenance other than what Abraham Maslow (1908-1970), the "human needs" psychologist, cited as priorities—air, food, drink, shelter, warmth, sex and sleep. The philosopher was probably right and all of Man's needs are the same.

There were "hermits of the mountains" long ago, hermits that lived when the Native-Americans referred to Mount Washington as "Agiocochook." It was Dr. Jeremy Belknap, who in 1784 suggested the name, Washington after the general, but not yet president, George Washington. Belknap was a noted historian and George Washington was not president until the year 1789.

The remainder of the Presidential range, six peaks (sans Mt. Washington) in total, was named in 1820 and later. Several hundred millions years ago, the contiguous range of peaks (from 4,300 to 5,700 feet) were formed from the pressures of the earth and the heating and cooling of granite during the Pre-Cambrian and Jurassic periods. Granite, by name and composition, consists of quartz, sodium and potassium—rich feldspar, mica and hornblende. Because "granite" is specific for various forms of stone, it can also vary in color and composition. Magma, deep in the earth, cooled slowly during volcanic activity yielding hard stones that were both multiple and varied in minerals and composition.

Silica is a predominant component and pressure over time, glacial or otherwise, created the "granitic" or "granitoid" layers that resulted in the New Hampshire nickname, "The Granite State."

The uplifting effects of volcanoes shifted the earth, generating peaks that were probably higher than today's mountains. It was the glacial activity that scoured the tops of the mountains that we see today, moving huge boulders to unlikely places and gouging out the ravines, great cirques that made the mountains seem unbalanced in physical appearance. High winds, cold temperatures and icing yearly created, for posterity, tree lines that are riddled with low scrub pine and fir—all of which can withstand the harsh winters of New England.

People inhabited the tops of many of the mountains since old stone huts and foundations remain and preceded the recreational hikers of modern times. Those adventurers of old were "hermits/ loners" in a way, living with perfect views of the perilous landscape in both the most favorable and the foulest of weather. Interspersed between the stony mantles of ledges and crevices, wildflowers return in June and July across the region, blueberries as well.

Halfway up the slope to the Mount Washington peak lay Hermit Lake at an elevation of 3,898 feet. The Coos County lake harbors fish and other wildlife that people have lived off of for generations. It has, in the past, sustained the nomads of yesteryear who ate the wildlife, drank and fished the clear blue water to survive.

A group of men from Lancaster, New Hampshire, led by Ethan Allen Crawford in 1820, named the other mountain peaks after prominent men and presidential notables. Besides Washington, the remaining mountains were named Adams, Jefferson, Madison, Monroe, and Clay, the last of which may become Mt. Reagan in the future. The process to change the name began in 2003. Other peaks of note became Webster, Franklin and Pleasant, all prominent figures in New Hampshire.

* * *

"English Jack" was the most famous and well-known hermit of the White Mountains. Born in February 1822 in England, he died in New Hampshire in April 1912. John Alfred Vials (Viles, Vial), known as English Jack, was only a part-time hermit since he welcomed visitors to his cabin at Crawford Notch. He referred to his home of wood as "The Ship" for he was a seafaring man in early life and only lived in the remote abode during the summer. The home was also called, the "House that Jack Built" or "House of Jack" in later references by historians. Winters, he spent with friends elsewhere.

In summer, he lived off the land—eating snakes, small animals and fish. He was said to have harbored a small aquarium by his front door. He would fish, catch and store in the aquarium the meals for later.

At least one photo, published in historical references showed Jack as a Santa Claus-like figure with a large white beard and mustache, bright eyes and a one-time handsome face. In the photo, he appeared to be wearing a felt hat. Very much the recluse but only seasonally, he drank fresh water from local streams and brewed a concoction of hops and roots, a beer-like cocktail, *au natural.* His home was located some nine miles from the main road but hikers found him anyway. They sought him out. He sold pictures of himself as postcards as well as handmade trinkets fabricated from the woods. Since he mingled with people in winter, he was able to earn a living selling photos and booklets based on his life's story—*his* version and a unique life indeed. Upon his death, they found that he possessed some $1,440 in assets. Perhaps he was an *occasional* hermit to some, one with an entrepreneurial spirit.

Unlike Festus Gravel, who lived in the woods fulltime, English Jack was more social and civil in demeanor. No one knew Jack's politics or political bent or even cared, but many knew Festus's radical views. Festus could fall over just "leaning right." Conservatism and Federalism were his values.

Life had not treated English Jack kindly however, and his tale of woe is worth mentioning here. He was London born and orphaned at

12-years-of-age. Destined to be mariner, he hung out by the docks in hope of securing a job as a cabin boy on a ship. When his initial attempts failed and he was forlorn, he met a young girl who had been separated from her father. After resolving the issue to the joy of both the father and daughter, Jack spent time with the Bill Simmonds family who took him in, cared for him and admired his courage and thoughtfulness regarding the lost girl. Simmonds, a seaman, took a liking to Jack.

His wish came true when English Jack was offered a cabin berth on a Simmonds tour at sea. The good ship, *Nelson,* took them to the Indian Ocean and beyond, but hurricanes and other foul weather landed them shipwrecked on a small island where fresh water was scarce and they had to survive on mussels, crabs and snakes.

Captain Bill Simmonds died and an American ship and crew rescued Jack. He was the lone survivor of four people who were stranded, a strong mate for sure and well seasoned by then. Bill's wife had died as well and Jack's friend, "Young Mary" had been sent to a workhouse. She had no parents left.

Jack got Mary out of the workhouse and into school we are told, and he paid for her board while he was off to Hong Kong on another ship. Returning from his voyage, he then learned that Mary, his beloved, has passed away in his absence, just one month earlier. Jack was devastated, since they had grown up together and were engaged to be married. His life would forever change from that point on.

While in the Navy, he prayed that his life would be lost in battle for he was miserable after her death. He ended up in Africa where, unlike the modern day Festus Gravel's of the world, Jack fought to free the slaves that he encountered. Festus, you must realize, was a bigot, a southern one in origin and ideology.

English Jack sought out explorers in the frozen north as well and later ended up leaving London and immigrating to America. He settled at Crawford Notch in New Hampshire and worked the emerging railroad, a navvy of sorts, while hunting and trapping for food. For money, summer visitors to the White Mountains purchased his souvenirs while he spent "off time," in the "fall" of his lifetime, with a family at Twin Mountain during the winter months. Winters were too harsh in the cabin.

"The Hermit of the White Mountains" was kind we are told, offering to help others who were orphaned. His own immediate family was probably long dead, for in his later life he never found a living relative in the United States.

The book, *Our House of Jack* by Concobar (Daniel P. Connor) in 1912 is a fitting testimonial to English Jack. The author talks of Jack's travels, venturing into the surrounding mountains of Willard, Webster, Avalon, Field and Jackson, all within view of his home.

Concobar talks of Jack's wealth, (once $5,000 in a bank) and his oddity of walking in the middle of the road or wearing odd fur hats. The self-constructed abode, "The Ship," built between the late 1870's and early 1880's, is shown in historical articles as a log and timber home, with its sides braced and fortified with angular lumber assuring that the walls would not fall outward, or the roof might collapse from snow pack.

He kept a "secret vow to Mary" consigning himself to self-exile, a recluse without companionship most days, but in her honor.

Love was the binding factor apparently that led to his life of a solo existence for the most part. Just like Festus Gravel, Jack survived without need of intimate company. Festus, a loner as well, despised intruders into his "space," English Jack didn't mind the curious hiker, male or female.

English Jack communed with nature, bear and deer, and even harbored a cub for a while—until the cub became an adult. When puberty and the breeding season emerged and the "call of the wild" prompted the normally docile beast to harm his master (or consider Jack as a meal), Jack, in self-preservation, took an axe to him!

Jack related tales of his life and times to visitors. He was an entertainer of sorts. He often recited poetry since he was very creative and a learned man, well read even in isolation. He was a "old salt" and ex-mariner and talked of being stranded while at sea, of eating berries and a diet of critters that crawl on islands, and of being saved from a sad fate on isolated islands, only later to emerge as a railroad man, "spiking the rails" for the turn of the century railroad boom.

Jack knew history and was aware of General John Stark under Washington's command. He read incessantly while alone and could converse intelligently about nature or the evolution of America, and the "freedom" to be a loner in the Nation we know today. He was an Englishman who admired America's secession from the British motherland.

When asked if he was lonely, he merely recited a poem of his life to anyone who would listen—a poem where he *shunned his neighbors who might steal his grub or borrow his tools and never return them. Why should they know all your "biz?"* he would ask. He wanted to remain alone in "The Ship" until, as he often said, "I drift 'cross the *bar*," he offered, explicitly implying his inevitable mortality. "The Ship," in the poems, was his *house of wood*, landlocked in a remote forest of flora and fauna.

Concobar, the author, philosophically compares and parallels English Jack's life to "how circumstances control one's life 'with the ideals that we set for ourselves.'" Jack found that "sacrifice" was his greatest *service* . . . and "love" was his highest *freedom*.

And so with this introduction, one realizes that there are many hermits in this world, some even in New Hampshire, who desire to control their own destiny with the necessities that Maslow iterated and preached in his psychological hierarchy of human needs.

Like English Jack, Festus Gravel sought out a similar lifestyle but one with a different agenda. People don't have to live in cabins in the woods to be hermits. Festus Gravel chose that life and herein we begin to know his convoluted road and solitary journey in the woods of the White Mountains. The smoke from the fireplace may be the same, but the message in the sky reads differently—for those who march to a different drummer.

Chapter 1

It was autumn and the foothills of the New Hampshire White Mountains seemed innocent enough, having been previously well traversed in history, often leaving footprints engrained in the forest floor from the early Native-American hunters and indigenous travelers that extended in time from the colonists to the inhabitants of a modern 21st century. Hiking trails to the north were basically the remnants of the Appalachian Trail.

The Appalachian Trail extends from Springer Mountain in Georgia to the Highlands of Roan to Kadahdi, or Bethel, Maine, some 2,175 miles. Conceived in 1921 by a forester, Benton MacKaye, the trail was completed in 1937. The New Hampshire portion of the "A.T.," as hikers call it, extends some 161 miles, with 117 miles through the White Mountains. The elevation can vary from 400 to 6,288 feet. Hikers who deviate off the trail can pass through wooded areas that have never been traversed by "Man" in modern times. In that regard, people have been known to be recluses in the darkest portions of the woods, although the occasional hunter might stumble upon them by accident, or after being disoriented or lost—the intentional exploratory deviations from normal hiking trails through the Presidential range.

The impending rainstorm that had been predicted to arrive this one particular day and blanket Mt. Hoosac with torrential water by afternoon was ominous with swelling and swirling clouds. The black clouds were enormous in magnitude, almost as if the heavens were ready to envelop the landscape below with torrential rain, lightning and thunder. It was to leave behind a rain barrage, just as it always had in the past, especially on notoriously rough mountain "rock."

The repetitive event was once familiar to the Algonquin nation and the subsequent colonists that followed two centuries later. The cloudbank was dark and foreboding, swirling with the wind and creating a gale-threatening atmosphere that would scare any hiker or climber with its inherent horizontal rain. This one particular day was not a day to be in the woods alone, or to be traveling with less than adequate protective gear from the elements.

A natural granite overhang or cave would be the only protection for someone escaping the deluge and high winds that often bent the stands of birch and pines in a direction with that of the storm. Trees seemed to scream out in agony and creak and moan as if they were ready to split in two. Some were.

The rustle of the leaves in fall was a constant sound of distress as they fought to hang on to the maples and oaks in autumn. They turned precariously upside down in resistance to the prevailing weather, exposing their ventral, lighter shade of green under inclement conditions.

Tall pines of deep green creaked, while their soft branches split and fell to earth with a thunderous sound. They were weak compared to the mighty hardwoods. Small brooks began to swell from the runoff of the surrounding hills, eventually merging like small capillaries that followed and terminated in the larger veins of gullies and streams.

The landscape was still the same, rocky cliffs with lichen encroachment in stony crevices, a parasite that shriveled in the sun and cast a gray-green hue when viewed in the dull shade of late day—an overcast, afternoon sky.

Granite has always been forgiving yet strong when time and weather often chipped away at the mineralized cliffs and boulders deleteriously causing the stone to become more porous. It has always invited the runoff of water or winter ice formation that expands in low temperatures. Ice would act as a wedge of enormous pressure akin to what a logger might use to split the hardest of woods from felled trees—convoluted, grainy and dense hardwoods that resist the pressure to split. Ice expansion can move granite.

* * *

Festus Gravel was a nomad, a man who had escaped society and became a lone wolf of sorts. Festus had no real family, at least none that anyone knew about. His origin was from the south where his parents also grew up, yet he had been in New Hampshire for more than five decades.

They weren't really parents to him in the traditional sense. They were uneducated, prejudiced, and often bigoted showing little respect for minorities and the downtrodden. Festus had once found a ring in his father's belongings, long after the old man was dead. It was associated with the KKK, an "executive member" symbol of the fraternal organization.

Festus knew that there were titles for the Klan's upper echelon, some of which were named Night Hawks, White Knights, Grand Dragon and the Imperial Wizard, the ultimate leader. His father was probably a Night Hawk as best as he could determine, especially from the symbols and markings on the ring.

Festus was not a member of "The Invisible Empire," as it was referred to, but his ideology didn't stray far from their agenda, even in modern times. Numerous books had been written of the Klan's conception, infancy and maturation in the United States. It was homegrown so to speak, and bigotry was eventually its fuel for expansion, nationwide. Its humble beginnings were however in the South.

The KKK was originally a social club of Confederate Army veterans. After the war, they wanted to rebuild the South and protect the women and children from the soldiers of the North.

They never accepted defeat and accused the Union Army of raping their women after the victory by the North. At first, the Klan's mission was one of protectionism and *not* a mission of outright bigotry toward blacks or other ethnic entities.

There have been three different periods of the Klan. Formed in 1866 was the Reconstruction Klan, which evolved after the Civil War. They opposed the Republican Party of the time. They often acted independently and had no "central" oversight or control. They ruled by terror in the South, lynching blacks or ironically whipping white Republicans. They often kept black men from the polls, which affected the overall results of elections in the 1800's.

By 1872, the Federal government stepped in to help quell the movement and officially banned the Klan.

The World War I Klan emerged in 1915. It spread to the North from the South and included portions of the Midwest states. That, and their Southeast history, was the apparent movement that *attracted* Festus's relatives to their agenda and mindset. Other subunits reached as far north as Maine in New England, with some elected officials in Congress actually represented from the Northeast. Even presidents of the United States were implicated as members of the Klan.

After WWI, cross burning was introduced as a tool of intimidation to non-members. Burning crosses and bonfires lit up the night. By 1920, there were three million Klan members nationwide.

The Great Depression in the 1920's emerged and quelled the movement once again and the U.S. Government abolished the "wearing of masks/hoods" by members. They enacted laws that prevented the KKK from operating "in covert secrecy."

About 1920, the NAACP, a black organization, emerged for the first time to counteract the violent KKK's agenda.

In 1922, Hiram Evans became the Imperial Wizard of the reemerging KKK organization. The members, at that point in time, favored a *white Protestant* nation, claiming that all other religions were un-American. The U.S.A. was claimed by the KKK to be an "American-American" organization, not of other ethnicities i.e. Italian-American, African-American or Jewish-American. Roman Catholics were not *part of this country,* in their mind.

The original colonists were Protestants and America was to be *a Protestant country,* based on *history* and the Klan's prejudiced agenda, forever. The hatred spread.

The Klan hated socialists and communists, homosexuals and any ethnicities that were not considered American-born in their eyes. The Klan overlooked the fact that their *own* relatives came from England or from central Europe and Scandinavia. If you were not American-born, Caucasian and Protestant, you were not "an American," at least in their way of thinking.

In the 1920's, protests of the group and a dwindling membership waned, eliminating the *second* Klan.

It was in the 1940's when the Klan once again emerged from its old remnants, organized in part by activist Samuel Green. Festus's father knew Green. He possessed old documents and membership cards that implicated that his own father was close to the new, *third* reorganization. As more states banned the Klan in general, its membership, although robust, dwindled again for the third time. While the 1960's civil rights movement grew and flourished, the Klan still had some 20,000 members, but no *central* leadership.

The lack of an organized movement hampered the sustenance and agenda of Klan members and new followers. There was no apparent continuity or leadership between member organizations or subunits of the KKK around the nation. Although imploding *en masse,* some people remained covert but active members in secrecy.

Prominent well-to-do businessmen members were influential; some were bankers, executives and socially active people that hid their membership from the public. At night and at regional meetings, they would attend critical gatherings to review plans and agendas for gaining new members and revitalizing the dwindling organization. New recruits could join for a mere ten dollars and secrecy within the group was paramount.

Festus Gravel never became a member of the Klan but he had books on the Klan's history stashed away in his father's trunk, a heavy wooden baggage box with leather straps and an antiquated, rusty lock of old—a family heirloom of sorts. The books, now faded to yellow, were his father's collection and Festus read them ardently; studying their inherent principles and ideology—an ideology that fueled a potential *renegade* nation and disillusioned anarchists.

He knew that the organization led to the formation and ties to other white supremacist groups like the Skinheads and the Aryan Nation. Festus was "right-wing" in principles but did not desire to become part of those tribes. He perceived them as sordid individuals—many of whom felt that America could only be inhabited by true, natural born, Americans. They defined the "classification," and modern day immigrants from Europe and Israel were not part of *their* America.

For years, the Klan marched on Washington to show their "might" and collective agenda. They wore the traditional garb, but without masks—masks that were outlawed.

In later years, the well-established NAACP, a group that was organized and who often confronted them with verbal and sometimes threatening attacks, counteracted the Klan. Surprisingly, in most cases, the Klan members would *back down*, violence was reduced and many prominent Klan members went into hiding. The Klan members feared massive exposure and rebuttal from the public, their masks having been removed.

Members of Congress were accused of being members and some came forward or "came out" to address the issues. Eventually, "Washington, DC" as an entity, had no tolerance for the Klan or their intimidation of their fellow citizenry.

What evolved over time however, were spin-off organizations that remain to this day—those *members in secrecy* that remain bigoted, anti-Catholic and anti-ethnic groups that have emerged in the new millennium. Almost Nazi-like in stature, they continue to vocalize and spew hatred and an "unorthodox nationalism" that intimidates civil citizens across the country. Small bands of common thinkers still emerge from time to time to remind us of the hatred that "Man" can impel on his fellow neighbors but with vitriol.

Festus was a hermit, a solo voice in the woods—a man with a preconceived ideology of his own; some of that idealism was fashioned from his father's subtle input and influence, often tainting Festus's rational thinking as he aged.

He preferred his upbringing and philosophy to be that way, and his political views were akin to Republicanism, but to a greater extent, the "extreme right-wing." He never wore his father's ring knowing that people might notice, probably invade his privacy and label him as evil, and more than a hermit, one who should be ratted out—perhaps even labeling him as a modern day, despicable Klansman from the past. He didn't draw attention to himself knowing that he was in the minority, especially in the North.

A recluse, he was not friendly and even viewed himself as a modern day isolationist. His life and *home* was the mountains, and except for a stray dog or two, he had no need for human interaction or materialistic humankind for that matter. He despised authority, government intervention and restrictions and controls of any kind, by the police or other authorities. He wanted to live free of impediments and the rules of law. As a *free spirit*, he had no constraints and paid no taxes to anyone.

His gray beard said it all. He resembled "Father Time," was thin as a rail and appeared fragile. One wondered how he survived the winters since his home-build shack was not insulated except for some simple mud as mortar, often applied to the corners of the small square building which was fashioned from felled and hand-honed hardwood. Locals, in the surrounding towns at lake level, knew of him from rumors, torrid folklore, hearsay and exaggerated tales, causing hikers to avoid the general area of his squatter's property.

There were implied fake threats of death to trespassers, and posted signs of "No Hunting/ Trespassing," by a man who seemed unbalanced at times and unpredictable in demeanor.

His age had impaired his vision, so that if he *were* to exercise his 2nd Amendment rights with an antiquated rifle or "take a shot at someone" in self-protection, he would probably miss the intended target. No one dared to challenge his protective demeanor with respect to his life or property. He was viewed by those who occasionally encountered him at the dump or in transit, as an odd duck. Accidental encounters by hunters further fueled the perception that he was a loner, a bit introverted and unorthodox in his survivalist behavior. He was.

Festus was not privy to everyday newspapers or current events except those that he found at the nearby dump—often outdated. He relied on a faded copy of the U.S. Constitution and the Bill of Rights as a *bible*, not that he completely understood the Forefathers' intent or language all that well. The documents, or portions thereof, were posted (with four nails) on the wall of his shack. *His* America was an *old* America—200-years-old in doctrine. He escaped modernization and most communication by maintaining the minimum of necessities or staples in his abode—it was a crude but minimal existence, but uncomplicated.

Festus burned animal fat for candlelight. He would heat it until liquefied as oil. His water supply came from a nearby brook. He was long immune to *Giardia intestinalis*, a waterborne parasite of animals that could often cause serious diseases of the intestine and body of humans. He drank from the stream without boiling the water. The disease when rampant caused fatigue, nausea, diarrhea, cramps, dehydration and a foul-smelling stool. Untreated, it could last from weeks to months. Small protozoa from animal droppings being the culprit. He seemed immune from the infection, which might debilitate the normal person. He was a survivor, and rarely ill.

Festus's need for clothing was minimal. He bathed and washed his garments in the pool that he had dug in the nearby stream. Personal hygiene was optional for him; he had no one to impress and Mother Nature could care less about his body odor.

In winter, he would boil water outside in a large, cast iron kettle used to cleanse his clothes—a wood fire heated the hot water. Inside the cabin in winter, he would dry the clothing near a stone fireplace or in summer on a line of rope outside.

The rainfall began at 3 o'clock as predicted. He was not privy to the forecast since he had no television, radio or recent newspaper. He "knew the sky" after having had decades of studying the heavens visually, and the prevailing winds and cloud patterns.

Retreating to the cabin doorway, he sipped botanical tea, which he had created from local green berries and edible leaves. The dented, amber-stained tin cup looked like it was from the Revolutionary War in origin—perhaps it was. It came from his father's old trunk, perhaps one of his great grandfather's possessions.

The rainstorm came straight down and eroded channels in the earth near his cabin. He was used to nature's runoff and he dug trenches in the ground channeling the water away from his cabin. The channels had been layered with stones from the local streambed. Self-sustaining survival was his life and *modus operandi*. His home seemed to withstand all inclement weather.

A rain barrel sat to the side of the homestead, where fresh water from the roofline and eaves drifted along the makeshift log-to-log roof channels and was captured ingeniously in vinyl pipes, then into the wooden-staved circular drum—perhaps a drum that aged whiskey in the past. Bands of metal strapping, two inches wide, held the oak barrel staves together. The water inside swelled the wooden segments prohibiting leaks from both the sides and bottom. The vinyl piping was refuse from the dump, mere leftover construction material.

To him, it was fresh drinking water without any metallic or mineral taste as opposed to tannin-infused autumn water he garnered from the nearby stream. He preferred the barrel water to that of any brook or pond source. The ponds were for fishing and obtaining other game for food, not necessarily for water resources or consumption.

A hermit in the real sense of the word was *more* than being a human survivalist. He had also dropped out of a normal society for a reason. He had horded for years what he felt he needed to maintain his simple lifestyle should the nations of the world destroy one another.

Festus Gravel was a one-man army against conformity and a self-serving individual of the highest order. His fellow man was irrelevant to his life. Festus's mindset was different. He actually envisioned that if he were to be the last to die if the world collapsed or imploded, he would make it. In many ways, he had been delusional or paranoid for years but contented in his uncomplicated life.

Chapter 2

The year was 1809 and it was the 31st of July. History recorded it well when a man and patriot, New Hampshire's favorite son, other than Daniel Webster, was responding to an invite to a reunion of the Battle of Bennington of 1777. General John Stark was the invitee and he was elderly and seriously ill. He was plagued with chronic rheumatism for many years. His regrets to the reunion organizing committee (in written form) were referenced in a footnote toast that accompanied the detailed letter of why he could not participate. The toast was, *Live free or die. Death is not the greatest of evils.*

He was New Hampshire born and a "maverick" in the eyes of many statesmen and military leaders of the day. His poetic words would eventually become the official motto for the state of New Hampshire in 1945, commensurate with the end of World War II. The famous quote would honor him forever, often taken out of context.

Stark had been invited to the 32nd reunion of the famous 1777 battle by the Sons of Liberty and destined for celebration on August 16, 1809.

In his letter from his "Quarters" in Derryfield, he penned an inspirational correspondence, which was well thought out and "enabling" to the men that had admired him for decades.

Stark seemed as patriotic in his old age as he was previously during the original battle, with a profound reflection and literary reiteration of beating the British in '77. He was proud of his own leadership, a commander of many men and battles, each of which impacted the Revolution and the eventual defeat of the British. He was the *first* to carry the 13-star flag into battle.

He was very old at the time of the correspondence and reminded the organizing committee that he was close to death.

"My friends and fellow soldiers," he began, to the inhabitants of Bennington and its neighborhood, "I am fourscore and one-years-old and *the lamp of life is almost out*," he said, reminiscing. Thanking them, but declining to attend, he continued, "the infirmaries of old age will not permit." It was apparent that he was a tired and broken, old man.

Undoubtedly, his fans and fellow soldiers were disappointed by his implied absence but his lengthy letter of inspiration energized them.

"I never was worth much for a show," he mentioned modestly concerning his looks, citing that, at his age, *they would not be impressed*. "I am not worth seeing now."

He reminded the organizing committee of the reunion, that "the men of Bennington had not learned the art of submission or been trained to the art of war." He compared his men to the British invaders of liberty saying that "undisciplined freemen are superior to veteran slaves." His own militia had been formed of rag-a-bond civilians, farmers and field workers, but devoted to the cause and trainable. They became a homegrown militia by proxy!

Stark reinforced his "worldly values" from the historic war and in the same letter to his admirers.

"I am now the friend of the equal rights of men, of representative democracy, of Republicanism, and the Declaration on Independence, the great charter of our National Rights . . . and of course the friend of the indissoluble union and Constitution of the states."

Stark emphatically reiterated his convictions that "this (referring to the U.S.) is the only spot for liberty . . . the only Republic on earth." He asked for the *women* attending the reunion to be as patriotic as well, just as they had been in '77 when they dismantled beds to obtain the cord needed for binding the hands of, and for escorting, the enemy away.

He asked that all attendees be *good sentinels*, since he feared that the Tories had *infiltrated* the new government even 32 years later. He feared that their influence would "squash the Sons of Liberty" if they were not abated. Paranoia was evident. He never wanted them to let their guard down against the British.

He sensed his death was forthcoming but in reality that would not be until later in 1822 at age 94. In his closing in the letter of 1809 he seemed to be a *fatalist*, citing, "Till I go to the country from which no traveler e'er returns, I must soon receive my marching orders." His letter to the committee, his friends and fellow soldiers had a simple P.S. suspected to be on a separate piece of paper (now lost):

"I give you my volunteer toast, *Live free or die. Death is not the greatest of evils.*"

He was and remains today admired by historians, Civil Libertarians and conservatives who regard him as a demigod.

Festus Gravel was a marauder of sorts and had read of Stark's war policies—he knew of his battles in the earlier French and Indian Wars, Revolutionary War and his presence at Bunker Hill. Stark also participated in central New Jersey with General Washington, and particularly in battles around Trenton. The ragtag regiments of New Hampshire supported the Massachusetts battle groups that ended up in Boston, New York, New Jersey and Pennsylvania, by foot and by horse.

Until recently, modern historians had paid little attention to Stark, his life or his contributions to the inception and establishment of this great nation, America. He did not call attention to himself but, to this day, he is acknowledged through granite monuments and honors in New Hampshire, Vermont and other states that were part of the American Revolution.

The only historical books and documents that Festus kept for posterity were stored in his father's wooden trunk, which resided in one corner of the cabin. He read by day mostly and when he was bored by inclement weather. Over and over again he would recite the quote of Stark, with no one around to hear him. It was ingrained in his mind like the Pledge of Allegiance. It was his morning prayer "to live free," a mantra he proselytized before stepping out into the wilderness to hunt for game or fish.

He often quoted Stark's other famous saying, *"Yonder are the Hessians. They were bought for seven pounds and ten pence a man. Are you worth more? Prove it. Tonight the American flag floats from yonder hill or Molly Stark sleeps a widow!"*

Was Festus insane or delusional in his old age? Had dementia set in even though he was in decent shape for a nomad in the New Hampshire woods? His mind was sometimes sharp but he digressed to a state of catatonia when depressed, often repeating a call to battle even when there was no war to fight.

Obsessed with *freedom*, he felt that man would encroach upon his land and territory enforcing laws, rules and constraints. He despised taxes and avoided discussing them or paying them for that matter, most of his life. New Hampshire had no income tax and no sales tax. Basically, Festus felt that there should be no taxes on *anything*. He had no recent job and never formally owned property. He was merely a squatter who desperately existed in a modern world of pleasures and laws for which he had no desire. He was not materialistic in any respect and just wanted to be left alone. He was a lone *sentry of the past, and in his delusion, a John Stark marauder,* but with a different agenda than Stark.

Chapter 3

Festus was supposedly a descendent of a U.S. president, he once boasted to close friends in his youth. As an adult, he had laid claim to that fact and touted that he once lived near where John Stark grew up in Derryfield, now the city of Manchester. How he got from North Carolina to New Hampshire nobody knows. The president to whom he referred to be of Republican orientation, like Stark, but Festus no could longer remember which president it was. Few people believed him anyway.

For sure, Festus's relative was not Abraham Lincoln since the self-ascribed recluse was bigoted all his life. In his youth, he had been a proponent of segregation, even though he was now a northerner. One would have thought that he had more compassion, but his upbringing was more like a southern racist. His completion of school to the junior high level was an indication of a limited formal education and his constant physical fights with his peers granted him permanent leave of the institution as a teen. He incited trouble for he was a bully in his youth. Festus feared no one, but his own evolving government.

Comparatively, and up until his death, Stark feared the British and the French as well. History records that Stark always felt an intense distrust for the British even after America was formed. He had fought along side the Brits in the French and Indian Wars, but *against* them in the American Revolution.

He surely had no issues with his newly formed government, unlike Festus Gravel.

Job-wise, Festus was a welder for a time as a young adult, often fabricating metal into obscure sculptures that never sold. Having relegated himself to a hermit, he was now a man who was cautious and protective of his squatter's rights. The land really belonged to the state of New Hampshire but some of it bordered on land belonging to a shoemaker in Boston, a man who fell on prosperous times before going broke in the Great Depression. Where Festus now resided was on the border of a large undeveloped estate and protected state land.

He was surrounded by some four thousand acres that were virtually pristine, untouched and protected from common trespassers, except hikers. People illegally hunted on the land without a license for there was little law enforcement or Fish and Game oversight in the overgrown pine and birch natural environment. It was too dense and vast to cover especially in winter, and rarely was there a forest fire to abate. For most hikers, it was a convoluted journey to get there, but Festus knew shortcuts that were traversable and familiar to his needs.

On this one particular Saturday morning he emerged from his hut, the door of which swung open with a groan from the lack of lubrication and the rusty hinges of old. He peered up to the sky and then between some encroaching maple trees. They were in the process of denuding their leaves—an annual event of autumn color that was now waning.

The crisp autumn air caused his breath to be seen as steam, for autumn was in its quarterly stage of transition from green-yellow leaves to crimson and orange and then brown.

The previous night had harbored a fading crescent moon, a thin fingernail image behind the clouds that dominated the sky. The nearby stands of white birch were stagnant and pristine often clustered in twos and threes and interspersed with dense green firs and ash-colored poplars.

In the distance, Festus heard a helicopter at an incidental angle above him. It was early morning but the rotors pounded the air into a cadence-like drum, a lub-lub-lub sound of the chopper's low flight, a sound, which was bouncing and echoing off the hills. Soon the logo on the side of the aircraft came into view. It read "State Police."

They were often summoned to retrieve injured hikers on mountains inaccessible by foot, foolish "granola types" in his mind, who easily lost their way even if they had a compass. Their commune with nature was often perilous and ill-planned.

The state of New Hampshire had always used Bell Jet Rangers, Model 407, and a helicopter that featured a high-tech single engine that is produced by Rolls Royce. They utilized the same craft for the apprehension of suspects on the run.

The 250-C47B, turbine engine was extremely reliable in the industry. The aircraft had a Full Authority Digital Engine Control (FADEC), and a fuel management system that required little maintenance. The State Police had found it to be a cost effective flyer for rescue and S.W.A.T. related missions.

The four-blade rotor provided for a smooth ride with superior hover performance and air speed. This particular State Police aircraft I.D. (N366SP) was emblazoned on the sides of the machine and clearly visible from the ground when there were open spots in the early morning fog.

Its austere presence in the sky "implied business" to offenders of the law on the run, especially with a capability of an airspeed of 153 mph (246 km/h) and a flying range of 380 miles (612 km). Its quick maneuverability was unsurpassed. An open side door with officers pointing automatic weapons could send a chill up and down the spine of perpetrators, especially when the mission called for apprehension of convicts or felons in the Granite State.

Capable of holding seven passengers, today's flight was occupied by two officers and one civilian pilot. The pilot was not a sworn New Hampshire State Police officer, but an experienced chopper pilot who was not involved in law enforcement directly. That was left to the men in the back of the bird, specifically trained to seek our criminals and violators. Those being pursued might hide for a while, but the police and chopper had features and equipment to locate them over time. A large spotlight hung from the bottom of the aircraft cabin. It was the ultimate tool in darkness and in search and rescue operations.

Festus could hear the rotors pounding the moist, heavy dead air. Normally a quiet machine, the low-pressure atmosphere and light rain made for a repetitive pounding sound that reverberated everywhere. On a clear day, the composite material in the rotors suppressed the engine noise and air compression.

Festus, standing in limited clothing, heard the helicopter pass over . . . and then move on to the east. They would surely circle back if they noted unusual movement or activity. Festus Gravel hoped they would merely keep going. He was unaware of any issues that needed police surveillance.

Festus was wearing one of his three pairs of underwear, the other two were hanging from a line near the brook. They were soaked again, since he had washed them the evening before the rain had arrived unexpectedly.

What were the police looking for? Or who, for that matter? There was silence for a couple of minutes. The air was heavy and quiet but for the rustle of leaves.

In the distance, Festus could hear two voices in the woods to the west. He was cautious and reached for a pair of WWII binoculars by the door. The case was camouflage green in color, with a leather neckband. They were 400X in power and could easily see anyone approaching, except for the fog. *Were the police there for a rescue or chasing someone that had escaped from a local limited security prison?* One existed some fifteen miles from his home and Festus knew that the "walk-aways" were a common occurrence—those inmates that were considered low security risks, and having committed prior misdemeanors.

They sometimes breached the trust of the facility management and made a run for it. They never got very far before being recaptured. Intelligent criminals they were not.

Festus reached for a nearby shotgun, one that had been his father's. It was old but still worked. He kept the 20-gauge near his bed or near the door depending on whether it was day or night. The barrel of the gun had been modified and was shorter than normal—a sawed off scattergun of sorts. That way, birdshot spread out in a wider periphery.

The helicopter now off in the distance, seemed to pan the area hovering at 200-foot increments in altitude and then slowly turned 360°, perhaps to get a better view of the mountainous area and general landscape.

Again, Festus heard voices, men it seemed; voices that increased in volume with accompanying heavy breathing, as if someone was out of wind and on the run. They were. The woods were misted in fog created by the rain and the cooler air over a warmer ground. At first, he couldn't see anyone in his line of vision.

"Who goes there?" he shouted toward the mist, as if he was John Stark and speaking to an impending evil, or opposing, military force. There was no response from anyone in the lowland fog—the voices were silent. It had sounded like two men, young men.

"Who goes there?" he repeated, his heart now racing.

Again . . . there was silence.

"Identify yourself!" he demanded, raising his weapon almost to eye level. He squinted, but saw no one. Then he heard mumbling.

One man shouted, "Go . . . run!"

All of a sudden a pistol emerged from the fog and the shadow of a man appeared with arm extended, and quite indiscernible as a figure. Festus wasted no time in pulling the trigger. There was no hesitation and he felt his hand and body go cold as if he had shocked himself by the aberration of the intruder's weapon.

He considered his land his own. He felt violated and responded immediately.

A shot echoed off the hills and one voice went silent. The other one screamed, "Jesus! No!" Birdshot rustled through the trees where leaves were remaining. There was a groan and a thump and the sound of someone taking off through the brush. A rustle of leaves on the ground could be heard in the distance, perhaps the sound of someone high-tailing it in the opposite direction. The helicopter was at enough of a distance as to not suppress the nearby voices and gunfire. They were only partially muted by the sound of the chopper's rotors in the distance.

A series of granite boulders offered an obstruction of Festus's view from the hut, and he now feared that his warning shot in self-defense had seriously injured someone.

Again he looked at his hands. They were shaking from the brief encounter. He placed the long gun against the inside door jam and residual smoke from the barrel and the smell of sulfur remained in the moist air near the entryway. His heart was racing. He closed the door slowly, feeling weak in the knees and sat silently in a nearby wing chair to gather his thoughts and catch his breath. He felt light-headed and was afraid to go outside to see what had happened. *Where was the other person?*

Had he taken his freedom of the 2nd Amendment a bit too far? He knew his "rights" but he had never injured or killed anyone before. Festus sat staring at the door and pondered if the police had heard the shot. The rapid paced scenario became a simulated movie in his mind. He no longer heard the pulsing drone of the helicopter's rotors. They had perhaps moved on to another peak or location.

There was no sound from the woods either. He decided to sit and wait for his heart to settle down. His pulse raced. He planned to venture out as soon as he was able to regain his composure. His eyes were still wide from an adrenaline rush. Above his armchair, in which he huddled, was a framed picture of General John Stark and his wife, Molly. He did not move an inch but merely stared at the floor which was half composed of dirt and non-matching slabs of wood. A doctor, had there been one present, would have said Festus was catatonic, or experiencing apoplexy.

There was still no sound or movements from the nearby woods, no moaning, and no crying. The helicopter was long gone and, except for the rustle of the trees in the rain and the scurrying leaves in the fall wind, there were no other out of the ordinary sounds to startle Festus.

He finally rose and cautiously peered out of a side window, backing off quickly as to not be seen. A wood fire, abating the wet chill of the day, crackled nearby. He shook in fear.

Chapter 4

During the history of the colonists and emerging colonies, including Massachusetts and New Hampshire, the militia of the day (with sometimes rag-a-bond recruits) often volunteered for action during the French and Indian Wars, the Battle of Bennington in Vermont (then New York State) and at Bunker Hill in Charlestown, Massachusetts.

General Stark was a strong colleague of the then, young George Washington. Regiments from New Hampshire grew out of the central and southern portions of the state and marched, or rode, to Boston. They were as feisty as anyone who fought on the battlegrounds of New England, New York and New Jersey, in particular the New Brunswick and Trenton areas, and then it was on to Philadelphia with Fort Washington and the Delaware River being prominent battlegrounds before the year 1776. Stark managed to venture and ride south himself, a difficult task in those days and an arduous trip, travel-wise.

Stark was a "maverick," a marauder in his day, and to this day often inspiring liberty advocates and "Freestaters" or modern day extreme right political radicals in the 21st century. They admired him first for his bravery and fortitude and later for his quest for freedom from the unwelcome British invasion.

Attempts had been made in the early 2000's to encourage the Freestater (advocates of liberty) or libertarian thinkers to migrate to the Granite State. Although there was a desire to grow to 20,000 of these modern day marauders/recruits, the followers of the professed 1st and 2nd Amendment "mantra" only generated 500 or 600 members or residents in New Hampshire over a two or three-year period.

The concept was and remains to saturate the state of New Hampshire with voters that would elect Libertarians or right-wing factions in critical presidential, state and local elections.

Festus Gravel was not one of them, per say. He was homegrown and considered Stark's history and place in the world as *significant*, without instigating a specific revolution *against* a growing United States government. Festus was not interested in forming a "new Stark militia" in New Hampshire. He was merely a lone wolf in a movement of "Stark pretenders" that idolized, to this day, the U.S. Constitution—a bible to them and not meant to be altered by modern applications or revisions two hundred years later.

* * *

Barnaby Stillwater, Esq. was a local lawyer in the Lakes Region of New Hampshire. His office was located near his home, which was on the border of Laconia and Gilmanton. Stillwater had long been a proponent of civil rights law but he also was a perpetual student of Constitutional law. He was graduated from the George Washington University School of Law in D.C. and had been in practice for some 37 years. He was a pillar in the community, and a model citizen.

Stillwater had focused, in particular, on the constitutional aspects of the 1st and 2nd Amendments and how the framers of the U. S. Constitution espoused their thoughts to the general population of an emerging nation. Stillwater was of the predisposition that both amendments in the Bill of Rights were *abused* in a modern society and often taken out of context after some 230 years of this nation's history.

His colleague, Attorney Tom Moore, another respected attorney, but one that attended law school in Boston, was of the perception that those particular amendments were to be taken *literally* and that there was "no magic' in what the Founding Fathers had meant when they penned them on parchment.

The opposing views of the two men often lead to heated but civil discussions over a casual Friday night beer in a nearby tavern that had once been a 1890's train depot. The discussions were intense enough arguments that voices were raised but they were always *civil* in discourse. The discussion points were academic anyway.

After decades of discussion, debates and review by the U. S. Supreme Court in Washington, the justices at the highest levels always deferred to the rights of citizens to free speech and the right to keep and bear arms, under almost *any* conditions. Their interpretation in a modern world caused much debate and consternation. *What would the Framers have thought?*

"You can't claim that the 2nd was meant to apply to modern day weaponry, like Uzi's," Stillwater vented between sips of beer.

"Sure you can. Apply the rights," Moore would argue. "Arms are arms and the people can protect themselves as needed."

"The Founding Fathers never knew how the country would evolve," Stillwater persisted. "You can't say that the colonial weaponry of single shot muskets, that took a couple of minutes to reload and were for the formation of a *well organized militia*, applies to *today's* modern weaponry and gun rights."

Moore responded in kind and in an elevated voice, "Barnaby, a gun is a gun is a gun. They kept the amendment simple. All weapons applied to their thinking back then."

"The amendment was to have the citizenry protect themselves *from a government* that went awry! It was not to shoot your neighbor if he crossed your damn stone wall, Tom!" Stillwater insisted.

Stillwater became agitated at the thought that Moore was taking the 2nd too *literally* and universally.

"How do we know what they meant? They left it open to interpretation," Moore added, drinking a pilsner in one full swoop. "I'll have another, Mike," he bellowed to the bartender.

Stillwater shook his head.

"The country was young then. Read what they wrote. The wording applies to an "army of people" protecting themselves from a *government of tyranny*. Then drive over to that ammo shop on Route 9, where the good ol' boys hang out, and tell me which weapon on the wall of the shop applies to protecting the citizens from our current government in Washington or in our statehouses around the country."

Moore sat back and cogitated. He laughed.

"There are some people that hate any government. They hate taxes. They hate rules," he gestured, wildly. "They hate the infringement of government into any personal affairs of the state. You know that. They don't want their arms taken away by big government."

Stillwater shook his head in disgust, as if in pain. "For Christ's sake, no one is taking away their arms! People say Obama wants to do just that. Just look at the morons on the Internet who claim he wants to curtail their rights. They're fanatics. We all know that would violate the 4th. They're just pissed that some Libertarian didn't win the election of 2008," he emphasized.

"Some weapons just need some restriction," continued Barnaby. "They have no place in society, or in a home for that matter. There are people right now that are allowed to take their weapons into a Starbucks in Virginia . . . Jesus! Starbucks doesn't want to be a policy maker for Washington. I guess Starbucks doesn't care about customers that are threatened by this measure and neither does 'opencarry.org.' Those are pistols that are concealed! I'll be damned if I'll patronize their stores! Even students at Colorado State are hiding handguns in their pants and going to class. President Clinton achieved a limited assault weapons ban in 1994; especially of AR-15s and TEC-DC 9's but in 2004 Congress did not extend it. Senator Feinstein tried. Gun companies redesigned weapons to create loopholes as to what was specifically labeled an 'assault weapon.' Some automatic military weapons need not be in the hands of the average person or child for that matter. Ya can't encourage the extremists and minorities in political thought, bordering on dementia, to hunker down in the rolling hills of the White Mountains and hoard weaponry, water, cans of food and medicine and wait for the day when they attack *en masse* the Capitol in Concord! Some Libertarian views encourage just that, Tom! At one point people could carry weapons into the New Hampshire State House. It was legal!"

Stillwater sat back and rubbed his eyes as if he was tired from a grueling week of court cases and the ongoing argument with Moore.

"Jesus Tom, study the laws and Supreme Court rulings. The U.S. vs. Miller in 1939, where the court ruled that the 'obvious purpose of the 2nd was to assure the continuation and render possible the effectiveness of the "state militia"—the National Guard. In Illinois in 1983 (Quillici vs. Morton Grove) the court ruled that there was no 'individual' right to keep and bear arms. In 1991, Supreme Court Justice Warren Burger referred to the 2nd as 'the subject of one of the greatest pieces of *fraud*' and that the NRA has misled the American people. As late as 1999, the courts decided that the 2nd refers to the right to keep and bear arms *only* in connection with a state militia. There have been 32 cases on this issue since the Miller decision."

Moore mentioned the 2008 case of D.C. v Heller where the U.S. Supreme Court ruled that an individual has the right to possess a firearm for private use in *federal* enclaves. Barnaby retorted.

"The ruling did not address the same freedom in the states, however," he offered, "like guns in the State House in New Hampshire.

Moore didn't immediately respond, but one could see he was *looking* to respond. He knew that if he did, they would be there for hours, arguing. He had much to do that weekend and needed to get home. He also knew that all fifty states needed to ratify any changes in amendments to the U.S. Constitution and that was virtually impossible to accomplish.

Changing the 2nd as Stillwater wanted might involve other amendments that would be infringed—those like the 4th, 9th 10th and 14th.

Moore considered Stillwater's principles noteworthy but he saw him as an "idealist" with pragmatic concepts that would be hung up in the U.S. Supreme Court for decades, or millennia. Still, Moore respected his partner's opinion. He just didn't want to stay all night and argue what he considered to be a useless point, one that could never be resolved over a beer.

Mike, the bartender, appeared tableside. He wiped down the surface while clearing away the dead soldiers.

"You guys need another?" he offered, sensing the intense discussion of the past few minutes was at a lull.

"Cease fire?" he quipped, and then smiled.

"Nope," said Stillwater, reaching for his coat, "we've solved all the world's problems for today," he voiced, smiling at his colleague, "No more beer needed. My buddy here is *crazy*."

"I gotta go anyway. I'll pay *this* tab, this week," Moore added, graciously.

The two men stood and headed for the door. It had begun to rain and their cars were in separate, but nearby parking lots. They shook hands, laughed for a moment at their previous discussion and headed for their respective vehicles. Stillwater's SUV was a Cadillac Escalade and Moore's car was Lincoln sedan. Both were fairly recent models and black in color.

"'Night, Tom," said Stillwater, smiling from a few feet away.

"'Night, Barnaby . . . have a good one," added Moore. "Say hi to the wife."

"You too . . . see ya Monday mornin'."

* * *

The sirens rang out within four minutes of the men leaving the bar and café. Stillwater lay motionless and hemorrhaging next to his vehicle, his car keys locked in his hand and the driver's side door partially open. The interior overhead light illuminated the body, which lay crumpled on the nearby asphalt, his $600 suit stained with bright crimson from a wound to the head initiated by a small caliber gun. The scene was gruesome and yet serene under a yellow street lamp. A mist prevailed over the body.

The assailant(s) had fled on foot and disappeared into the nearby stand of trees that lined the darkened corner of the parking lot. Attorney Moore, unaware, had already departed from the other parking lot.

Moore would get the shocking call from the police within minutes, a call that his partner had been murdered. It would be the worst weekend of his life and a distressful call from authorities that would change Moore's life from that point on, and . . . forever.

One of the things that the police noticed upon their arrival, aside from the victim who they tried in vain to revive, was that one license plate was missing from Stillwater's car. Two screws that held it in place had been removed, a simple task with a portable power drill or common screwdriver. The screws were still on the pavement. The "tag" was a vanity plate similar to the remaining, second license plate on the front of the vehicle. Perhaps the perpetrator or perpetrators were startled and had little time to remove the second one.

The Stillwater vanity plate, registered on file, read: "AMEND2." Those in the know, especially colleagues in the legal profession, were sure that it referred to the 2nd Amendment and Stillwater's advocacy, ardent support of the desire to see the U.S. Constitutional amendment "amended" once more to reflect the needs to restrict firearms that were either deemed illegal, or potentially violent in a modern day society. It was clear that some "freedom advocates," or NRA proponents might take offense to the suggested message on the front and back of his car.

His legal partner, Moore, had warned him that the plate might be inflammatory to some gun advocates, but Stillwater "stuck to his guns," so to speak, offering the proposition that the 1st Amendment rights protected *his own* free speech (written voice) in the matter. It was academic to him and few people would know what the plate meant anyway, he surmised. He was dead wrong . . . and now deceased.

* * *

On all New Hampshire license plates is the motto, "Live Free or Die." It was adopted by the state of New Hampshire in 1945, in tribute to General John Stark.

Stark, whom Stillwater idolized for his patriotism and impact in the Revolution, was born in Londonderry, New Hampshire in 1728. A marker by the side of the road also denotes the general area of his birth, just off Route 28. He died after a stellar career as an officer in the militia, the American Continental Army. Known for his brilliant strategy under George Washington in 1775, Stark was a self-made military man, but a common farmer, who married Elizabeth "Molly" Page in Dunbarton, New Hampshire. Somewhere in between battles, he was able to raise a family of eleven children.

Admired by the State of New Hampshire, historians and the public, Stark grew up in Derryfield (later Manchester) and his boyhood home remains to this day on Elm Street. His father built it in 1736.

The Stark family was of Irish and Scottish descent and Stark's parent's journey to the New World was perilous in, and of itself.

Many residents of New Hampshire are unaware of the origin of the motto and object to this day, to the mantra on their plates. The motto replaced the state's previous acumen that read, "Scenic New Hampshire."

As a battle cry to extreme politicos of the "right," this particular motto has been the mainstay of their efforts to protect *all* personal freedoms, as outlined 200 years ago.

Stark would be aghast to know how often his famed footnote has been *misconstrued* or *misrepresented* in modern day tributes to his revolutionary cause and surname.

Some peace activists have objected to the motto on license plates and have challenged the court by covering up the motto on their own plates. The state courts ruled that no one could be prosecuted for *hiding* or *covering* the motto or deeming it objectionable by some citizenry. By nature, it almost incites rebellion, for the phrase is forceful in impact and a written exclamation—a call to arms in and of itself. Peace advocates despise the motto.

Stark served in Rogers' Rangers in the French and Indian Wars and was later a colonel at Bunker Hill during the war with Briton. Two months after the Battle of Bennington, he was made a Brigadier General, only to retire in 1783 as a Major General.

Stark's bravery as a *maverick* actually preceded the 1777 Bennington battle but was exemplary in 1752 when, at one point, he was captured by the Abenaki Indians while trapping animals along the Baker River near Plymouth and Rumney, New Hampshire. He was taken to Quebec and his valor tested against a band of Indians with sticks in hand.

He ran the gauntlet and survived! He was so agile that the tribe adopted him as a member of their own until a government agent from Massachusetts traveled north to find him and paid the Indians the equivalent of $103 Spanish dollars to free him. He then returned Stark to New Hampshire. John Stark's respect for the Native-Americans and Canadian Indians never waned.

General Stark died May 8, 1822 and his bravery and service in the military has been revered in the state ever since. His "Minutemen" division from New Hampshire participated in many of Washington's battles of the American Revolution, including in New England and south.

Stark is buried on his farm—land that eventually became a state park. Statues and monuments that attest to his valor and contributions militarily, as well as achievements and bravery, are located particularly in Vermont and New Hampshire.

* * *

A note left at the death scene—at Stillwater's final living moments, further complicated the investigation of the apparent Stillwater murder. It was a piece of paper, with individual letters cut out from a variety of magazines and glued in place to read, "Live Free or Die."

In effect, John Stark's motto had once again been used to instill an offensive battle cry for someone or some persons who most likely objected to Stillwater's beliefs.

The note seemed to reaffirm the intent of the person who took the missing license plate. It was critical evidence with possible fingerprints or forensic data and was removed from the crime scene.

The police wondered if the evidence and perpetrator(s) knew Barnaby personally, perhaps from some court event or trial, or whether it was a random act of violence, or intimidation, gone afoul.

Stillwater's wallet and personal jewelry remained with the body, so it was unlikely that the *modus operandi* was one of robbery—that being theft of valuables for drugs or other material possessions.

Attempted car theft was ruled out because the license plate would probably not have been removed. The authorities were puzzled by the scene, note and motive. *Who would commit this crime?* The coldness of the act matched the crisp air of autumn—a chilling night at a scene of immense tragedy.

Chapter 5

The eulogy to Barnaby Stillwater by Thomas Moore at his friend's funeral and memorial service was profound and reflective of their long friendship. Moore had all he could do to refrain from breaking down in front of the family and friends of the noted and respected lawyer, Barnaby Stillwater, Esquire.

"He was a man of conviction," he cited. "He was a man who represented all people, the poor, the rich and the downtrodden, even Republicans," he added, for humor. The attendees chuckled, knowing he detested that political party.

"This senseless act of violence is the antithesis of what Barnaby represented in his daily life and in his legal profession. We have lost a great citizen and gentle giant . . . and I have personally lost . . . my best friend." His eyes welled up with moisture.

He stood silent for a moment gathering his emotions before spending another ten minutes eulogizing his colleague. People in the front of the church, mostly relatives, were sobbing at the elegy.

Judges, lawyers and state officials attended the service for Stillwater and Moore was now without a partner in a law office that was respected for its integrity and dedication to the rules of law.

Moore was now without his closest friend and confidant, a person who challenged his cerebral mind on philosophical, judicial and intellectual issues, especially when they had friendly discourses over Constitutional law. The fact that they were close, family close, meant Moore would have to debate someone else in the profession to keep his keen mind stimulated. That fact had never entered his mind since he was almost similar in age to Stillwater and always thought, due to ongoing medical issues that he would be the *first* to go. They chided each other as to who was in better health. Stillwater was heavier but Moore had a genetic, familial history of cardiovascular disease and diabetes. That didn't matter now, he thought. Barnaby died, not from illness or old age, but from a callous, intentional gunshot to the head by some two-bit thug.

Following the burial of Stillwater, Moore returned to his law office the very next day and sat in Stillwater's brown leather chair behind his desk. He pondered the task of carrying on without his friendly adversary. An impending event or two, piles of unread legal documents and other incoming mail sat on top of Stillwater's desk, and next to the telephone. The message light was blinking. Numerous calls needed to be returned.

Stillwater had taken on two new court cases in recent weeks. One was a "freedom of speech" issue and another was a slander/ libel case. Were they anyway relevant to the crime at hand?

How might they be related to the senseless murder? he wondered. *Had Stillwater taken on a case that endangered his life? Was he representing a lunatic that was disgruntled? Who would have killed his friend, and worse, for what reason?*

Moore was perplexed by the missing license plate from Stillwater's SUV. It implied that someone who defended the 2nd Amendment, (in its most literal translation), might be culpable for the horrific murder. The police were of that mindset, even with little evidence to go on. They had no real leads at the time of Stillwater's burial. Barnaby Stillwater, Esq. had no known enemies in his personal or professional life yet someone had a vendetta against him. That was the prevailing theory for the police and Tom Moore.

Chapter 6

Mustering up his strength (and bravery) after firing the shotgun into the woods aimlessly, Festus Gravel exited the cabin and slowly walked over to the large boulder on his property. The fog was lifting. He pointed a reloaded shotgun straight ahead. The old man could see a lower leg and boot lying in plain view. The closer he moved toward the massive granite boulder, the more macabre the scene appeared.

Nothing moved.

There was a mist of fog about two feet above the person. There were two ball caps on the ground but only one person lay in the new fallen leaves of red, brown or yellow.

A man in his late 20's or early 30's was dead on the ground. There was no one else around. Festus slowly scanned the area. The sight of the man—motionless, shocked him. *Was the person on the wet leaves playing possum?* He poked the body with the gun barrel. Again, nothing moved and he panned the area, 360°.

Festus's breath hung in the air like a cloud. He peered at the victim, while the chill of the autumn day made his own body shiver from the revelation that he had "hit" someone when he fired, and actually *killed* someone. *It was a warning shot,* he thought. *Just a warning shot.* He had no idea who the person was.

Where was the other person? That *other* voice he swore he had heard. The second baseball cap was evidence of another intruder. *Did they not see or read the "No Trespassing" signs posted? Was the other man hiding out in the mist, ready to pounce on him?* He shook in fear.

"Jesus Christ," he uttered, in shock and sadness. It was no one that he had seen before, even as the casual hunter . . . or hiker in the woods.

"What the hell . . . ?" he continued to mumble, softly. His hand was gripped tightly on the shotgun, trembling from fear. He leaned over and noted that the buckshot or pellets had penetrated the man's chest and face. Dried blood spots prevailed like acne.

The color of the victim's clothes was a dull olive green and beige collage, almost military-like and not bright orange as a hunter might wear. A pistol lay to the side of the deceased person, a foot from the now motionless hand.

Were there in fact two people? he wondered. Festus had heard two voices but at his age he was unsure. Maybe the other person had run for help leaving his hat behind on the ground.

The second hat lay some distance from the dead body.

There was a Budweiser logo on the front and it was red in color with the number 3 emblazoned on the lid. The person, either male or female, was an obvious Dale Earnhardt Sr., NASCAR fan. The dead man's hat was next to his head. It contained a military logo for MIAs on the front panel and was black in color with white lettering. The hat had taken some "shot" from the gun as well and the man's face bloodied by the spray of the gun. Festus stood silent, staring in horror.

For a random shot "in the name of self-protection," Festus had unwillingly killed an innocent person, and the other person had probably skedaddled to save his own life. *Who in the hell were they?* he wondered.

A slight wind through the trees was all that Festus heard, branches creaking and the occasional leaf swirling about the ground. Knees shaking, Festus walked aimlessly back and forth—first right, then left, then right again.

Festus sat on a smaller boulder and stared at the carnage on the ground. A light rain began to fall around him. The body lay in wet dirt and leaves. Soon it would be mud. He noted that the dead man had a camo-colored knapsack that lay askew at an angle to his body. The body was positioned on its side and his legs and arms seemed Gumby-like, spewed in different directions like a rag doll.

Scared, he slowly rolled the man over onto his stomach. He opened the pack and peered into the depths of the green canvas sack. A change of clothes and some limited food and snacks were apparent at the top of the knapsack. A water bottle rolled out and a pack of Marlboro cigarettes. Tucked vertically in the back of the sack was a single New Hampshire license plate that read, AMEND2.

Festus stared at the vanity plate and thought it odd, but nothing unusual registered in his mind.

His first concern was to hide the evidence (the body) as soon as possible. That included the deceased man and the knapsack. On second thought, he considered keeping the license plate and the backpack in the cabin, at least for a while.

After a few minutes, Festus's heart rate and breathing returned to normal. He became more rational. He knew the exact place to bury the dead man. Festus needed to complete the mission and quickly.

The hermit knew of a small area that formed a shallow pool from the nearby brook—it might provide potential camouflage and secrecy. In the back of his cabin was a shed with a two-wheeled hand truck that had decent balloon tires. He kept the tires inflated with an old bicycle pump. The hand truck would prove helpful in moving the body without leaving a "drag trail" of bloody evidence should someone return to investigate. It would take Festus the next two hours to accomplish the task.

He pondered the events carefully and concluded that the helicopter must have been looking for the two men. Now there was only one on the run, and no helicopter could be heard in the area. The low ceiling and fog probably postponed the search.

* * *

Festus Gravel did not exist solely on his own, by fishing and hunting. Wintertime was rough and the deep snow sometimes prevented him from seeking his own meals from the woods and drinking water from nearby sources. The rain barrel froze annually.

A mile-and-a-half below the cabin was the town dump, located at the base of Mt. Hoosac. A small stream ran close by and Festus could follow the path even with aging eyesight. He only visited the dump in the off hours and after the front gate was locked. He entered unrestricted by way of the back woods where there was no perimeter fencing. His only competition, for useable dump items i.e. leftover food from restaurants, was that of the occasional raccoon, skunk or infrequent bear.

The dump was really a "recycle center" that was maintained by the contractor, Recycle Management. The fact that it was a recycling center made it no more pleasant than any other dump in the summer heat and humidity. The autumn chill and brisk temperatures reduced the putrefying odor—an advantage for dump-pickers. The degradation of the garbage was less volatile than in summer, but still unpleasant.

In this recycling center, garbage ended up in one pile and was deposited in and around a shed where a front-end loader placed the mixture into large trucks for transport elsewhere. The wasteful mass from humanity was relocated to a facility with a massive furnace, somewhere in a remote, nonresidential area of the state.

Residual outdated food from grocery stores could then be reclaimed or found palatable before the transfer to another facility. Outdated breads, pastries and produce helped maintain Festus's body mass and energy in winter.

Separate metal waste bins harbored recycled paper and newspapers by the ton. Bottles and cans were in separate containers as well.

Each visit to the dump meant Festus could read a varied selection of news from local papers. Some editions were out of date, but others were as recent as the day before. If the papers appeared in reasonably good condition, he knew that they were *recent* editions. News was never that far off if he frequented the refuse center often.

His life seemed uncomplicated until the shooting. Days, months and even years meant nothing in time to him. Neither did holidays or celebratory events and local festivities.

He planned to visit the dump the next day, in hopes of reading of any events that required the State Police helicopter surveillance above his cabin area. Maybe, just maybe, the police were seeking the two individuals that had transgressed onto his property.

Newspapers would help him discern the issues at hand and what he might be dealing with in the coming days, police searches or otherwise.

He feared that more intruders would descend upon the mountain. He knew that his solitude would soon be interrupted.

Chapter 7

It was Sunday and the Saturday night before Festus had not slept well. It was clear that he was anxious over the events of the last day—those that had resulted in him burying someone on "his" land that eventually would be missed by relatives or friends. Surely, someone had to know that one or two persons had entered the woods in recent days and that one of them did not exit. *Where did the one who escaped go?* he wondered. *Was he wounded as well? Hiding?*

On Sunday, Festus had heard a helicopter in the distance but it never approached the area of his homestead. The rain had subsided. The previous night, he awoke at least four times, once to pee and the other times he thought he had heard searchers, perhaps "phantom searchers" in his mind.

He was still antsy over the fact that he had a dead body on the property. He knew forensic investigators had ways to detect blood on the ground or used search dogs that could find cadavers. He wasn't stupid but he still feared the worst. He needed to find a recent newspaper from Saturday. He would need today's as well, but that might require another journey to the dump the next day.

No one was around at the recycling center. He had managed to venture down a back trail early in the morning. He spotted the overflowing containers of newspapers. Saturday's collection of local street refuse was enormous. He dragged his two-wheeled hand truck into the woods and scoped out the landfill area in detail, before scavenging. The gate was locked as usual. He entered the back area where there wasn't a fence. He was tired from the hike down the mountain and waited to make sure that no other trespassers appeared near the trash bins or the refuse pile. People were known to jump the fence in the off hours.

The newspaper bin in particular was near the back woods. An occasional inland seagull or crow pecked at the rubbish pile in search of any bits to eat. Festus, in leather Timberland-like boots and rawhide laces, stepped gingerly toward the dark green bin—the most recent load was from a nearby town's weekly collection. Some papers lay windblown and strew across the ground around the dumpster. Many were wet and compacted, sticking together like *papier-mache*. Others were dated news and a variety of colored advertisements from supermarkets and pharmacies.

The smell of two-day garbage impregnated the air around him. Garbage odors were pungent and ever persistent. Even in cool weather, the recent pile was over a day old and would not be transferred to another recycle site until Monday or Tuesday afternoon.

In time, he managed to find portions of newspapers from the last three days. They were not in any order by section; A, B, C, D or E but through painstaking precision and sheer luck he was at least able to find local news specific to the surrounding towns, towns that were in close proximity to the recycling center.

He was approached by no one while he dump-picked, and saw no other animals besides the feral birds that seemed to scatter at the sight of him. They brazenly lighted on adjacent dumpsters patiently waiting for him to depart.

He found a discarded antique wooden fruit box. He thought it useful. Attached was a label of a California grower—painted peaches and a landscape of art from a Central and Sacramental Valley producer. He thought all peaches came from Georgia. Not so. The box was clean and sturdy and was well constructed.

He compiled a representation of recent papers in the old fruit box and spent a few additional minutes searching for scraps of outdated food from the local restaurants and grocery stores. There was more than he had anticipated, including fairly fresh produce and breads that were most likely only "days old," but edible.

One pile of waste was from a local McDonalds where leftover French fries, wilted salads and overcooked burger remnants or chicken parts were "free protein" for him. They had been previously cooked, but apparently went unsold over time. They were dried out patties, but he had found and eaten them before. None of what he collected even came close to moldy. It was essentially "fresh garbage."

He headed into the woods using the same path he had used to descend. The wheels of the hand truck left no discernable marks in the woods. He was careful not to make the load too heavy.

The sky looked threatening. It was about to storm again and any tire tread marks would be obliterated by the next day's natural runoff of mountain water. He scanned the sky and hoped to make it home before the deluge.

* * *

Festus had built a fire in the cook stove. His wet clothes were hung nearby, drying. He added wood as needed to help dissipate the damp air inside. The increased wind was chilling as it howled and rattled the windows. Festus managed to consume some of the products of the dump scavenge and his belly became distended over his waistline.

The box of newspapers sat to the right of his bed. Under the light of a lantern, he painstakingly perused each page of the local news.

Most of the newspapers were from the previous Wednesday to Saturday. Any news sections not relevant to his quest were used as fuel in the stove, that being sports sections and advertisements. Anything that would implicate the date of his trip to the dump he burned to ashes.

A Friday edition was virtually complete in content, including separate sections for NATIONAL NEWS, SPORTS, ARTS, BUSINESS and LOCAL happenings. It looked like it hadn't even been read. Festus had noted that section B was LOCAL news but the front page of section A contained breaking news stories from the previous day or two. One story was about a murder—the Stillwater event.

The prior funeral for Barnaby Stillwater was listed in the obituary section, with lengthy; multiple columns, which included a picture of a casket and six pallbearers emerging from a private church service the day before. A flag-draped, mahogany casket was held level as the men descended the stairs following a High Requiem funeral mass. An entourage of men dressed in black suits and starched white shirts, most of whom were professional businessmen, balding and well seasoned, looked somber and mournful. They were obviously close friends and business acquaintances, or even relatives of Attorney Stillwater. He was a Vietnam War veteran and an honor guard was representative of the corps. They stood at attention as the coffin passed.

Festus read of the account of Stillwater's murder and the man's life, obviously cut short by a senseless act of violence. He noted that the police had leads concerning one or two individuals who reportedly had been seen at the general crime scene. The descriptions matched the intruders on his property!

The men had on baseball-like caps according to one witness who had noticed men in dark clothing and jeans running from the crime area.

The sound of a gun had occurred and had been heard by another witness near the train station cafe.

The extreme darkness of the evening, with little moonlight visible and subdued lighting near the parking area, prevented the witnesses from adding more details to their accounts. The perpetrators of the crime were purportedly men in their 30's. The police deemed the approximation of the villains' age by the witnesses subjective at best. They had no *definitive* proof of how old the suspects were.

Festus Gravel rubbed his cheek numerous times, and then stroked his jaw with an open hand. His thumb and forefinger were spread apart across his chin, as if he was in pensive thought. He knew that the person he had buried had been wearing camo and a baseball-like cap as described in the papers. A change of jeans was in the backpack.

The news article elaborated further on the fact that no money had been stolen and Stillwater's Rolex remained on his wrist after the murder.

A license plate from the lawyer's car had been taken. It was noted in the article that the vanity plate read, AMEND2. Festus almost fell over from fright. The license plate was the same one he had in his possession.

"Holy shit," he blurted out. "Them were the guys that iced this lawyer," he said to himself. "They friggin' killed this guy. I knew they was bad." His command of the English language was obviously poor and became virtually redneck when nervous.

Festus stopped short. He could hear a helicopter. Whoever they were looking for that morning had not yet been apprehended. He now knew where *one* was. The passing chopper hovered over a nearby clearing and Festus was sure that the State Police were about to land and search the area where he lived, perhaps on foot. He was savvy enough to know that missing persons in the woods of New Hampshire were easily tracked, or rescued by Fish and Game personnel, not the State Police. The State Police offered tactical support.

The Fish and Game officers were mobilized and utilized if hikers and mountain climbers were in dire straights, usually on the highest peaks. They were needed when people were ill prepared for severe weather. The adverse effects were often generated by fog, rain, snow or high winds. Rescues could be perilous for both the victims and for rescuers.

Moments later, the helicopter moved to the west and Festus breathed a sigh of relief. *Were they gone?* They may have noted his chimney smoke from the fireplace or wood stove; a stove that provided heat in the chill of autumn, as well as a hot surface to cook his meals.

In the news articles he noted that a stolen car had been found abandoned in a remote parking lot near the base of the mountain—his Mt. Hoosac. The license plates had been removed and the car hidden in dense brush of pine boughs and bittersweet.

Few other details of the vehicle were provided in the news article. The VIN for the car matched one that had been absconded in an adjacent town, and was reported missing to the authorities by a local owner.

Festus assumed that the State Police were searching for the thieves in his geographical area, an area fairly close to his cabin. Ledges, caves and overhangs could provide refuge for the suspects. The police were focused on those possibilities.

Shells from a small caliber weapon had been retrieved at the scene of the Stillwater crime. The caliber cited in the new papers was the same as the pistol that Festus had found by the dead man—the man he had shot and buried in a shallow muddy grave. It was a 9 mm, the kind police use in their job, in addition to a .38.

Chapter 8

Festus emerged from his hut to check on the now swollen stream. In the isolated portion where he had buried the man's body, there was an absence of accumulated water that should have pooled. The fallen leaves had created a dam elsewhere. The ground had soaked up much of the torrential rains and the excessive run off. He scanned out the area where he had buried the physical evidence.

He was startled and nauseated when he saw what appeared to be a hand or fingers sticking out of the ground. There was jewelry on the ring finger and the color of the hand had darkened in death *Rigor mortis* was apparent. He leaned over and wrestled the ring off, sticking it deep in the pocket of his overalls. The swollen, bloated finger did not give it up easily. It grossed Festus out as some skin ripped off the bones.

Jesus, he mumbled to himself. *What the hell?* The persistent rain had quickly eroded some of the dirt away from the shallow grave exposing the part of the body, mainly the left hand and cupped fingers. He took the ring out of the pocket, his hands still covered with muck from the mixture of dirt and leaves. He rinsed it off in a pool of water.

Upon initial inspection of the jewelry, he could see an inscription on the inside of the ring. It was not a wedding ring. He would need his reading glasses or a magnifier to decipher the initials or words.

Undaunted by the morbid appendage, he nervously reburied the hand with his foot, scraping and callously pushing the semi-stiffened body part into the mud with his boot.

He thought that he had buried the torso deep enough in the ground, but the storm had carried some of the dirt downstream, both earth and small pebbles. Leaning against the shed was a flat piece of heavy slate he had acquired from a nearby ledge. Festus placed it over the location of the interred hand and newly repaired soil. There was little chance that any future rain would uncover that part of the body again.

* * *

Festus Gravel knew from the newspapers in the dump that someone had killed a well-known lawyer in an adjacent town. He now suspected that the man he had shot in the mist, and buried near his cabin, was one of the alleged perpetrators of the crime. The unique vanity plate was the clue. He also realized that the authorities would contact the owner of the stolen car, the one that had been left hidden in the dirt parking lot at the base of the mountain. The link between the wanted men and the automobile was inevitable. No wonder the helicopter focused on the general area of his home, he thought.

Festus, putting two and two together, realized for the first time that searchers would again be in the general area, and for an extended period of time—clearly seeking out suspects who *might* be on foot. They had no clue that one was dead.

The helicopter was just the beginning. They would now be combing the area for clues! That meant that his home and the surrounding area would probably be a *focal point* for the search. There was also a good chance that he might be sought out and interviewed by the authorities. He was unsure as to how he would handle the encroachment, if strangers were to be around his self imposed exile and land. His life was about to be disrupted but he did not know to what extent he would be involved. He feared the worst.

Aided by the light and flickering shadows of an oil lamp, Festus lay back on his bed and pondered the day's events—cautious and reflective of the confusing uncertain details. He stared at the ceiling of logs and intermittent mortar, hand-packed insulation between timbers, consisting mostly of mud, shredded paper, straw and twigs. When dried and hard, the mortar above his head appeared like horsehair plaster, mimicking the wall covering of an old Victorian home.

The insulation technique was that of some Native-American tribes, particularly in the Southwest—members of tribes who often used nature's creations to protect themselves from the adverse elements. They combined raw materials similar to the construction of a bird's nest. The composite seemed to hold up in the rain and snow reinforcing the ceiling of the cabin. Leaks were easily repaired with nature's provisions and the occasional trip to the dump where leftover construction materials and building waste were readily available. Corrugated roofing was an alternative, but sometimes plentiful from completed construction sites. He covered his small shed with the plastic or steel roofing.

The dump materials were free for the taking and stacked in a designated "metals" pile or in plastic bins, and Festus was appreciative of local contractors who were wasteful—those builders who threw away materials that, when combined, seemed sufficient to build a new home from scratch.

Chapter 9

General John Stark was a motivator from his earliest life in the wilderness. He was characterized as a man with blue eyes and prominent features, an extended nose and sharp jaw line. He was of average height and spent his early years as a hardworking lumberjack and farm worker. His later duties as an adult in the militia would enable him to be a brilliant tactician and excellent General.

Many of his contemporaries felt that he exhibited the prowess to anticipate what his enemies would do in battle. As a strategist, he often outsmarted the enemy forces and leaders, taking unusual approaches to surrounding the British and supportive mercenary Hessian forces. This was amazing since Stark oversaw an untrained militia of citizens while the British had a formally trained "army."

General Washington was fond of Stark and often confided in him by correspondence. Stark's rank was dependent on how many troops he raised. At one point there were a thousand under him as a colonel.

Festus Gravel had taken American history in school when he was young. Surely few people knew who Stark was back then. Gravel didn't even grow up in New Hampshire. He was southern born and his parents were uneducated. Festus left school at age 16 and hung out with the wrong crowd when he was bored because they were entertaining peers.

His father grew peanuts or soybeans on a local farm. His mother was a homemaker, primarily raising Festus and his two brothers. The brothers never married, or relocated north. Festus hitchhiked from the South at age 19, mainly to escape poverty. He never went back to his roots. His influence and peers were those people who were staunch believers in the U.S. Constitution, basic "flag-wavers" of the 1950's and 1960's. They took the words in the document *literally*.

He managed to enter the U.S. Army in his early twenties and all he had learned to date, as an elderly man, was Army life, survival and discipline, ingrained in his brain from drill sergeants and Army formality. Once out of the service, he became a nomad—he had no real caring relatives or close friends. His brothers lost track of him.

New Hampshire appealed to him because of its remoteness and his ability to be a loner when he wanted to be. Anyone who met him in passing found him odd, almost antisocial and distant. He expected nothing from anyone and offered nothing in return.

Festus "drank" a lot in his 20's and 30's, almost dying one night in an alcohol-infused car accident. Whiskey and beer were his staples, homemade at times. As he aged, he cut back on the liquor but did not eliminate it. He never reapplied or regained his license to drive.

Anything that he drank for pleasure, he made himself if he could. Applejack was easy since New Hampshire had many apple trees where he often stole bushels of the fruit from local orchards, fermenting the brew each fall.

He would freeze the fermented mixture of smashed apples, water and natural yeast from apple skins in a barrel. Festus later tapped the center of the wooden keg and out would pour a concentrated liqueur (applejack) that was virtually 100% ethyl alcohol with a hint of apple flavor, generally consumed as a drink for sipping.

It took little effort to get high or drunk on the amber liquid.

He would "cut" it with apple juice or water. The homemade concoction required no preservation. It was preserved by natural chemistry—the highest proof of alcohol attainable. A trace of methanol remained in the brew, harmful but unknown to Festus. It could literally make you blind.

As an excuse to drink, he would toast General John Stark frequently, sometimes daily. The bizarre ritual was all he knew at the end of the day or week. He drank out of boredom.

Festus was a recluse and his daily agenda was almost the same daily itinerary. His lack of interaction and communication with people caused him to talk to himself, and he did that frequently, especially after consuming the homemade liquor.

* * *

Festus Gravel was born on August 28th. Oddly enough, he shared the same birthday as General John Stark. Stark was born in 1728, however. People born under that sign are Virgo in astrology; they are creative, intelligent, impatient, analytical and quick thinking. Festus had some of those qualities but lacked discipline and strategy, qualities that Stark possessed.

The only real common connection between the two men was their military service and ideology, albeit two centuries apart. Stark was, by definition, a *maverick, one who refuses to abide by the dictates of, or resists adherence to, a group—a dissenter.* Festus Gravel was a renegade calf, a field stray from the mother, and Festus was independent as hell.

The fact that they shared birth dates inspired Festus to be a patriot, a freedom fighter, often quoting or admiring . . . even idolizing Stark. Festus, as a young man, studied Stark's life—historical notes later edited by Stark's offspring and his grandson.

The Starks were of Scottish-Irish descent with a name that was akin to *strong* and *rugged,* as in the Germanic sense. Archibald Stark, the father of John, left Ireland with his wife, Eleanor and their children. They sailed to Boston Harbor in 1720. There was famine, a poor farm economy and highly contagious small pox in the country of origin.

Stark's father wanted a new life for his family. Their first three children unfortunately died from the plague while at sea, and received a watery burial in transit. This devastated the parents—physically leaving behind their children to the depths of the ocean, and in God's hands.

The Starks and their shipmates were rerouted to Maine because of Boston's fear of the dreaded contagion.

It was only later that they were able to settle in what is now, Londonderry, New Hampshire, referred to then as the town of Nutfield. John Stark was born eight years after the perilous trip from Ireland.

The Stark family weathered a variety of contagious diseases up to, and including, the 1730's. Many other immigrants, some 1,500 in number, died from the plague(s), many victims of which (one-third) were innocent children. Many of the Irish immigrants perished during that time period, a travesty since there were no cures for the various pathogens they encountered.

Festus Gravel never had that challenge with fate. His parents did not emigrate from a foreign land under dire conditions. There were no plagues in his life. When he was young, there was polio that could have affected him, but he managed to escape that virulent contagion and Dr. Jonas Salk and his vaccine saved many peoples' lives in the 1950's.

A young John Stark managed to develop friendships with other children, some of who were thought to be Native-American children. Little is known of John's early life or interactions in historical accounts. He later learned the language of the Abenakis who captured him in

1752. He respected the "Natives" of his parent's new land and learned from the customs of the local tribes.

In an effort to mimic John Stark's bravery, Festus Gravel had tried to learn Native-American languages or words that Stark may have used for communication. He had a sheet of common words that described objects and nature. Because there were no tribe members to converse with, his desire to speak the language fluently waned. Any remnants or descendants of Native tribes resided north by the Canadian border, and were inaccessible to Festus in his reclusive life. He traveled nowhere.

Chapter 10

The police fervently continued the investigation into the murder of Barnaby Stillwater. A prominent citizen and lawyer had been brutally murdered and for no obvious reason. The motive was subjective at best, but leaned toward his philosophies that were controversial.

The town folk were in fear not knowing the reason for the murder or if the perpetrators were still at large and still in the area. Chief Colin Randall was fastidious in his endeavors to find the culprit or culprits. Stillwater was a friend of the police department as well, having prosecuted many villains in the past.

Tom Moore was just as passionate in helping with the investigation. He felt that the political views and political orientation (anti-conservative) of his partner might have been a motivating factor in his violent death. It was a political election year, both locally and nationally, and Stillwater was not shy in expressing his alliance to traditional Democratic ideals. His letters to the editor and OP/EDs in regional papers emboldened his opinions, formally stated on paper in "black and white."

Some locals with leanings to the right, the far right, often chided him but out of ignorance. They spoke from emotion and often failed to write coherently, when in fact they probably should have researched their prevailing facts in more depth and detail before assailing him.

Stillwater would respond with follow-up letters, but in a manner of eloquent prose—"chopping them off at the knees" so to speak. He finally realized that he could no longer educate the *stupid* or *ignorant*.

Moore continued to seek his own evidence and met with the police behind closed doors.

"I know of no enemies per say," he offered, with certainty but regret. "There was no indication of threats to the office or to him directly—nothing pertinent in the office mail or files for that matter."

The chief sat back and tapped his pencil on a pad of lined paper. It was a yellow legal pad. Occasionally, he looked at his notes and then at Moore. He had a list of questions that he had prepared in advance for the lawyer, afterthoughts from the last meeting.

"Was he ever threatened at home?" he asked of Moore. "I mean, was his family threatened or he, personally? Might you know?"

"Not to my knowledge," Moore added, rubbing his eyebrow nervously while trying to recall.

"He never mentioned any issues."

Moore continued.

"There was the recent stealing of political signs off his property," he stated, "but that happens to everyone most probably. It's political vandalism by opponents, or kids."

"Signs?" asked an officer seated at the table. "What signs?"

"Yah, you've seen them. Ya know . . . stealing yard signs for candidates that you don't support. Kids and people do it all the time, especially if you don't *support* who is running or those that differ from you in political views. It's common practice, basically vandalism by boneheads that think that by removing them it will help their *own* candidate."

The chief responded. "Did he tell you that the signs were gone? Did he say who he thought took them?"

"No," offered Moore, "he really didn't have a clue, that is . . . Attorney Stillwater."

"Perhaps it's relevant and then again . . . maybe not," said the chief. "Kids will be kids, but on the other hand, adults can be vicious and stalwart in their political views. Stealing is *still* a crime even if some 'nut job' comes on your property and takes something like a temporary endorsement sign or not."

The chief sat back and looked out the window. Leaves were flying in all directions. The day was cool and the foliage distractingly beautiful. Maples and birch were showing off their Kodachrome "pallet" as they always do in autumn. New Hampshire, like Vermont, was a Mecca for tourism in the fall. It was revenue for the state when visitors drove hundreds of miles north just to go "leaf-peeping." This year was no exception. It was a spectacular show of color since there had been much summer rain and the colors were vibrant. In dry spell years, the reds, yellows, purples and oranges were often muted—but not his year. As the chief became engrossed in the colors, he heard the conference door open.

The interview of Tom Moore by the chief of police continued further when Detective Dave Sims appeared in the room. He was impeccably dressed in a blue uniform, tall in stature and in great physical stature and shape. After the introductions, Dave spoke about a theory that he had—*was Stillwater shot because of his license plate that read AMEND2?*

"Attorney Moore . . . did Barnaby Stillwater often interact with people who voiced their displeasure over his license plate—the one that is lettered 'AMEND2'?"

"Sure . . . all the time," he offered. "Some people were civil about it and others were not. They chided him on occasion. Some respected his opinions on gun control and the wishful restrictions of assault weapons."

Sims followed up.

"Did they threaten him or try to steal his license plates, might you know?"

"Not to my knowledge, detective."

Moore pondered the question a bit more.

"Wait . . . now that I think about it . . . perhaps once. Someone tried to pry off the plate but failed, as I recall. Last year. Maybe they liked it or maybe they didn't. Some plates are stolen because people like the words or initials—they see them as collectibles or as adornments in college dorm rooms for instance."

The detective rubbed his forehead lightly with his hand. A pencil was stuck between his first and second finger and frown lines appeared on his brow as if he were perplexed or maybe interested in further information.

"Possibly . . . but some people argue erroneously . . . that *gun control advocates* are also against the U.S. Constitution," Sims offered. "They claim it's a constitutional right that is guaranteed by the 2nd Amendment. Gun lovers seem to *broaden* what the forefathers wrote and extend it 'to the right to keep and bear *any* arms.'" He chose his words carefully. "The advocates forget the part about 'a well regulated militia,'" he added.

"I know all too well," exclaimed Moore with a sigh. "I have often had to defend those *rights* in the past, sometimes with reluctance. Gun owners in this state think that 'the right to keep and bear arms' precludes any other restrictions, and the NRA supports that claim. They are against any gun control laws, however modest."

"Right," added Sims, "the NRA interprets the U.S. Constitution differently than most folks. They distort what the forefathers were referring to, and they distort the judicial rulings that have occurred in the last 200 years. The NRA has disregarded court cases at the highest level."

Moore was well versed in the amendment. "Look, the 2nd Amendment was quite specific: 'A well-regulated militia, being necessary to the security of a free state, the right of the people to keep and bear arms shall not be infringed.'" He sat back while Sims thought of the meaning—a historical phrase that was *militia* specific.

Sims responded,

"Yes. They often forget about the 'militia part' citing that the *people are* the *militia,* therefore the whole country of citizens has the right to arm themselves with anything."

Moore added, "Surely, the whole country back then was not a militia. Each of the states had their own militia; there were citizens who were *ordinary* folks who did not serve *full time,* but were 'part time' soldiers." He hesitated and breathed deeply.

"The militia definition is the *crux* of the problem . . . and Barnaby knew that. 'Well-regulated' referred to the training of such *part-timers,* since the militia personnel supplied *their own* arms and practiced military exercises away from home. If outside forces or people stirred up rebellions, the militia would curtail it. They were essentially the first army in a way . . . the first 'National Guard.'"

Sims agreed. "Today, people think it applies to them as *individuals* when in fact they are not a *militia,* but individual owners who want the *same* rights."

"The population or populous was not a *militia* any more than it is today . . . the military was *separate* from the residents, so the amendment has been stretched and misinterpreted to include the general population, *unfairly.*"

Moore added to the premise—that the militia was a "selectively trained" body under the Constitution.

"In the 1770's and later, the militia was basically young, 18-year-olds. Some were a bit older, perhaps up to 45-years-of-age, and generally able-bodied whites. It was not meant to describe *all* citizens, male, female, kids and hunters!"

He shook his head since he was aware that the 2nd Amendment was probably the most abused of all the amendments of the U.S. Constitution.

Modern day debates and discussions had actually *distorted* the intentions of the Founding Fathers. They had no clue how the nation would evolve in a modern 21st century America, and with a mass of 231-million people.

"There was a specific *Federal* army," mentioned Sims, who was knowledgeable.

"In many ways, the 2nd Amendment was proposed to prevent the Federalists from disarming the militias in the new 'states.' Since the U.S. no longer has 'militias established by citizens,' the amendment is *obsolete* in many ways. Perhaps that's why Barnaby wanted the 2nd Amendment, amended again!" Moore was duly impressed with the officer's knowledge.

Chief Moore interjected a comment.

"Gentlemen, the motive may have been as simple as some nut job or two opposing 'a license plate?' Is that what you're implying?"

Moore was quick to respond.

"Probably so, since Barnaby had that plate for decades. Renegade constitutionalists with right-wing political leanings often took offense to Barnaby's mission—the wishful changing of the U.S. Constitution. Although he was not a judge or member of Congress in D.C., he felt compelled to speak up and out, locally, on behalf of New Hampshire."

"For that he was shot?" asked Sims, with disgust. All of the men shook their heads in dismay. The prevailing motive was merely an unproven theory at this point. No one really knew why Barnaby was killed but evidence of Stillwater's beliefs supported a working theory for his demise.

Chapter 11

Rebecca "Becky" Godkin was in her senior year at Lakes Region High School. She was popular with classmates to say the least, primarily because she was stunning, levelheaded and outgoing in personality. She had inherited her mother's facial features and hair; therefore she was blonde with blue eyes and displayed a firm jaw line that was almost Christie Brinkley in anatomical structure. Her profile was however more Michelle Pfeiffer in likeness: a stunning portrayal of youth at its finest, as well as virginal innocence.

Becky was a cheerleader and fancied the high school football quarterback with whom she had been a classmate since junior high. He had moved to New Hampshire from Westport, Connecticut, a community of affluence and influence. Todd Baylor was equally as handsome with blonde hair and rugged features that most high school cheerleaders desired as a mate or boyfriend. If toy dolls were to be made of the couple, they would be the typical Ken and Barbie, except that both students were bright, scholastic achievers and on the honor roll.

Any Friday night in fall was high school football season and Becky was captain of the senior cheerleading squad.

The Saturday after one of the most winning nights in football against rival, Penacook High, came fast and against a well-organized and experienced team. The Lakes Region team had trounced the opposition 35-7 and both Becky and Todd had celebrated the victory at a friend's home—a post game party. They were obviously in love, perhaps "puppy love" at this stage in life, but both had remained virgins to date. She had been raised Roman Catholic and he was Protestant. Todd's father was a successful and prominent IT computer businessman from southern Connecticut—with ties to the banking industry in New York City. His office was actually in New York and he commuted from Connecticut before they moved to New Hampshire. Stressed from the New York work atmosphere, the father needed bucolic New Hampshire. He retired just before turning 50-years-old. The Baylor's were now a family unit again and any anxiety dissipated.

On Saturday morning, Becky and Todd had agreed to hike the local range near Mt. Hoosac. They had prepared themselves well for the hike, stuffing a backpack with water bottles, a bag of trail mix (granola-like packets) and sandwiches for a picnic. They had hiked the range before and noted key vista points in the past, often wandering off the beaten path to see views of the Lakes Region and water bodies other hikers were less familiar with.

"Look at that cliff on that ridge," she said, pointing to the vista overlooking a pond. "Let's sit up there for a while," she added, longingly. Todd agreed that they could access the ridge with some ease. They wore hiking shoes with thick soles for gripping the steep and jagged incline. Dressed in jeans and warm vests, they observed their breath hanging in the chilly air.

"Follow me, babe," she offered, "I can see an open clearing and this path seems to get us there fairly directly—a shortcut perhaps." Her ponytail swayed back and forth with each step as she trudged up the hill, a path that was framed by aging pines and oaks at least fifty to seventy-five-feet tall, pristine old growth in a fairly uncharted area. Todd followed her, often gently pushing and stabilizing her while placing his finger in a belt loop of her jeans. He was no fool. The view from behind her was enticing. If there was a finer butt in high school, no one knew of it and Becky was not one to hide her attributes. Her jeans were tight, not loose, and she loved to be noticed, especially by her boyfriend. They were actually too tight for hiking, but the fabric was stretchable, designer-like and accommodated her every move.

In twenty minutes time, they both were winded but were able to reach the plateau they had noticed from below—it was shy of the summit but still a mountain peak worth investigating and pursuing; it offered a perfect vista of the western peaks and foothills of the White Mountains. The rocky ledge was slate and granite, with many areas that had been eroded or flattened over time, including open spaces and smooth surfaces that had been warmed by the sun in the early morning. Bug season was over and the dew on the low blueberry bushes and golden rods sparkled in the sunlight.

Becky reached for a water bottle, Aeropostle '87 in brand, but refilled with home refrigerator-filtered water. They quenched their thirst with gulps of the cool, clear solution. The view was magnificent—a clear day with vistas forever.

The couple was only a mile from Todd's car, an SUV, which he had parked in the same lot that had been used by the two strangers that Festus had encountered.

The Festus Gravel cabin was only 1,000 feet or less from the resting point, and not in direct view from the teens own vantage point on the ledge. Numerous pines and hardwoods blocked a view of the hermit's cabin. His fire in the woodstove had diminished that morning hence no real smoke was visible from the makeshift chimney.

Festus awoke that morning and had stacked some wood that he had felled and split in late spring when the climate was more reasonable. The wood was almost dry even though the recent rains had been prevalent. He used a brown plastic tarp from the dump to cover the stacked wood. He anticipated a cold winter this year so an appropriate number of cords were already accumulated.

He had a keen ear in his old age and often could hear voices that resounded off the nearby hills. He knew that hikers liked the fall season; they ventured into the woods and he avoided them as best he could. He found their banter and laughter irritating—disruptive of his solitude.

This particular morning was no different and he could hear a boy and girl off in the distance. He placed an open hand against his right ear to enhance the volume of their conversation. Their voices were garbled but he knew people were nearby. Festus had seen other teens on the ridge in the past. He referred to them disparagingly as "horny little harlots," for kids were *not* his preference, *nor* to his liking.

When the leaves had fallen, there was a distant view of the ledge especially if he walked a bit to a select vantage point on his property. The ledge was a "lover's leap" secret place where kids made out, or could pet or have sex. He had witnessed it before and Festus, being a loner, was keen to be a voyeur of sorts.

Festus had few women in his life and satisfied his own sexual desires over the years by taking matters into his own hands, or hand. He possessed a few copies of Playboy from years past. Having positioned himself strategically below the ledge with a pair of binoculars, he sat on a boulder and scanned the ridgeline. With one pan of the binoculars he spotted Becky and Todd sitting above his hidden vantage point. In due time, he would be entertained.

* * *

Police Chief Randall and Attorney Moore postulated that the motive to kill Barnaby Stillwater was deeper than most people had presumed. Somehow, the motive seemed to be related to gun laws and rights and issues where the common person desired any kind of weapon that he or she wanted. The advocates often used the 2nd Amendment to empower themselves and justify the possession of anything with firepower.

Having had a conversation in the bar with Stillwater shortly before his demise, Moore reminded the chief that in 1939, the U.S. Supreme Court emphasized that the "obvious purpose" of the 2nd Amendment was to "assure the continuation and render possible the effectiveness" of a "state militia." Later in 1969, the Supreme Court upheld New Jersey's strict gun control laws and, in 1980, the court supported the ban of felons possessing guns. The Court reiterated prior interpretations in the 1960's and, later in the 1990's—which a modern day "militia" referred to what is now known as the "National Guard."

"Illinois went further, chief," he touted. "One town in Illinois passed an ordinance banning handguns, except for the military, law officials and gun collectors. Boy, did that piss off a lot of people. A plea to the U.S. Supreme Court in 1983 was declined, so the law remained."

"Holy shit," the chief responded. "That had direct impact on the state's right to keep and bear arms, at least in that case."

"Yup," Moore added.

The chief was inquisitive. "Is that what Stillwater wanted to do?"

"Not sure, chief . . . not sure. He was adamant about seeing the 2nd Amendment changed, even at the local or state levels. He had witnessed too much violence with kids shooting kids, and kids killing adults—often with their parent's *assault* weapons. Take for instance the historic Columbine shooting and another in Littleton, Colorado just this year, in early 2010."

"He had participated in a couple of "children's cases" in juvenile court. Some were eventually tried as adults and held accountable for their premeditated deeds."

The chief tapped his pencil on a notepad. He was jotting down important facts, an attempt to relate the death of the prominent attorney to a prior gun violation case in court. He could think of none in the recent past. He wondered if the perpetrator or perpetrators were prior clients of Stillwater, or perhaps opponents to his ideological agenda. Did Stillwater have known enemies from older court cases? No one knew.

Both men needed to research additional New Hampshire criminal weapons cases and mandates on gun rights, as well as Stillwater's previous personal case load. There could be a link.

They agreed to meet again, later in the week. Moore wanted to review Barnaby's court cases of recent note—ones that might further elucidate why his colleague had been targeted specifically, and intentionally killed. Revenge was often a motivator in other national gun-related cases.

Moore never felt robbery was a motive, but he wondered if Barnaby had long-term enemies, unknown to him personally. No one knew if there were predisposing issues. Moore surely had no knowledge of any—he had worked closely with Stillwater.

Attorney Moore left the meeting at the police station. The chief stepped outside to smoke a cigarette. He had tried to stop smoking in the past and today's stress was just the kind of day to enable the habit.

His hand shook in the chilly air. He was frustrated by the lack of promising leads, except for an abandoned car that had been spotted by searchers. All indications were that the Stillwater perpetrators had used a stolen car during the crime and after the horrific event. *Were they hiding in the woods? Had they used the car lot as a diversion and then 'thumbed their way' out of that geographical area?* The parking lot was near a major highway across the state. They could have "blown town," and be long gone.

* * *

Becky Godkin buried her head between Todd's neck and shoulder as a sign of affection and for warmth. They sat close enough together on the granite precipice so that little wind could pass between them. She was in love and his arm was behind her, hand gently patting her back. They were teenagers who planned to go to college the following September. Although they were true to one another, both knew that love required frequent interaction and companionship.

College often challenged existing relationships, as each person would meet new and interesting people from around the nation. There were concerns that they might drift apart over time. After all, "absence makes the hearts grow fonder" . . . *but for someone else,* was the caveat.

"Do you think we will still be in love a year from now?" she whispered, with trepidation and sadness. She faced him and rubbed his cheek softly with her hand.

He sighed and reassured her that his love for her was true, no matter what. She responded in kind—a pledge of commitment.

"Nothing will change, honey. If I go to UNH and you go to another school in New Hampshire, we can get together on weekends, and often. Our love will grow stronger. We'll both have cars."

She smiled, reassured by his thoughtfulness and sincerity.

"That would be wonderful. I don't want to lose you. You being a football star will have many girls chasing you all week long," she said, tenuously, and with remorse.

"How can I prove to you that I love you?"

Todd kissed her cheek and embraced her from the side. She turned and whispered in his ear.

"I want you to make love to me, right now . . . here in our *special* place."

Todd was startled by her comment but his desire for her had already manifested itself. He felt a rush, warmth between his thighs, and she was quick to enhance the moment by fondling his jeans and stimulating him, smiling directly into his eyes.

"Are you sure?" he said, with reticence. "We haven't done that before."

"I know," she replied. "But I want you to always desire me . . . and only me. I'll prove my commitment to you."

Without much hesitation, they caressed. They simultaneously unbuttoned each other's clothes, first their shirts and then their pants. It was lust. She had brought a blanket, albeit a small one, picnic-sized, tucked neatly in her backpack. It was intended for use in their picnic on the ledge but neither one cared much about food at this point in time.

The blanket was an impromptu "bed," like the well-known lyrics of the Mary Chapin Carpenter folk song, *This Shirt.*

She crouched in her bra and panties, then stood slowly and looked around for strangers or hikers. Apprehension set in. There was no one in view as she crossed her arms in front of her bra for privacy. Becky was insecure and afraid. She wasn't on contraceptives, the pill or otherwise, but assumed naturally they would have intercourse. He had no protection either.

In the heat of the moment, she didn't care. Lust, excitement and innocence prevailed.

"Are you okay with this?" he asked, softly. He stood directly in front of her. "Are you afraid?"

"Not really," she said, kneeling and facing him. She was gorgeous. Todd knelt as well. He was in his underwear and obviously aroused. They lay back on the blanket and kissed, first simply, then repeatedly with intensity. Passion prevailed.

"Will it hurt?" she asked. "I'm not sure what it will feel like. I hear it's painful the first time. There's blood and all, my friends have said."

"I don't know, honey . . . I'm not experienced," he commented, somewhat embarrassed by his lack of knowledge.

While they kissed, they fondled each other, innocently beginning to giggle in unison. Apprehension and excitement grew for them both.

She stopped abruptly, in fear of someone being present. He looked around cautiously to reduce her anxiety.

"Did you hear that?" she whispered, blue eyes wide open in fear. She turned an ear to the woods nearby. There was nothing. "A noise . . . thought I heard a noise," she voiced, with concern. There was no one.

"No. What did you hear?" He was scanning the area for visitors, animal or man. "I heard nothing."

"I thought I heard someone," she said with some paranoia, "voices!"

He listened once again more closely, cupping a hand to his ear. He said nothing for a moment. His eyes wandered back and forth. He squinted as if his visual acuity would be better.

"I don't hear anything," he repeated. "It's probably the wind in the trees, the leaves."

She began to relax. "Just nerves, I guess. I'm nervous," she said, coyly. Moments later her undergarments lay to the side of the blanket and he was undressed as well. She had worn an enticing thong for underwear and Todd was stimulated even more when he saw her in the nude. She was statuesque, a supple figure akin to a Roman goddess. He had dreamt of this vision for months. It was now reality.

Becky guided his body slowly between her thighs and for the first time in their lives they were linked as one entity, a symbiotic, undulating combination of flesh as if they had practiced the rhythm before. They hadn't.

They seemed to know what to do and yet "nature" choreographed every motion, that being the natural impulse of human desire.

The cool air didn't bother them. The warmth of the moment made him climax ahead of her but he did not stop after the moment of ecstasy. He kept her pinned to the ground and repeated the motion until she smiled.

He let her passionate moans reach a crescendo and she experienced her first, real orgasm—the first of two that were moments apart.

He smiled, self-pride in pleasing her.

She gasped for breath but Becky sighed and exhaled a long, warm mist that hung in the air, and then seemed to dissipate into the atmosphere. He kissed her gently. She held on to him firmly.

After the exhilaration, she experienced an inner pain in her lower abdomen. She had lost her virginity, a moment in her life not to be forgotten, and deep in New Hampshire's woods. He hugged her closely as she grimaced, eyes closed for a moment. She held her breath and the pain subsided.

There was a faint, but gentle smile on her face as they lay side by side in the autumn air, fingers intertwined tightly until their knuckles were white. Sweat formed on his forehead and between her breasts. The passionate dew glistened as he comforted her with words of affection.

"That was wonderful," she responded, out of breath. "Can we do that again . . . soon?"

Todd, surprised at her desire, placed his hand across his bare chest.

"Give me a minute, hon. I need to catch my breath. You are the most beautiful thing I've ever seen."

"Thank you. You are an Adonis yourself," she responded.

Becky rolled over and lay on his chest. There was a tinge of blood between her thighs. He had experienced the crimson color on himself. She straddled him again, sitting erect. She took advantage of the opportunity, being coy and sexy. She was a vixen and deserved round two.

"You are somethin', football man."

"So are you, my love," he replied, smiling at the thought of her renewed desire. "It was worth the wait."

She closed her eyes, "Yes . . . worth the wait. I have given myself to you, to you alone."

The sun appeared as incidental light from the west and shone down on them directly. Her body was warmed by the sun, her back directly illuminated by its infrared rays. The chilly wind had subsided and they embraced, whispering sweet nothings. It was approaching late afternoon and the light would be fading fast. Autumn meant shorter days as winter approached.

They knew they had to start for home, and before the sun set. Each of their cell phones had recorded voicemails—they never heard them ring. They recognized the familiar numbers of home.

Becky knew her parents might check on her since they had been gone for hours. Parents get concerned when their children pursue woodland adventures. Sometimes cell signals can be lost or absent and that worried her father tremendously.

After dressing, they held each other like newlyweds. They stared at the landscape of a nearby mountain. A helicopter was noted in the far distance as they descended. They feared their escapade might have been noted. Both kids laughed at the sight of the aircraft, thinking the worst of a potential close call. The authorities, however, never saw the sensual encounter on the ledge.

"This moment I will remember forever," she voiced, in innocence. "I knew you would be the one."

He smiled proudly and agreed. They were still kids after all. He felt like a king, a man, yet he remained speechless. He was in awe of the experience and kissed her.

A hundred yards below and to the left, sequestered in the woods and pines, Festus put away his old military binoculars and headed carefully down a familiar slope to his cabin. He grabbed branches as he stepped to insure his stability. The sound of the helicopter had startled him as well, as he stood close to a giant pine trunk for camouflage. He feared that the State Police might spot him. He remained still for a while, and then moved closer to the cabin. The helicopter was a safe distance away.

Festus had observed the young couple from the beginning to the end of their lovemaking. He was a classic "voyeur," a hermit devoid of female companionship. The scenario of the entangled couple was better than any porn he had seen in his youth, and he was now aroused from the encounter. He closed the cabin door and latched it securely, all the while thinking of their passionate encounter on the granite ledge.

Their impromptu and primal tryst was beyond his imagination. It was as if a button went off in each of their brains encouraging them to perpetuate the species, or at least practice the motions.

Becky was foregoing her stoic Catholicism for a moment of thrills, but would later experience guilt and an obligation to confess her lustful sins to a family priest. Father "Joe" had known her as a child and now as a young adult. He had advised her to wait with respect to sex. *What would he think?*

He probably knew her voice in the confessional. She worried. She rationalized "the intimate moment" in a self-protective manner. *How could God be mad at what they did?* She had proven her love to Todd in the only way she knew how. That made it okay, in her mind. It was love.

They had taken no precautions in pregnancy prevention, and neither of them had discussed the timing of her menstrual cycle, an unknown that could surprise both of them if a child was conceived after the irresistible experience and transgressions of youth.

Festus Gravel, now physically *excited* by the unexpected view from afar, a view that he had experienced occasionally in the past with other teens in lust, fantasized and eventually achieved a climax to his own satisfaction.

He had no woman in his life and he was much older now. It was unlikely he would ever personally experience sex in the future. There was no chance anyway that he would ever feel what the young couple had felt. It was love, passion and the loss of innocence.

He fell asleep shortly after his fantasy was completed. He knew that the woman he observed naked would remain in his mind for a long time.

Festus had watched her stand and meticulously dress in the open—on nature's granite mesa. The teens were unaware of the view Festus had from afar and assumed that no one else was around. They were naïve and wrong. He had been their sole audience throughout the sensuous encounter.

Todd and Becky locked arms as they descended the hill and Todd discovered a local hiking trail that would take them to the parking lot. She continued to lean into his shoulder and Todd's thighs were still throbbing from the sensual motion they had both experienced. It was a new experience for both of them. They were both anxious to repeat the act in the future. It was a "slice of paradise" in teenage terms. The kid's virginity was lost simultaneously and the age of innocence was gone, forever.

Chapter 12

John Stark was ahead of his time, even ahead of Abraham Lincoln, when it came to his compatriots and neighbors. Stark believed in "the equal rights of men" and stated so in his apologetic letter of 1809 to the Battle of Bennington Reunion Committee. Festus Gravel never knew that aspect of Stark and his compassion for all people, and all colors.

Festus Gravel was a maverick as well, like Stark, except he was a selfish maverick. He was a recluse for a reason. He never really got along with people and he sided with those politicos that read into the Constitution and the Bill of Rights a "literal" translation that was at times irrelevant and outdated hundreds of years later.

Times had changed and so did the United States government. It was more complicated with 230-million inhabitants and multiple ideologies, and ethnicities.

His only acquaintances in life were renegades of sorts, including men similar to the ones that he had shot in a foggy and limited light situation; he was of the same ideology as them but less violent and less radical in thinking. Festus was not aware of their radical association and wondered a couple of days later who the men were and why they had breached his posted property.

Festus was crass and often told people who didn't agree with his opinions that they were fools and unpatriotic. He alienated himself from the norm and his only friends in his adult life were people who were less educated, or performed menial jobs. Some were avid NRA gun fanatics. The 2nd Amendment was their "culture" and their expression of freedom.

Often they took actions to the extreme, especially when confrontation was imminent or apparent.

Festus Gravel sided with people who did not conform to authoritative rule, regulations, taxes or common decency and civility. Decades earlier, he had stood in crowds of fellow "constitutional" ideologues, especially at military gatherings, or American Revolution reenactments and limited VFW functions, but only on national holidays.

The constitutional fanatics were pseudo-wannabee-modern day Forefathers. He was young and wore his hair long then, often standing back in the shadows of the crowds; crowds that were overly patriotic in dress and demeanor.

Unlike General Stark, Festus had become a bigot, a man who was an obvious racist. He frowned on Jews, African-Americans or people from the Middle East—innocuous Muslims, not the terrorists that were extremists. He was ignorant.

Until his death, General John Stark feared that England might again encroach upon America in their attempt to suppress the "new" republic. He felt they were trying again to curtail the newly conceived and emerging government's growth and sustainability. Stark, however, did not show any bigotry and he fought with men of color.

Festus was unaware that it was "men of color" who built the White House and other prominent memorials of granite and marble. New Hampshire marble was present everywhere in D.C. and they played a role in its creation.

Festus, an ignorant man in many respects, only saw men of color as dirt, of lesser value than Whites, and obligated and relegated to slavery, similar to the controversial times during the birth of America (1700's-1800's).

He thought their blood was black, not red, an ignorant concept since all men were equal in body and soul according to General Stark. They were also equal in biology and the human genome. *Homo sapiens* was still, *Homo sapiens* and *God-created, Black, Yellow or White.*

Festus also condoned the Black mans' subservience in a scenario similar to the fate of "Uncle Tom." The pejorative term, "Uncle Tom," was condescending to African-Americans who were dimly viewed in a famed novel by Harriet Beecher Stowe, known in modern literature as *Uncle Tom's Cabin (1852).* They were *a people* who were dominated by "White" Americans. Uncle Tom was the main character in the book, a book that Festus never personally read.

Today, an "Uncle Tom" refers to black people whose views might be detrimental to African-Americans as an entity, especially with reference to politics.

Stowe's book played a role in the Civil War, and was based on the opposition to slavery and the prejudices against *Blacks* in general. She was ahead of her time.

Abraham Lincoln met Stowe in the 1850's and said, "So this is the little lady who made the big war." But Stowe never intended for "Uncle Tom" to be denigrated. In contrast, the book became an anthem for the anti-slavery movement in the United States.

Festus Gravel never studied Stowe's work in school so his "preconceived" ignorance was "bliss." Even more appalling is the fact that there are many bigoted Festus Gravel's in the United States to this day.

* * *

Robert "Bobby" Cummings, age 29, was one of the two men who had haphazardly come upon Festus's cabin in the woods. Bobby was a troublemaker, beginning in his teenage years.

He had already removed from his wounds some of the buckshot with a Swiss Army knife—that shot which he had received from Festus's shotgun.

He was a survivalist, self-trained.

After the incident, Bobby had made his way down the mountain, and hid out for a day near the local dump. He planned to thumb his way west to Laconia, "The City by the Lakes."

For an hour, repeated drivers passed him by. Finally, a passing truck driver gave him a lift, noticing that the passenger had been injured. Dried and stiffened blood, dark in color, permeated Bobby's jeans. The passenger said nothing about his wounds but willfully accepted a ride from the gentleman.

"You alright? You're bleedin' man," the driver offered, with concern. "You hurt yourself?"

"I'm fine," replied the injured man, cupping his thigh. "I got injured in the woods; fell off a small ledge into a crevice, into some blind ravine while hikin'. I managed to get poked by some branches. The leg is healin' okay."

"Looks like you were bleedin' pretty good, son. 'Liable to get infected," the driver added. He was concerned.

"Do you want me to take you to some local clinic or hospital? It's not all that far from here." The sympathetic truck driver thought the wounds looked more severe than Bobby had mentioned. Bobby shook his head, no.

"Thanks, sir. I'm fine. Really, I'm fine," replied Cummings, frequently looking out the passenger side window.

The truck driver said little more and in a matter of fifteen minutes dropped Bobby Cummings off near historic Veteran's Square, a memorial park with monuments dedicated to all war dead as well as those still living—those participants in "all" military campaigns.

Bobby thanked him profusely and hobbled to a nearby public restroom to clean up. The injuries were still oozing crimson when he walked. Much of the pain from the multiple pieces of buckshot had subsided, that is until he hyper-flexed his knees to get to the restroom. No one was present in the bathroom, but the stench of pee on the floor suggested that the facilities were used by transients, much like himself, and often. He gagged at the odor of intense ammonia.

The injured man was able to wash much of the blood off his skin and pant legs. He used a hand dryer on the wall to warm and dry his jeans.

The facility was not heated and the autumn air chilled. He was hungry but wanted to avoid the public knowing full well that he was back in the town where he had shot the popular lawyer. He hadn't expected that fate with the driver!

The town was quiet and no one was on the main street. He saw a nearby Dollar Store and bought some generic Band Aids for a dollar and some change—also a newspaper for .50 cents.

He traversed some residential streets off of the main drag and to remain inconspicuous—an attempt to get to a local highway (Route 3) that would eventually take him to the I-93 Interstate.

The sun was setting in the late afternoon and his persistent thumbing paid off as (finally) a passerby in a pickup truck gave him a lift to the nearby town of Tilton—an eight mile ride west. He hitchhiked to southern New Hampshire by way of Route 93 S, and on to Route 101 W.

The car he and his buddy had left behind had already been removed from the parking lot at the base of the mountain. It was impounded behind a chain-linked fence at the police station. The authorities noted that it had been stolen locally and traceable to the date of the Stillwater murder. They scoured the vehicle for evidence.

Bobby Cummings was destined to rejoin the group of "Freestaters" in southwest New Hampshire. There was an annual gathering of the Free State Project (FSP) continuing the next few days in the town of Jaffrey. There he would be among acquaintances of a similar mindset and could change clothes, destroy the old bloodied clothing in a bonfire, and mingle unnoticed within the mass of revelers that celebrated "liberty" in their *own* ideological way. The non-conformists, unaware of Bobby's torrid history, would be his acquaintances for the week.

* * *

The town of Jaffrey is near the Vermont and Massachusetts borders; Vermont is to the west and Massachusetts lies to the south. Jaffrey is easily accessible from Route 91 in Vermont, Routes 101 or 202 in New Hampshire, or from Route 2 in Massachusetts, all major conduits.

The Grand Monadnock mountain region surrounds Jaffrey and other small communities. Elevated at 3,165 feet, the popular range is attractive to hikers during the summer and autumn months.

A local Native-American presence (the Sokoki band of the Abenaki tribe) existed there for 10,000 years and prior to the colonists and modern "Man." Archeologists confirmed their presence in history, in New Hampshire and Vermont. They were hunters and farmers, a tribe that grew squash, beans, tobacco and corn. They were free-spirited survivors utilizing the three nearby lakes for water sources and the mountains for hunting game.

One lake, Lake Contoocook and its tributaries, flowed north toward Concord, New Hampshire—one of a few rivers that do so in the entire United States. Most rivers flow south.

The colonists came to appreciate the mountainous area. Some came from the seacoast, Portsmouth in particular to the east. Lt. Seth Wyman in 1706-07 was the first colonist to climb Mount Monadnock. Others would follow, realizing the value of the land and local waters for fishing, farming, hunting and food production.

The population of Jaffrey borders on 5,500 inhabitants; the township was established in 1773 in Cheshire County. Patriots from Jaffrey, some 52 in number, served at Bunker Hill during the Revolution and later in the War of 1812. They were active members of the John Stark *marauders* and military—those that represented and fought at the Battles of Bennington and Saratoga.

Stark commanded many farmers and tradesmen from all over the southern portion of the state. Bennington, Vermont was near Keene, and convenient to the band of patriotic militiamen. Stark utilized what he could for volunteers. He was a master at commanding hundreds, if not thousands, of troops from any geographical areas that bordered with central and southern New Hampshire.

Formerly a possession and township of Massachusetts, like much of southern New Hampshire, Jaffrey became part of New Hampshire in 1741 when new geographical boundaries were mandated and approved by King George. The township became "official" in 1773, shortly before the Revolutionary War.

Today, the quiet community touts a safe and healthy lifestyle, and draws retirees and people who desire solitude, the New Hampshire woods and New England colonial history. There were mixed emotions when the "Freestaters" invaded the area for their annual ceremonial gathering. It was viewed as somewhat disruptive for the quaint little town, but a financial boost to the economy.

Historically, famed literary writers have found solitude and inspiration in Jaffrey. Noted authors, Hawthorne, Emerson, Kipling and Thoreau climbed Mt. Monadnock.

Emerson called it, "the new Olympus" and Hawthorne thought it to be, "a sapphire cloud against the sky."

The reason for the vivid description is well known; the top of the mountain is windblown and lacks hardwoods and fir trees, yielding pastel hues of indigenous rocks and boulders smoothed by time, inclement weather and history.

Granite rocks can appear as distant shades of gray, blue, deep green and charcoal.

Hawthorne was perceptive, for at a distance, the mountain peaks appeared to him to be a condensed cumulous mass held against an untainted navy blue sky.

Jaffrey is the only geographical place in the world that claims that particular name as a town. It was named after George Jaffrey, who *never* set foot in the town. He was from the coast, Portsmouth, and a Masonic proprietor who invested in land everywhere. Little is know of his political leanings or any Libertarian views. He probably had nothing but the foresight to buy valuable land.

Historically and uniquely, the murder of a prominent doctor in that town has "scarred" the community and tainted Jaffrey for many years. It remains an unsolved mystery to this day.

Dr. William Dean was murdered in 1918 and the sad event is claimed to be a dark moment in the town's local history. Perhaps the spirit or mystery of the torrid event in the town attracted the modern day followers of General Stark's mantra to that area. Outwardly, they appear as free-spirited as the colonial patriots and their descendants, those that followed Stark chronologically but deviated drastically from his philosophy.

The colonists for "liberty" were not only relegated to the males or patriots of the day. The women of Jaffrey played a role, supporting the troops, feeding and caring for them while their husbands were at war in the late 1700's, in Vermont and New York.

Much like Stark's wife, Molly, who did the same, the women raised their children solo while their husbands were absent fighting battles that continued on for months. The difference with Molly Stark was, that she actually went to Bunker Hill while her husband was fighting there. She stayed in Medford, Massachusetts during the crises. She brought her 15-year-old son, Caleb with her where it is claimed that she fought the enemy, along side her young son.

Knowing Stark's legacy, there is little wonder why the "Live Free or Die" mantra became the inspiration for the liberty advocates, including the FSP's desire to encroach upon the New Hampshire landscape. It remains a vain attempt to make the politics of New Hampshire more ultra conservative and Libertarian in principle.

John Stark surely did not call his men to arms for that objective. He might have found the modern day Freestaters' agenda in direct opposition to his ideology. Civility was paramount in his time, not anarchy.

Libertarians, on the other hand, feel that big government has encroached upon its citizens' rights—those principles established in the past. The majority of New Hampshire residents do not condone today's "virtual Libertarian militia." Festus and Cummings were by far in the *minority*.

New Hampshire, being open-minded, is cautious as to who may assemble or infiltrate into their geography, armed with alternative objectives, measures and influences on an already established democracy. Jaffrey in recent years just happened to be a small town caught in the fray.

Chapter 13

Festus Gravel was aware of the Free State Project. He had read of the organization from the occasional news articles on the emerging group, a group that desired to entice and assimilate new followers into their ideology. Their agenda was and remains an attempt to create a "new society" with an emphasis on "limited" government. The *maximum* role of government, in their eyes, is solely for *the protection of liberty, life and property*.

A recent event in Raymond, New Hampshire attracted FSP members to the town common. About forty protesters, some with guns, gathered in honor of a hastily arranged International Day of Peace, with a blatant show of unconcealed weapons, which to local resident's, was the *antithesis* of peace. An odd juxtaposition of two agendas.

A local woman resident wanted to organize the "yoga for peace" effort in September 2009, but the town fathers had rejected the request without more information from the yoga instructor as to what the proposed agenda was for the "gathering." The FSP members supported her efforts, and showed up *en masse* touting the 1st Amendment right to assemble.

The locals in the town knew little of the FSP members' objectives. It was a bizarre gathering to say the least and Festus was aware of the controversy, which he had read in a news article.

Obviously Festus already had property—that on which he resided as a squatter. Basically, he was "sitting there" free and clear of encumbrances like taxes and constraints of the state legislature. In New Hampshire, residents paid property taxes in lieu of a state income tax. Festus paid nothing and contributed nothing monetarily directly to society—he was a hermit and a freeloader.

The FSP members sought a reduction in *all taxes* and a reduction in regulations in general with a concomitant *increase* in individual rights.

They supported a free market system and a reestablishment of a Federalist government, constitutional Federalism. *Liberty* remains their focus of their agenda, yet the term remains ill defined and obtuse.

Activism by the FSP would eventually impact many states that are small—New Hampshire, at 1.3 million residents, was being influenced by potentially 20,000 FSP members, at least from a political aspect.

The FSP was already advertising in obscure magazines—advertising for new members to join nationally. Of those national publications, *Cannabis Culture* and *Liberty Magazine* were reaching people of a similar mindset.

Oddly, the FSP remains unconnected to any formalized political party and offers no candidates for election. The group does not fund campaigns. Some of their New Hampshire members have run for state offices under the guise of either Democratic or Republican principles, depending on which political party has the best chance of winning. In many respects, the FSP seems to lack impact—especially without influencing elections with "campaign financing" or backing a winning candidate.

Festus knew of their ideology but was traditionally "Independent" in his thinking. He sided with some aspects of their thinking but he also shied from other extremist concepts of the FSP Libertarian organization. He was a loner and did not participate in the political process.

The FSP settled on the state of New Hampshire as their "home ground" after much evaluation and research of states that were *tolerant* of others and their ideals. The "Project" desired a vulnerable state in the Union, where "change" could occur for "liberty-minded people," those who desired smaller government and less control over its citizenry. Basically, they wanted political and social radicals who followed their lead for the reform of America. New Hampshire qualified as a seedbed.

They liked the fact that New Hampshire had been rated one of the safest places to live in some national surveys, a state where healthy lifestyles were advocated and the economics were reasonable.

Jaffrey, the town of choice, met some of those ideals. It attracted the advocates because of its small size—smaller local government and limited intervention. Through the affinity of FSP members, especially from outside the state, the FSP hosted the annual New Hampshire "Live Free or Die Rally" each August. Their speakers touted radical change and a self-centered agenda, which included the firing of kegs of gunpowder, revolutionary guns and cannons, (some provided by the Revolutionary Artillery Company) and free on-site camping for attendees. They were John Stark wannabees.

Festus had read about the annual event in a stray news article. Barbecues and rock bands offered entertainment and camaraderie for the attendees.

Locals seemed immune or naïve to the agenda in their town, thinking perhaps it was a "reenactment" of the days of old, akin to the yearly Battle of Lexington and Concord revelers on the 4th of July in Massachusetts. The FSP event was in no way similar to those commemorations.

The "Jaffrey days" were filled with patriotic speeches of "liberty" as well. The speakers focused on subjects that included gun rights, the U.S. Constitution, testimonies to the New Hampshire motto by John Stark and revised, but "sensible," drug policies—sensible only to them. They fought any proposal relevant to I.D. laws, often screaming the "infringement of privacy rights." One's identity was none of the government's business especially when acquiring firearms, or the right to bear them.

Festus Gravel found the members' objectives to be bordering on civil discontent and anarchy. Festus hated confrontation, rebellion, confusion or the dissent of normal values in society. He loved the U.S. Constitution but saw the FSP as adversely influencing the U.S. Constitution's true meaning. Festus despised those who were belligerent renegades, ones with a selfish mission in a free society.

One member of the FSP was seen at a President Obama healthcare town hall Q and A meeting in Portsmouth, New Hampshire in 2009. The man's weapon was in plain view of the public, but at an outside gathering of a presidential speaking engagement no less. Even Festus assumed that the U.S. Secret Service was "tuned into" this lunatic. Carrying an open weapon at a presidential appearance was insane. *Was the man immune, or in denial of the history of assassinations of presidents in this country?* Stillwater would have classified the "renegade of liberty," a madman—an abuser of the 2nd Amendment and an illogical thinker.

Perhaps that was why Festus felt that he had to defend himself against strange visitors. He was paranoid about intruders whether they were local residents, or illogical dissidents.

In recent years, Festus Gravel had scared people off with warning shots from his cabin—shots fired high into the air. He never intended on killing anyone. Festus merely wished to protect the land.

Now, due to the recent killing of the man, he had to deal with the consequences of a body buried on his property. Confusion and remorse set in. He could not block reality from his mind, haunting him since the shot was fired.

* * *

Police Chief Randall and Attorney Tom Moore met again toward the end of the week. They had much to discuss relevant to the probable motive behind Stillwater's death. New data was emerging. They were aware of the August reunion of the Freestaters in Jaffrey. During the weeklong event, Randall had sent two undercover detectives to attend the final weekend of the "Live Free or Die" rally. The officers were dressed in jeans and T-shirts, a way to assimilate into the crowd.

That following Monday, they reported their findings to the chief, relative to the FSP's agenda and events. Chief Randall wanted Moore to know of the festivities and details of "the invaders."

Randall had been in touch with the local authorities in Jaffrey and utilized their input and intelligence relevant to the "new movement" in the state. The Jaffrey police were also aware of the recent Stillwater death and possible motive.

In the report by the detectives, it was noted that the FSP agenda and speeches had to do with the abolition of gun laws—any law that restricted possession, ownership or the "open carry" regulations of firearms in public. The police, actively investigating the Stillwater death thought that the attorney's demise might have been related to the recent events in Jaffrey. A direct link between the rally and the murder, however, was missing.

"Nice to see you again, Attorney Moore," Chief Randall said, cordially. "I have some updates on the gathering of the 'FSP invaders' in the southwest part of the state—especially those who attended from other states."

"Really?" Moore responded with interest, hanging his coat on a hook behind the chief's door. "How did your boys do for intelligence gathering? Any breakthroughs?"

"Some advances I would say—it appears that there were many 'handouts' at the festival," offered the chief. "Here's a couple for your perusal." The chief handed the leaflets to the attorney and Moore shook his head. "*Hard right* attitude, eh?"

"For sure," added the chief, with concern. "These loonies aren't in New Hampshire's best interest. Their Web site confirms their mission and ideology! The paper leaflets support their mantra."

Moore peered over his 1.50-magnifiers/reading glasses and began flipping through the pages of the handouts. It was clear from just skimming the paragraphs, without reading the details, that one knew the gist of the agenda of the gathering.

He held his glasses in his right hand.

"Looks like they know the state of New Hampshire gun laws pretty well."

The chief nodded in agreement and then stood slowly. He paced back and forth in the room while stroking his chin. He had notes in his hand, the synopsis memo of the detectives' observations from the rally.

"Ya know . . . they do know the current laws well," added the chief, "but it's hard to fathom how people *abuse* or misinterpret the 2nd Amendment. They never address the *militia* portion, just 'the right to keep and bear arms.' They pick and chose what they want to protect, as long as it suits them."

"True," added Moore, remorsefully, "these people are on a mission to walk anywhere they want with concealed weapons, just 'waiting' to *protect* themselves. They adapt the laws to their ideals, often out of context. They think it's their *right*.

New Hampshire has lax laws currently on the books. I have issues with their interpretation of the 2nd and their rally cry. We are not returning to a Federalist government. This country is not going to reinvent history. That would be lame!"

He leaned back against his chair and instinctively rubbed his thighs, almost with nervous anticipation.

It occurred to him that the death of his colleague might be related to the recent protest at the New Hampshire State House in Concord—the support of an old law to be able to "carry weapons" into the State House or other public facilities. Many Libertarians and opponents of stringent gun laws had done just that . . . walked into the prominent gallery with weapons. Earlier in 2009, some armed individuals in the House gallery stood and shouted at lawmakers. The gallery attendees were belligerent rowdies taunting the legislators. Legislators were scared to vote their conscience.

The visitors were not arrested. The advocates knew of a New Hampshire law which was *formerly* on the books—guns were *allowed* to be carried by anyone into the State Capitol." Moore was aghast.

"Can you believe that shit?"

"With a New Hampshire weapons permit, one could even *conceal* the weapon in those hallowed halls! There was a ban from 1996 to 2006—a ban that made sense."

"Chief, as recent as 2008, the New Hampshire legislature in this proud state, actually *defeated* a bill to "ban guns" in the State House. The crazy Republicans overturned the ten-year ban. The vote was 279 to 19, if you can imagine that.

In late 2009, Republicans once again challenged the ban after Democrats wanted the 10-year ban reinstated and actually approved new legislation."

The revelation made the chief shiver.

Adding fuel to the fire of discontent, Moore informed Chief Randall that there was no central database of "concealed carry holders" in New Hampshire. "Local municipalities kept their own records," he added. Randall was aware of most of the laws, having experienced recent issues that arose at local town halls.

"Basically, the New Hampshire law on the books reads, 'All persons have a right to keep and bear arms in defense of themselves, their families, their property and the state'—(NH Constitution Article 2-A). The Freestaters embrace that law to their advantage . . . for it means more "liberty." A person is not required to 1) pay a license fee, 2) to be fingerprinted, or 3) provide a DNA sample. To them an I.D. requirement is to be treated like a *criminal*. The sometimes ambiguous law and lack of constraints relative to firearm possession helps augment the FSP's recruiting of new members into the state of New Hampshire."

Moore elaborated a bit more.

"That day in 2008, the New Hampshire House chamber was packed with gun advocates. Barnaby Stillwater found the whole scene abhorrent since he actually attended the same session as a guest. New Hampshire state representative, Kjellman, a democrat from Henniker, and the only sponsor of *the bill to ban*, spoke in favor of restrictions. It made sense to the civil populous, but no one followed the Rep's lead for common sense and civility."

"Amazing," voiced Chief Randall. "I can't believe that they once allowed weapons in the legislative branch of this State's Capitol. I'm glad that was rectified in 2009. Barnaby would be proud of the new Democratic leadership."

"Barnaby Stillwater was aghast at the vote that day. He had been a strict proponent of gun laws for years," Moore added, with furrowed brow. "I see a potential link here."

He continued.

"I think that Representative Kjellman lost her subsequent primary bid after that, ya know, for reelection. How sad is that? She was well-intentioned but overruled."

"The Freestaters must have rejoiced that day," added the police official.

"Surely they did," added Moore, "for one guy, David Ridley, an 'anti-gun law advocate' claimed that upwards of 600 people packed the hall and gallery for the vote. They were unruly . . . a mob. New Hampshire is strange that way."

Moore leaned forward in the chair. He seemed perplexed. Chief Randall noticed the now melancholy lawyer and put his hand on Moore's shoulder.

"I know what you're thinkin', Tom. You think Barnaby's attendance that day might have resulted in his death?"

"It entered my mind," the attorney iterated. "Yes, it entered my mind that someone saw him there, or worse, chatted with him or overheard him express his views."

"Perhaps," offered the chief.

"He may have offered public comment and someone didn't like his views . . . the bastards," voiced Moore with distain.

"Let's not jump to conclusions too quickly," offered the chief, "we don't know that, that *one* public disruption at the State House was the cause of his demise, or if anyone knew he was there, let alone know his opinions in the matter. His death might have been a foiled alternate issue, a verbal threat gone badly. Barnaby may have physically resisted. We'll seek out more info on the Jaffrey rally, the State House protest and the transcripts and records at the 'gun law vote' from that session. There may be clues further elucidating a reason for your colleague's death."

Moore agreed. "I'll review the legal aspects as well, and the controversial state gun laws that affected the reenactment of the law."

Moore agreed, but commented,

"Basically, the current law applies to visitors to this state as well. Anyone, and I mean anyone, can carry a weapon in this state, even some rebel from the Confederate states of the past—ya know, the yee-ha's with gun racks mounted in their pick-ups. Some think they can create their own society! That . . . alone . . . is damn scary. Damn fools."

The chief rubbed his forehead.

"There's one caveat in all this gun law horseshit. The Freestaters think that *anyone* can have a gun and that the legislature of the past was on their side for a while. But, hang on," he offered. "I remember seeing a note in the laws relevant to the 'license to carry' regulations." He stumbled though some papers on his desk. "Yah, right here," he pointed. "In Title XII Public Safety and Welfare—Chapter 159 on Pistols and Revolvers, Section 159.6, it states: '*a license can be issued to a person,*' specifically with the caveat . . . '*that the applicant is a suitable person to be licensed.*'" He hesitated.

"Just who gets to judge who is *suitable* to be licensed? In my way of thinking, just about anyone can appear *suitable to be licensed* if they want to. Even 'whack jobs' can be normal and become actors during the application process and go ballistic later, and perhaps kill someone. They could cite that their rights and their life was threatened! It's all bullshit and fraught with loopholes."

"True," added Moore . . . "wonder who gets to psychoanalyze these people who may or may not appear *suspect* during the licensing process. With dozens of residential transplants coming into the state each year, to follow the 'call of the Liberty Bell' so to speak . . . who gets to determine their sanity and prior history as felons or criminals from other states in the Union. The state of New Hampshire is way too lax, it seems."

Randall scratched his temple and sighed.

"Good point, counselor . . . damn good point. It doesn't make my job any easier, or the job of my staff members who have to deal with these potential 'marauders.'"

Chapter 14

Festus Gravel had grown up with pets. Most were mongrel dogs for he generally despised the feline species. He found them to be far too independent for his liking and that annoyed him—a surprise since he was just as independent in many ways. He was no different than them and perhaps felt they reminded him of himself. *Cats only come to you when they're hungry,* he mused. Dogs, on the other hand, always provided unconditional love and a response to a command. They could care less if the owner or master was fat, skinny, unkempt or poor. They loved the owners that treated them well—unconditionally.

Days after the shooting, Festus had acquired a companion dog that had wandered his way to the cabin during a violent thunderstorm. The dog shook and was soaking wet—it whimpered at the front door. Festus was half asleep through the thunder and lightening and approached the door slowly, peering through a crack in the wood. The thunder seemed to resound off the nearby mountains and valleys, and rattle the windows of the cabin. It echoed back and forth as he opened the door to find the dog distressed and cowering, as if it had been mistreated by a previous owner or was merely lonely.

With his gentle voice, the dog entered the cabin at his command. The animal was soaked and his tail was tucked between his legs, most likely in fear. The dog "sat" at his command. It knew the words, "sit boy" and began to wag its tail. It seemed to find comfort in his demeanor and was seeking warmth and protection from the elements—a cold autumn rain and wind. Shivering at times, he was appreciative of Festus's caring concerns and attention.

Grabbing a nearby towel, Festus patted the dog gently and then wrapped an old seed sack around him like a blanket. "It's okay, boy . . . it's okay," he offered. "You lost?"

The dog merely stared at Festus, tremoring.

There was a remainder of a fire in the fireplace—warming coals and the occasional flicker and crackle from a smoldering, fragrant piece of pine. It was warm and the dog seemed to relax and lie down near the hearth. The intermittent shivering of the animal ceased as he stared at Festus almost as if he was an old friend. The extra length of the seed sack acted as a bed for the dog.

"Ya gotz a name?" he whispered to the dog. "Huh?" he added, patting his head and stroking his hair slowly between his ears. The dog did not respond to the question. There wasn't any collar or I.D. on the dog and his fur was matted around his neck where one might normally be worn.

"Name? Guess not," added Festus, patting his head gently. "Ya must be hungry, boy," he whispered. "Need some *food?*"

The ears of the dog stood up at the word, *food*. He was familiar with the question and responded facing Festus, tail wagging. His tail swept back and forth like a windshield wiper and his head was cocked to the left.

"You know the word . . . *food*, eh?"

The dog was dark brown in color with black glossy highlights, almost Shepherd-colored in appearance but noticeably retriever in facial structure. The breed was more akin to a "Lab mix" and the eyes were deep brown like chocolate. The canine was a sorrowful sight after a suspected terrible night in the adverse elements.

Festus repeated the question. The dog's ears perked up again and he tilted his head, this time to the right. Festus could tell it was a male from the wide jaw line structure and large paws. It had been neutered at some point and the animal was sedate as if he was extremely fatigued from a long journey.

Without a name on a collar or an owner's address, Festus decided to keep the animal for a while. He needed company and the feral animal was in need of immediate warmth, affection and attention. One paw was bloodied, as if it had been punctured by a sharp stick or jagged stone. Granite would cause that injury, stone often becoming sharp as a knife when chipped or broken.

Upon closer examination of the foot, the dog whimpered but was not resistant to Festus's gentle handling of his paw. The animal licked the wound and Festus's hand.

"Not too bad, boy . . . as far as I can see."

Festus decided to feed him first, basic leftover meat scraps and some water—meat that he had dried in the shed as jerky. He decided to clean the wound later with an herbal solution that he used on his own cuts. He created and stored his own "salve" just for these moments, unexpected superficial injuries.

"Here ya go, buddy," he offered, setting a bowl of preserved meat by the dog's side. The dog ate as if it had not eaten in days.

After the dog finished and consumed a bowl of fresh water, Festus tended to his wound.

First he cleaned the abrasion gently with warm water. He had a topical botanical "tea" of sorts; one that he kept in a jar on the shelf. It was a concoction of plants, including witch hazel plants and willow bark, an herbal paste that he made by boiling the leaves and twigs of the famed witch hazel plant. He often used it on himself to reduce the redness in his hands, especially after chopping or splitting wood. It seemed to reduce the swelling and alleviate any pain, heal sores and ulcers and treat insect bites. The New England Native-Americans used similar preparations. An oral version as a warm tea was used for dysentery.

The dog didn't mind the attention and licked the paste on his paw until it became unpalatable.

Festus knew it to be bitter, having mistakenly tasted it himself by accident—chapped lips. Festus was not a fan of doctors in general, but he had recipes for "what ailed him" most of the time. A book of natural remedies from the 1960's sat on a shelf, many pages dog-eared.

"There ya go," Festus said, consoling the injured animal. "You'll be okay. It's only superficial and the blood is gone." He spoke to the dog like a veterinarian would in a veterinary clinic—soft and reassuring. In the warmth of the adjacent burning embers of the fireplace, the dog blinked repeatedly and then relaxed on the floor with a massive sigh.

Comforted by the seed sack, he subsequently fell asleep, tail curled back toward his face. Festus added a log to the fire and then retreated to his reclining chair.

"It's no wonder you're tired," Festus said softly, "can't tell how long you been wanderin', but you sure look like shit, boy." There was little response from the dog—merely a contented blink of the eye or two.

Festus relaxed and stared at the flickering fire. He leaned back observing the dancing flames. He stared at the contented animal. Festus felt useful for a change.

He now had a friend.

"Can't call ya 'boy,'" the old man said, "we'll have to name ya something' . . ." He rubbed his forehead as he thought of an appropriate name, one that was fitting and appropriate after an uncanny adventure in the wilderness. He reviewed names he had heard in his youth like Buster, Pal or Blackie. He sat forward and placed both hands on his knees with excitement.

"I got it! You can be . . . ah," he hesitated, almost forgetting the name.

At that same moment, there was a bright, bluish-white flash through a window and a loud crack of thunder that followed! Festus startled himself and the dog looked at him like he'd been shot. The dog stood in fear and next to Festus. He circled once and lay down again, comforted by Festus's presence and immediate consolation.

"'Thunder,' will be your name!" he said, with conviction. "Yup, Thunder! You're don't look that fast to be called 'Lightnin'." The dog raised his head as if the word was recognizable and then laid back down, slowly.

"Yup. 'Thunder' it is, from now on," Festus reaffirmed, stroking the dog's head and chin.

To Festus, it was a *stray* and could stay with him for as long as it wanted. He decided he would fashion a leash in the morning. There was rope in the shed and a piece of light chain that could be a noose-like collar.

Together, they would venture to the dump to find leftover food, provisions that the dog would also find enticing. Festus needed to keep his own food stash for himself. He couldn't afford to waste his supplies on an animal, even a companion dog or otherwise. Winter would be long this year and with much anticipated snowfall, perhaps a hundred inches total. Trips to the dump for scraps would be fewer and fewer. As long as he wouldn't starve, he would share his supplies with "Thunder."

* * *

In the local newspaper, a 2" x 2" black and white notice appeared a day after Festus found the dog at his door. It was a *Lost Dog* ad in the classified section: *Reward: Lost Dog, Answers to the name, 'Lucky.' Black/Brown Shepherd/Lab mix, Reward, Call 535-0020*. Festus would not see the ad. A photo of the dog's face accompanied the listing. In surrounding towns, there were posters of the missing animal tacked up on telephone poles, an attempt by the owner to alert residents to help find and return the lost pet.

Chapter 15

The day after the dog had appeared at the cabin, Festus heard the sound of a State Police chopper, near the mountain peaks. It was circling the area and he again became apprehensive of its presence.

Unbeknownst to him, the helicopter was heading for a landing on another mountain peak, to the north and at a reasonable distance from his abode. The top of the adjoining mountain was flat granite with little brush or fir trees. There were no obstructions to the pilot's approach and intended landing. They had rescued hikers there in the past, a natural landing pad with plenty of clearance for the rotors to rotate freely, unobstructed.

The granite peak had been flattered by time and abrasive weather, and was almost a perfect landing spot but the pilot did not want to chance it this day due to winds. The prevailing strong winds from the north would topple the craft if a sudden gust appeared out of nowhere, thereby endangering the aircraft and crew.

The civilian pilot was Rod Emerson, well known to the area as an experienced pilot and a veteran of the Vietnam War. He had flown Huey choppers in 'Nam, and in and out of Saigon, to and from the battlefields. He dodged and survived rifle fire from the Viet Cong (VC), a military group of the National Liberation Front (NLF).

Emerson could maneuver the ship like a toy, almost ballet-like in inclement weather. He had been shot at in Vietnam and wounded by snipers but always managed to make it back to base with his aircraft and soldiers.

Once a chopper he was piloting burst into flames after landing at a M.A.S.H medical unit. He received one bullet in the shoulder while flying and that earned him a lengthy scar after removal of the round, as well as the commendation from his commanding officer—a Purple Heart.

Wind gusts increased perilously as he approached the site. The pilot decided to hover a few feet off the ground, turn the nose into the wind and hold it steady. Out of a side door leaped two men in darkened jumpsuits. They were camouflaged in olive drab clothing with black highlights. Their backpacks included supplies and weapons, standard issue protection and munitions for S.W.A.T. team members.

The tactical team was different from a standard "search and rescue" police team, one that often traversed ravines and crevices or was dispatched to assist wayward or injured hikers in the White Mountains. Generally, the day-trippers were ill-prepared for inclement weather or were seriously injured requiring a quick descent from a mountaintop, precipice or ledge.

There were heart attack victims or novice hikers, minimally trained in survival techniques, stranded nights on remote or perilous mountains that often became chilly or freezing cold. Starting a simple fire in a rain-infused environment, or seeking adequate shelter, would be a significant task for any neophyte who wanted to climb a peak for the scenic views. Their daytime dreams of adventure often became nightmares of peril.

This "team" was different. They packed serious *heat* to defend themselves. They were on a different mission.

South of Festus's mountain property were parked two vehicles, both "Official" in nature. One was an SUV and the other a 4X4 pickup truck. The State Police and the Fish and Game officers were acting in tandem. The parking lot was the same one that the stolen car had been located, parked in a remote corner. It was a half-mile from the town dump as well.

The authorities were obviously looking for someone with the various law enforcement agencies assisting the flying tactical unit, but on foot.

Festus was unaware of the close proximity of the police and Fish and Game teams below his land. His plan that day was to visit the dump and take the dog for the quick journey for supplies. They would scrounge the area for whatever might hold them over for a week—plus new utensils, old pots and pans and outdated or expired edible food from restaurants. Festus Gravel knew what days local restaurants tossed their leftovers. He could recognize the type of trash bins and colored garbage bags that they used.

People were wasteful, he often thought to himself. He benefited, *since their trash, was his gain.*

Many provisions could be frozen in winter, naturally. Breads, some deli meats, and outdated cans of food could be stored as well, since supermarkets tossed out perfectly palatable consumables. If the product was outdated, the *real* expiration date was often four-six months longer than that printed on the package or label.

Food providers always underestimated the expiry dates, mainly because of 'freshness claims.' It didn't mean that the food was rotten or moldy. Expired dates on cans of vegetables and fruits would probably last another year or more.

All of his nutritional needs were free for the taking. Picking through the bags and boxes that were from Shaw's or Market Basket supermarkets yielded him lots of treats that made the long winter survivable. Those supplies, combined with what he hunted, trapped or shot (rabbits, turkeys and other feral animals), allowed Festus to survive better than most needy people on food stamps. He was a marauder, a hermit and sustainable through years of self-serving experience.

An outdated jar of peanut butter would provide protein, fat and minerals, all nutritional elements needed for the coldest of winters. As for nutritional value, the dump acquisitions often matched or exceeded prison "cuisine," and Festus had spent a small amount of time incarcerated as well.

His life was a book of stories but there were few people who had heard of his experiences or tales. They would go unmentioned to his grave, unless someone laboriously searched his personal history over the last forty years.

Today, the timing of his dump visit with the dog would be to his advantage. His absence from the cabin, while the authorities roamed the woods, was coincidental and timely. Festus was unaware of their investigation on foot.

* * *

The Lakes Region of New Hampshire harbors the occasional political fanatic who dwells on the past political dominance in the state—mostly Republican stalwarts.

Traditionally, New Hampshire has boasted of its stiff conservative views, those based on a historical perspective from the days of the Revolution. John Stark was part of that period and the state was predominantly Republican for decades. Now the Democrats were in office and the majority rule in Concord.

One local New Hampshire station WCON, AM radio, (touting conservatism ala Ronald Reagan) emerged from and hyped the local philosophies of the New England Republican Party, but to the extreme right.

Over the years, different conservative "hosts" of the Saturday program on politics evolved. More conservative discussions *enabled* a belligerent, accusatory and uncivil forum. It became a weekly critical assessment of many politicians elected locally, statewide or nationally. This small band of vocal irritants was nothing more than abrasive, wannabee "political analysts" targeting all Democrats each week. They praised Sarah Palin and Ron Paul in national campaigns. They were into Tea Party politics.

The hatred for anyone who condoned "taxation as a way to pay for social services" was always a target or a repetitive dialogue for discussion. Verbal and written critiques in Web site blogs made it easy for them to spread their venomous accusations without legal recourse from the accused. It was slander and libel at best. They screamed at opponents of differing philosophies on the airwaves, as if they were protected under the 1st Amendment free speech rights, under any condition. In that regard, hate speech was prevalent.

Although libel and slander could be implicit in their attack agenda, few listeners of the radio station paid the "vocal marauders of vitriol" any mind. They were considered lightweights and political curmudgeons by local well-experienced politicos, often touting ill-informed stagnant ideas for social change, not *real* solutions for positive change. Conservatism had changed drastically without a uniform, consistent message.

T.J. Crowley was a crusty old radio show host, one who took his "liberties" and freedom of speech to an extreme, beyond literal. He "hid behind his microphone" weekly, selecting callers-in by sex (avoiding women callers if he could), and by preferred political bent. His right-wing agenda each week was based on his interests in the current events of the week—usually a review of controversial newspaper articles generated his fodder for an "open" discussion.

He dissed healthcare reform, global warming, gay rights, taxes and social security and Medicare. Guests on the show enabled his political leanings, and implied bigotry ran high. His guests objected to, or ranted about, unnecessary social services for the less fortunate, illegal aliens or people who spoke a language different from English. The hosts generally bitched and blamed Democrats for everything, especially the newly elected Dems and their alleged fiscal agenda of spending.

"Good morning dedicated listeners," Crowley would start each week's show. "Here we are again Saturday morning, and we promise you a great show. We have a few guests who you will enjoy, I'm sure."

He always started with the same intro—pleasant enough until they got into politics and blood pressures skyrocketed. Crowley always took two Lisinopril before going on the air. His blood pressure elevated anyway.

"My guest host this hour is Tom Taggert—you know him locally as 'Terrible Tom' since he stirs up the community pretty good, eh Tom?" Crowley chuckled. Tom jumped in.

"Good Morning, T.J. Great to be here, as always. What do we have for today?"

"Today Tom, we will discuss the recent murder of local Attorney Stillwater, news that has dominated the papers and local TV this week. It seems that the authorities think that Stillwater's death is related to his 2nd Amendment views."

Tom Taggert smiled and then snickered.

"I'm not real familiar with his views T.J.," Tom teased. Behind the microphone, Taggert smirked, tongue in cheek. He surely knew of Stillwater!

"Now there ya go again, T.J.," he said, mimicking the breathy Ronald Reagan voice and demeanor in debates, "what proof do the authorities have that Mr. Stillwater was killed by dissidents of any gun restriction laws or amendments? Sounds subjective and fishy to me. You have a gun right?"

"Yes I do. I've always had one or two."

He then answered the question. "That's their take, at present, Tom," added T.J., with conviction. "The police seem to be leaning that way."

"You all out there in the listening audience are aware . . . I take it . . . that Mr. Stillwater was a proponent of a *new* 'amendment to' the U.S. Constitution's 2nd Amendment. His license plate on his big ass SUV reinforced his ideas, which they claim was a vanity plate, AMEND2. That apparently stated his views—at least publicly."

"True," added Tom. "Seems as if one of the license plates was missing from the vehicle that night. He was last seen leaving a local pub—that vehicle being his personal SUV when he was 'allegedly' murdered."

For the next two hours, callers and the hosts of the radio show recapitulated the dastardly crime, and chided Stillwater for his take on gun control and any needed revision to the amendment. The verbal discourse showed little respect for the prominent lawyer, his views or for his untimely demise. It was as if they felt he had *positioned* himself as a target, and *deserved* the fate since he wanted to modify what the Forefathers had decided was to be law, two-hundred-years earlier.

The local radio personalities were attempting to gain notoriety, as if they were the next Rush Limbaugh or Sean Hannity. They were neophytes and miniscule players in a modern world of Web-streaming and international political blogs twenty-four-hours a day.

Their radio station did not broadcast very far. Local listeners to the morning show were area die-hard fiscal conservatives, or nothing at all! There was little room for opposing views.

The radio personalities were not trained in political science, the U.S. Constitution or even knowledgeable regarding "traditional conservatism" and its evolution in the U.S or UK. They relished in the fact that they were known as *instigators*, frequently confronting state and local politicians that had run long and hard campaigns to represent their constituency. Local politicians were legitimate candidates, but the butt of their jokes. T.J. and Tom had never run for any political office themselves.

Self-centered, opinionated and narcissistic, they relied on their listeners of like-mind to foster and inflate their *own* egos. To the egocentric radio hosts, anyone who supported the "down and out" or who were liberal in view, was a villain in society and absconding others' hard-earned money to pay for the misfortune of the downtrodden.

There was no Democratic-equivalent radio station or weekly forum to counteract the abuses of the ultraconservative local radio show.

Radio "chat" and blogs were not needed since the Dems were far more civil in their letters to the editors, notes on blogs or other media viewed or read by political junkies, including fiscal conservatives.

T.J. and Tom merely liked to hear themselves talk and stir up the pot about nonsensical issues. They were coined "teabaggers" disparagingly by local moderates and the "left"—an un-welcomed term for Tea Party advocates.

Poverty, war, healthcare, infrastructure issues and social services required constructive input, not destructive rhetoric and disparagement by the "right." Each week, they whined and bitched about everything and many locals were sick of it.

Listeners to the show, who were fans of the hosts, were of no real consequence in the local general elections. They were a minority and too radical in ideals to gain acceptance of the bold, caustic and unorthodox political positions.

Criticizing or disparaging Barnaby Stillwater was not acceptable to the general listening public. That type of vitriolic behavior was left to Limbaugh and his cronies; they felt—those national TV and radio entertainers making 50-million-dollars-a-year.

There was little humor in the sad event where a man was killed unnecessarily. Disparaging the dead was disrespectful and insensitive, especially to the non-fans of the weekly show.

Murder was murder and no one deserved to be killed for his or her staunch ideology or political beliefs—debated maybe, but not murdered. America was founded on opposing opinions and the eventual resolution of conflict by majority rule, not bullying, tyranny and anarchy.

This one particular radio show discussion, relative to Barnaby, generated a furor of local call-ins who could not accept the two radio show hosts' insolence and disrespect.

Barnaby had been buried two days and was hardly cold . . . in the eyes of many listeners. The motives for, and perpetrators of, the heinous crime had yet to be identified or found. Leads were few in that direction and the radio show personalities implied that it didn't matter who had instigated the crime, Stillwater was trying to eliminate their basic God-given rights "to keep and bear arms." Anyone who didn't follow the U.S. Constitution or Bill of Rights was a traitor in their eyes.

This "literal" approach to an interpretation of U. S. Constitutional law was rampant in many parts of the United States. Some ultraconservatives virtually preferred the radical mantra akin to the old KKK or Nazi followers, those who once had no tolerance for any opinions other than their own.

Festus Gravel's father had been one of those men in the years that advocated violence and rebellion, especially against Blacks. His father loved guns, from pistols to automatic weapons. European weapons appealed to him—those with huge firepower. He had his own unique arsenal for years, anticipating a predestined doomsday or a Communist takeover of the United States. He grew up in that era of fear. Bomb shelters were the rage.

The radio show hosts had other topics on their gun agenda this one bright Saturday morning. Much of their discussions involved New Hampshire's restrictive gun laws, Charlton Heston's NRA proclamation "from my cold dead hands" which he shouted at the 129th NRA convention in 2000 in Charlotte, NC, as well as a recent story in the newspaper involving an *accidental* shooting with an automatic rifle. A child had been killed firing an errant Uzi and people were outraged.

"Now, I suppose, they will want to ban anything *automatic*," screamed T.J. "People don't understand that it's *people* who kill people, *not* the weapon."

Tom Taggert concurred. "It appears to have been an accident."

"For those that have not heard, Dominic Spano, a responsible father and his 12-year-old son, Michael were at the Westfield Sportsman's Club event in Westfield, Massachusetts. Allegedly, the father and other men have been charged with manslaughter in the death of eight-year-old Christopher Biziij who accidentally shot himself in the head. Prosecutors said the boy should not have been allowed to use the weapon. The recoil was too great."

"Ridiculous!" added Tom, "a police chief hosted the gun event and was charged with manslaughter. It was a controlled, authorized gun show event."

An irate caller was outraged by the broadcasters' naiveté, and pointed out that the kid was being supervised by a teen, not an adult, and that the gun club/ expo rules stated that "Adult supervision would be provided." The caller mentioned that the police chief and club were indicted on four counts of furnishing a machine gun to a minor. They should be held accountable.

"I blame the father," touted T.J., "not the gun. Although the father was present, he stood ten feet behind his son taking pictures, for posterity."

"Nice photo of your kid dying," stammered Tom, cynically. "The father was stupid, obviously. Don't blame the gun."

The caller reiterated that the Uzi is a military weapon, not a hunting rifle or target pistol. "It was designed by the Israeli Army for Israel's "special forces." It can fire 1,700 rounds per minute. It was not intended for recreational use, target shooting or for killing game. The kid had no business shooting it, even in a controlled range! The recoil would require the assistance of an adult to stabilize the weapon."

The radio hosts disagreed with the caller's viewpoint until they found out that kids at the gun show were *only* supposed to shoot .22's. They backtracked and tried to change the subject.

Callously, the hosts claimed that Barnaby Stillwater would have "maximized" and prosecuted this particular unfortunate case had the incident occurred in New Hampshire. It was all hypothetical and subjective. They saw Stillwater as an albatross against gun rights, a person who would have "profited" from the child's death by "ambulance" chasing.

The caller was outraged and continued.

"The child was only four-feet-three-inches tall and weighed sixty-six-pounds. *Small* weapons are known to have less recoil than larger automatics," the caller argued. "That was pointed out by the authorities. The recoil of an Uzi would point the weapon's barrel at the child's face in milliseconds, especially if a child is light in weight. The tragedy has outraged *everyone* . . . but you guys!"

The hosts cut the caller off.

"This kid had adults nearby. Blame them, not the club and Uzi," touted an unsympathetic T.J. "Why prosecute the policeman who coordinated the event and others that shoot responsibly? Everyone is protected by the 2nd Amendment, even the "kids" of America. The right to keep and bear arms does not say how old one has to be."

With that, the call-in board lit up with lights flashing, all from dozens of people that wanted to take T.J. and Tom to task. They were called various obscenities and unflattering names by irate mothers and fathers, hunters and gun advocates who felt that they were wrong on applying their interpretation of the U.S. Constitution to the callous loss of the child, and also to the Stillwater case.

The arrogant radio hosts could care less. They were indifferent and immune to criticism. They loved the hype and outrage. It garnered them more listeners and advertisers.

"Didn't you learn anything from the death of Mr. Stillwater? How many more children must die before they restrict automatic weapons nationally, even at gun events," screamed one concerned mother on the phone.

"Listen Pal, my lady!" commented T.J., "too many liberties have already been taken away over in the last two-hundred years. We don't need more regulations and bigger government, just people making sound choices with their kids. It was unfortunate, but these things happen from time to time."

The woman got in a quick statement: "Go to hell!" she shouted, hanging up.

T.J. reverted back to the subject of Barnaby's death, and the current inquiry into the suspected murder case. He focused little on any motivation behind the crime, but instead cited praise for the lawyer for "his right to speak his mind" before his death. That was a 1st Amendment right that the host's of the show wished to protect as well. That was akin to him speaking out of "both sides of his mouth" and the callers saw through his hypocrisy.

The show ended at noon with the switchboard on a console still lighting up like fireworks or a brilliant Christmas tree.

Local citizens were outraged at the show that Saturday morning and the insensitivity of the hosts in the recent passing of Stillwater, as well as the unnecessary death of a child by an automatic weapon, one he *should not* have had in his hands to begin with.

Area residents demanded that the radio show be taken off the air in the future. They wanted the hosts admonished by management.

T.J. Crowley and Tom Taggert would have "hell to pay" in the next few days, especially from letters to the editor and direct calls to the station manager. The comments and castigations rolled off the backs of the weekly hosts, like water off a duck's back. Their pompous attitude surpassed all reason.

The manager of the station felt compelled to call an *ad hoc* meeting of the radio station Board over the sensitive issue. The radio hosts had received their just reward—flak from the listeners and castigations from their advertisers, who threatened to pull out their financial support. The radio station Board of Directors compared their insensitivity to that of an insolent child. The hosts had crossed the line.

In a week or two, the Board promised the public a decision on how the controversy would be handled. This would not be the hosts only indiscretion while the board reviewed their callous behavior.

Chapter 16

The officers who descended from the helicopter traveled on foot and eventually approached the Festus Gravel homestead. He was at the dump and unaware of their presence at the cabin. The State Police had literally "scoped out" the self-made fortress from afar before approaching the left side of the building where dense pines were protective of their presence. They moved methodically, first to the back of the cabin and then to the right side of the building. Individual policemen, who came from the parking lot and traversed the woods, watched the door and windows, which were sparse in number.

Automatic weapons, typical of S.W.A.T. members, were clearly in view. Surely, the old man or murderers on the run would not challenge the authority with their hand weapons, or with Festus's own antiquated shotgun. Their S.W.A.T. weaponry could put multiple holes in someone in a few seconds.

Since the door was unlocked, one "Statie" kicked the door open, and then stood to the side of the doorway for self-protection. A second special teams officer, a large man who knelt near the doorway and right behind him, was a backup His automatic rifle was pointed inward, and directly at the fireplace area.

The leader rapidly and methodically panned the room left to right and then right to left, repeatedly, his finger firmly on the trigger of the weapon. His eyes were bulging from the excitement, an adrenaline rush. There was apprehension but no real fear. He was experienced and in command. He was known for his 20/15 eyesight and an expert marksman, even through his protective face shield.

The men noted that the rustic abode was vacant. *Could someone be hiding?* There was no basement or attic. They quickly search all alcoves and hidden areas near the bed and kitchenette. There was no one in hiding. Warm coals glowed in the fireplace, as if someone had occupied the cabin that morning . . . but had now apparently left the building. *Were they on the run?*

The central living area was warm and the stench of a moldy cabin permeated the air. Summer mold never seemed to go away and the pungent smell of earth was that of a partial dirt floor. It appeared to the officers like a cabin from the 1700's, yet it was surely not that antiquated.

The two S.W.A.T. members had no clue where Festus was. More than likely he had not ventured very far since the embers were recent.

They had heard of the hermit, a recluse of sorts, and one that bothered no one. The police had prior knowledge of Festus and assumed, rightly so, that this was his primary makeshift home. *Had the perpetrators whom they assumed to be on the run in the woods injured him? Was he involved in some way, harboring fugitives?* The officers took every precaution and saw no imminent threat.

Perhaps Festus thought that the helicopter was intimidating and hid in the woods, they surmised. In point of fact, he was dump-picking a mile from the homestead, with dog in tow and unaware of the invasion of his personal abode.

They search team left as quickly as they had arrived. Their mission was not to locate Festus; it was to capture one or two men suspected of the murderous crime of Barnaby Stillwater. His house was a potential hideout and *that* was their agenda—to seek out the villains. Had they examined the home more closely, the evidential license plate would have appeared in a nearby wooden box. It was the one that read, in green letters on a reflective white background, AMEND2.

They surmised that one or two assailants might find refuge and warmth in the woods, especially if a functional hunter's cabin was accessible. Festus Gravel's cabin seemed perfect for someone on the run—temporary safe harbor from the chill of a rainy, autumn season.

After an hour, Festus meandered through the woods and arrived home, dog in tow. The dog immediately sniffed the surroundings; head low to the ground like a bloodhound. The old man was unaware that anyone had recently been there.

The dog sniffed the ground near the door and rapidly paced back and forth as if a raccoon or another feral animal had been near the doorway in search of food. There were fresh human footprints in the mud near the door and also by the two windows. Festus suspected that the dog was aware of something, something unusual. It might be the authorities or a wayward hunter—but the dog was definitely onto something.

Festus noted that there were different sized soles and heels, and muddy imprints; he suspected that more than one individual had been there. *Was it the previous trespasser from before, the one he shot at?* Too many footprints, he surmised . . . *Cops!* he concluded.

He placed his newfound belongings and dump pickings at the front entrance and surveyed the property before entering. The shotgun was untouched near the entryway door casing. He was apprehensive and shaking, slowly panning the area completely—360°. He grabbed for his shotgun, just in case someone remained in the area, invading his *space*.

He heard and saw nothing.

The dog continued to run around outside, looking for new smells on the ground. The canine circled the pines and then the cabin a number of times.

"Here boy," he whispered. "What'cha got?"

The dog paid him little attention, busily retracing the odors back and forth until he ran himself into exhaustion. He whimpered, turning his head back at Festus periodically. He wasn't a hound but acted like one—a retriever with a keen sense of smell.

Festus checked the pines, and again noticed alien footprints. More than two sets appeared. He knew a military boot heel and sole from the fact that he had a similar pair in his house.

The damn police had invaded his territory, he surmised. *They had no right to do that.* Perhaps they were from the helicopter, which he had observed earlier. He cherished his freedom and liberties, to the death. He had already proven that, protecting life and property.

Were they lookin' for him or for the missing man? he wondered. He became paranoid knowing that a man was buried on his property in a shallow grave. He checked the brook, which had swelled from the rain . . . there wasn't any evidence that a body was there, no objects of the anatomy were protruding from the soil like he had observed the previous day. The slate was untouched.

The sound of the helicopter was long gone but he wondered if any of the police had been left behind to scour the hillside. He knew that they were trained to spend days and nights in the woods. *Would they return?*

Festus entered the cabin and grabbed his binoculars off a hook on the wall—he hiked to another granite precipice, slightly lower than where the two teens had recently made love. He knew the view from the ledge would allow for the observation of anything unusual, especially now that the leaves were on the ground. The deciduous trees offered little camouflage to anyone hiking or walking in the nearby foothills. Any activity would be readily apparent.

From that vista, he knew the general landscape like the palm of his hand. The binoculars aided him in spotting any potential or unusual activity in the area. He panned the area numerous times, sighing deeply in disgust. No one was apparent and he slowly headed back to the cabin, aided by the use of a cane his father once fashioned from a bull's penis and later bequeathed to Festus. Festus found it resourceful, novel and nostalgic. In the old days, it was a commonplace tool for elderly farmers.

He was exhausted from the roundtrip to and from the hill. He retired to his home to rest.

"Those bastards *trespassed*," he mumbled to himself. "Who do they think they are? I have a right to privacy."

For a moment he thought of history. *What would John Stark have done? Would he have allowed strangers on his land,* Festus asked.

John Stark was a revolutionary man but one with a sound mind. He did not mind neighbors. His principles were for freedom but he was respectful of others, even his military adversaries, the British and Hessians. Stark knew and respected the philosophies of his opponents. Officers respected one another. He was a *maverick*, strategy-wise, but he was a revered officer and appreciated that his opponents had agendas and missions of their own, and values. Their intent was not to kill one another. Capture, yes! Kill, no!

Festus Gravel had no real clue what Stark was like in Stark's time. He envisioned him as a man who put *freedom* above all other values. Little did he know that Stark was not a hermit, a loner or a renegade against authoritative government.

Had Stark not coined the term, "Live Free or Die," he would have probably gone unnoticed in history. Most people wouldn't care about his thoughts, his presence in the military or impact in history.

Festus Gravel was *no* John Stark, but Stark became his fantasy and alter ego in many ways. Gravel owed the world nothing. In that respect, he was and would be regarded in a modern world as a "quirk," a recluse or just a damned fool. *No man was an island.*

Everyone in this world is related to other human beings and to society. The Founding Fathers, the colonists and patriots touted religious principles and decency for the common man. They carried with them from England those ideals or ideology as well as the laws of the "old country" on which to formulate a new beginning, but . . . in a new land.

In that regard, Festus's disregard for laws and authority contradicted the values of John Stark's parents who ended up in New England as part of the historic emigration from England and the Isles to a strange new beginning.

Stark would have never tolerated renegade marauders. They were as much the enemy as the invaders from Britain.

Festus merely embraced and professed the principles of the colonists and statesmen—principles of note, but only the ones he "agreed with." To hell with religion and laws (local, state or federal) he thought, especially if they did not fit his own principles of life, freedom and liberty. Those were his guiding principles, along with an ill-informed or somewhat jaded history of the colonists, the Revolution and America's Forefathers. They desired a rational, cohesive government *of, by* and *for* the people.

The thought of a rational, cohesive government eluded Festus Gravel.

Chapter 17

The Jaffrey gathering of freedom advocates—the FSP attendees, inspired Bobby Cummings. He attended some of the festivities that week, and again on the following weekend while his wounds were healing. His numbed the pain from Festus's birdshot with numerous cans of Budweiser, but he lay low never discussing with anyone the issue in the woods to the north. He was still on the run for the murder of Stillwater.

He thought often of Ryan Cooper, age 30, his friend and fellow accomplice in the Stillwater case. He wondered if Ryan had survived the blast from the gun but assumed rightly, that he was dead. Ryan never moved after the shot was fired. Ryan was bleeding badly when Bobby took off. Bobby had fled rapidly to save his own ass. He never looked back to see if his buddy was okay.

This mission was not like in the Marines where comrades are not left behind. It was one for all and all for one. He sympathized with the plight of his friend if he, in fact, had been killed. Cummings rationalized and justified to himself that the greater mission was to protect the 2nd Amendment—that meant some people would get wasted along the way. In that regard, he was heartless yet he longed to return to the woods to see what had happened to his "buddy." Guilt set in. The more he thought about Ryan, the more he imbibed.

Bobby Cummings decided that he would ride north in the forthcoming days. He was waiting for the dust to settle first. Surely there were people at the Jaffrey gathering that might be heading that way, to the secluded New Hampshire woods or to Canada by way of Route 93 or northwest to Vermont by way of Route 89 in Concord. He figured he could "hitch" his way to the Hoosac mountain range and revisit the scene of the cabin shooting.

Bobby was aware of the general landscape and visual markers of the North Country especially after the encounter with the hermit. He had grown up as a hunter and was fairly well trained in survival skills; that is until the encounter with Festus Gravel. He strained to remember the features of the man who shot at him.

What Bobby didn't know was that Festus was also a survivalist. He figured out that the "other guy," the *second voice* in the woods, might return to seek out the whereabouts of his friend.

Festus was prepared for any adversary. He had backup ammo near the door. His shotgun was loaded and waiting, should the second stranger return. *He had no problem burying two people, if needed.* There was plenty of room on his squatter's property to hide another victim. He was arrogant in that respect and feared no one except, of course, the police in the helicopter, or the authorities on foot. They intimidated him by their sheer firepower, manpower and capabilities for back up reinforcements.

He knew they were now aware of his current residence and property. They obviously saw the perimeter of "No Trespassing" signs, but entered anyway.

Festus sat in his chair and patted Thunder. The dog had just eaten scraps that they had brought back from the dump. The "pickins" were good this particular trip and the dog lay contented on the floor, adjacent to his wiry master. The dog's belly was distended from gorging himself on trash remnants. He seemed relaxed on the seed sack. Festus could care less of its aesthetics since it was merely a buffer for the dog from the cold and damp floor.

A roaring flame in the fireplace had been enhanced by the addition of small logs that Festus had stored on the stone hearth.

The warming effect of the new fire made Festus drowsy, but his mind still wandered from the day's stressful events. He still feared the helicopter and wondered if the intruders of his home had noticed anything unusual. He stood and rechecked the AMEND2 license plate in the box of junk. It appeared undisturbed. The wallet with Ryan Cooper's personal information had been hidden behind a few old books on the shelf. Those history books revealed Festus's temperament and ideology and he was concerned that someone might know his opinions on government, just by their titles. Some of the books were incriminating, in and of, themselves—very political and bordering on extreme views. They courted militant tendencies and could be deemed threatening to those persons of opposing views.

"Damn," he mumbled to the dog, "gotta move that body, I'm a thinkin'."

The dog raised his head as if he understood, but it was merely a response to the fact that Festus had spoken out loud and directed his attention to his new companion. Eye contact was made. The dog's tail wagged responsively.

"Eh, boy?" Festus added to the conversation with himself. The dog didn't respond vocally but flipped his tail as if he understood his new master. The dog was not a "barker."

"Yup . . . gotta move that bastard in the morn," Festus reassured himself of the task.

"The police might find it by some method, like a 'smell dog' or somethin'," he voiced. "You dogs can find bodies," he said, smiling at the dog.

"Where I'm thinkin' of movin' that guy, they will never think to look. Should confuse even the best of bloodhounds."

*   *   *

The morning came fast and Festus was up at five o'clock when the darkness was slowly dissipating from the direct sun in the east. In the misty dawn, Festus grabbed a spaded shovel and started to dig a pit not far from the outhouse. The ground in fall was chilly and sometimes frosted in the morning but not yet frozen. Some leaves on the ground looked sugarcoated. Winter was still a few weeks off. Festus could see his breath.

Sweating, he dug the pit in rapid fashion as the dog sat and watched in wonderment. Each year he needed a new pit for the outhouse. The old hole would be filled in after he moved the tall wooden structure over a fresh pit.

A typical fingernail moon graced the door of the commode, hand-carved by the hermit. It was best to make the switch in pits when the air was cold. There was no odor to speak of, as opposed to summertime when the stench of excrement and urine was aromatic and foul, obviously from the heat and stagnant humid air of July and August.

The sound of the shovel and an occasional pickaxe hitting stone or gravel could be heard resonating off the nearby hills. Festus did not think much of that or worry that someone might notice.

In the distance, two members of S.W.A.T. were encamped within their overnight tents. One officer stirred and was awakened. He noticed the unusual clanking sound of metal against stone, early in the morning.

"Joe, did ya hear that?" he whispered to the other officer in a nearby tent.

"Sure did. What the hell was it?" he said, yawning.

"My guess is that it's the old man doin' some 'gardenin' or somethin' else with tools early."

"Pretty early for gardening," his colleague responded, lying still and leaning on one arm inside his tent. He cupped his hand to his ear to hear better.

"Kinda late for plantin' or too early for harvesting in this dim light. What's the damn fool doin'? 'Sure ain't a hunter makin' all that racket."

They listened again. There was a break in the noise from the other hill. Then it began again. This time it was distinctly in the direction of the cabin.

"Don't know, but we should check it out. Let's get crackin' and head over the hill."

"Okay. I've gotta piss first. This is too early for this shit." One of the men exited his tent to relieve himself.

The two troopers dressed in fatigues, assembled and rechecked their gear, and planned on leaving right away.

They had to walk a bit of a distance to get to Festus's cabin and in the morning light and mist of the previous day's rain, they were not happy about trying to figure out what the old man was up to at such an early hour. They had no intention of actually going to the cabin but wanted to observe his activities from afar so they could not be detected. For all they knew, it could be the suspects in the murder and not Festus Gravel at all.

Festus was ready to slide the outhouse to the side of the existing hole. He used a "Come-A-Long" winch and extra rope that he rigged to a nearby massive pine tree. He cranked the handle back and forth as it ratcheted along the gears, clicking, grinding and groaning. It was physics made easy . . . the wooden structure sliding slowly into position over the new hole. For lack of time, it was much more shallow than the previous one.

The odor was not that bad, he thought. He had added lye to the old pit every couple of months. Lye killed the bacteria and reduced the odor over a year's time.

Excess construction surplus at the dump provided him with some partially used bags of the chemical, sodium hydroxide. Most bags were left over from "end of project" construction sites. Aside from known tissue digestion, lye was used for the chemical peeling of fruits and vegetables, as a paint stripper, drain cleaner, the fabrication of soap and as a cleaning agent. Festus was aware that it digested feces.

Festus had accessed the putrid body of Ryan Cooper buried in the shallow muck of the previous day's rain. The brook had now receded a bit making it easy for him to unearth and drag the now darkened remains from the brook area to the old hole of the outhouse.

He used a blanket to transport it. The blanket left little odor on the ground. He wanted no physical or olfactory trail of the corpse on the ground, especially between the streambed and old outhouse pit. Festus covered his mouth and nose with a handkerchief. The stench of the remains was putrid, worse than animal waste or human excrement.

Prior to Festus dragging the body to the new burial site, the dog slowly approached the mass of darkened, decaying flesh and sniffed the remains as it exited the shallow grave by the stream.

Festus reacted quickly and firmly.

"Git back, boy . . . get otta there! Thunder, get back!" The dog cowered. He was not used to Festus yelling at him.

The dog backed off and whimpered. His face stiffened and his ears dropped low from the harsh command by Festus. He squatted low to the ground and Festus knew that the dog was not used to him reprimanding him. The old man knew he had breached the confidence of the animal.

He immediately stopped what he was doing and patted the dog.

"Sorry, boy . . . didn't mean to offend ya . . . sit over here. Come. Sit!" he commanded.

The dog obeyed and sat at a distance while Festus returned to his covert mission.

He dragged the body into the old pit, grunting and sweating. The man weighed about 160 lbs., he figured. It fell like a sack of potatoes or a rag doll into the abyss. It settled as a crumpled mass at the bottom of the hole mixing with a year's worth of human waste—a total disrespect for a human body—almost curling in, and upon itself—head over knees. The muddied corpse reeked while assuming a macabre position.

The hole was deep enough to accommodate a dead body, and he added more lye and began filling the pit with dirt excavated from the new hole. The combined odors of human excrement, lye and urine, and a decaying body, would probably confuse anyone, or any dog for that matter, from locating the remains. That was supposition on his part.

Festus threw more lye on the decedent, covering the visible brown skin with the white powder, excessive at times, to hasten decomposition. Festus dumped more dirt and then more lye, then more dirt and lye in layers. He buried the empty bag as well.

He was quick in his endeavor often looking over his shoulder with paranoia. He patted the ground and rapidly spread leaves over the old hole by using a broken rake with missing rungs, one or two of the center prongs broken off.

He sprinkled water from the brook over the already wet ground using an old watering can, thereby hiding the recent evidence of digging, the leaves marrying with the muddy mess as if nothing had happened.

With the commode in place over the new hole, Festus rolled up the blanket and tucked it under his arm. There was a reminiscent odor of death and bodily fluids on the blanket. He gagged. The dead man had relieved his bowels in death and stained the clothes, the residue of which permeated the blanket when he dragged it from the streambed to the old pit.

The streambed had quickly closed in the original burial hole with water, dirt and pebbles hiding the former spot where the body had been stuffed shortly after the gunshot had killed Ryan Cooper. Any evidence of a prior gravesite was eliminated by the stream's limited flow.

By the time he arrived at the cabin, Festus reacted to the stench of body and excrement-infused blanket with nausea . . . throwing up into a pail that he dumped into the new pit. He was repulsed first by the "visual," then the combination of the decomposing tissues and smells.

He entered the cabin and immediately placed the blanket in the fireplace, which was still roaring in the early morning. He burned the evidence as quickly as he could, and was relieved and even proud that he had *reburied* the man's remains so quickly. He surmised that it was a foolproof disposal.

The evidentiary blanket sent out black smoke from the chimney. It was a polyester and cotton mix, and the odor in the air was that of burning chemicals from the synthetic fibers and dyes and death. That alone could alert the police who were nearing the cabin after having walked through the challenging wooded terrain from their bivouac.

Festus returned outside and put away his shovel, pick ax and rake. He stored the rope and winch in the shed and then entered the commode and christened the new hole with urine. He had placed residual lye in the new commode. That would suffice for the next few months.

There was no fecal odor as yet, just a chemical smell, pee and vomit.

"Thunder" waited outside the outhouse door until his master was done. He whimpered once or twice, desiring entry, but greeted Festus as he emerged.

Festus whispered, "Shush! Quiet, boy!"

He had already accomplished one more chore prior to the arrival of winter—the new outhouse pit for the coming year. The other mission was to make sure no one would ever find the body. He felt confident that the placement of the dead man in the old outhouse pit was an intelligent move on his part. He was a survivalist and imaginative.

The dog stood and followed his master into the cabin. The dog lay back down by the fire to warm himself. He licked his muddy paws. Festus Gravel sat in his chair as if nothing had happened that morning. He closed his eyes feeling confident that he had achieved the final mission with respect to the dead man. He still needed to bring more wood inside and tend to the fire, but he would relax for a bit.

In the nearby woods were stationed the two state policemen. They had arrived within the proximity of the cabin twenty minutes after the new out house mission was accomplished.

Nothing appeared amiss at least from afar. From one-hundred-yards out, they scanned the cabin. They saw nothing to alert them to anyone who was working outside with tools. Smoke rose from the stone chimney.

The two men were not after Festus Gravel and had no clue that he had buried anyone on the grounds, especially in a privy pit over a year old. They were seeking the perpetrator or perpetrators of the Stillwater crime. They had no reason to suspect the bearded hermit in any deadly plot of Stillwater's demise. They watched Festus emerge for a moment grabbing additional dry hardwood. Nothing appeared out of line and they had no directive to intrude unnecessarily. It appeared to them that he might have been splitting wood, not gardening or breaking stone.

After casing the general area for an extended period of time, they retreated to their campsite and awaited the return of the police helicopter. They had no luck in locating any suspect or suspects on the run.

Festus, unaware of their presence in the nearby brush, heard the return of the aircraft. It passed over his cabin and disappeared down range. He later heard it depart . . . to the north of his home.

He felt smug. He hoped that they were gone for the day, and for good. He wondered what they were on to, but obviously feared the worst. *Would they return?*

The cabin was warm from the fire and he was exhausted from his labor. The late morning passed quickly. With dog nearby he fell asleep in his chair. Nothing seemed to bother him. He was once again a nomad—and to many proponents of liberty, the true definition of a John Stark marauder.

Chapter 18

Bobby Cummings did not seem to fear a return to the woods to the north. He managed to hitch a ride to Concord, New Hampshire and then secure another one to the Lakes Region, just off Old Route 3. The kid who gave him a lift was headed for Alton. In route, he bypassed most town centers that bordered the lakes. The area looked somewhat familiar to Cummings and at his request he was dropped off to grab a meal at a local diner. It was well off the beaten path. No one would know him. The driver, a young teen, merely drove on to Alton. In return for the ride, Cummings gave the kid a "joint."

"Thanks for the ride and enjoy the spliff," he said. The driver was ecstatic and phoned a friend of the benevolent rider and his good fortune.

"We'll smoke the doobie when I get there, man. This guy was awesome. A real southerner who grew his own shit."

It was a popular diner with a "Blue Plate Special" each day—a quick meal *du jour* created by a short order cook who had been there for over 30 years. There were few people in the establishment this particular day and he sat in an inconspicuous corner booth by himself. He ordered the corned beef and cabbage luncheon special and a Coke. A beer would have been better, he thought.

As he waited for his food, he perused the local newspaper, one that was previously read and stacked at the end of the soda fountain counter. He was anxious to know of any developments in the case concerning Barnaby Stillwater. There was a short article and a letter to the editor but little news on the apprehension of the suspect or suspects. He smiled to himself knowing the cops had no leads. The article did not mention the fact that the wooded area in a local mountain range was a place of interest. The authorities wanted to retain confidentiality in the investigation.

The police were in fact seeking *two* people in the crime; that became abundantly clear to Bobby. In his nervousness waiting for his lunch, he toyed with a solid gold ring on his hand, rotating it about his finger in boredom. He was anxious to move on and probably should have ordered the meal to go. The waitress sensing his frustration, checked with the kitchen help on the status.

The gold ring was similar in style to the one Festus had found on the body of Ryan Cooper. It was actually an identical ring, 14K gold embellished with a couple of small diamonds and nondescript lettering. The letters were small and worn, but legible. They were lined in a row and spelled, KKK. In addition was the word, *Liberty,* in script.

* * *

The police chief and a formal investigative committee met again with the detectives who had infiltrated the annual Jaffrey gathering of Freestaters, this time in private. The report by the undercover officers indicated that some individuals and speakers were distinct *proponents* of *unlimited* gun rights—some were also noted NRA advocates.

The prevailing murder theory by the authorities was that one of the attendees or "liberty" proponents might have had a reason to harm Barnaby Stillwater, that is if in fact they actually knew that he was a proponent of more stringent gun control. That position would be the antithesis of the Freestaters' desires and ideology.

It was conceivable that a right-wing advocate might think himself a hero by snuffing out a prominent lawyer who supported restrictions on gun ownership and possession. In point of fact, Stillwater was really only after increased control of *automatic* weapons, those firearms not needed for hunting or target shooting. Barnaby saw no reason why someone should own a BAR, an Uzi or an AK 47. Some of those weapons were used by drug cartels, those who fought U.S. border patrol agents and law enforcement officials who were outnumbered and overpowered by the nastiest of gangs to the south. They used weapons that could decimate a body. Border altercations often mimicked "war."

The chief detective gave a verbal, in depth presentation to a select investigative committee in order to augment and substantiate his written report. Attorney Tom Moore was a *pro bono* part of that investigation—a volunteer, but actively interested in all data on the crime.

"I saw no one in particular that might be a suspect," the head detective said, assuredly. "We hung out with the individual focus groups as best we could in Jaffrey. Many people were gun advocates but no one stood out as a potential perpetrator of such a serious crime as the death of Attorney Stillwater."

A staff member stood respectfully, and questioned the detective.

"You mean to say detective, not one person vocalized or focused on taunting New Hampshire representatives or prominent citizens that were anti-gun? That's amazing since they have been so vocal."

"No. No one, sir," was the response. "I heard nothing of that sort even around the evening campfires."

"It's hard to believe that when these folks gathered at night, smokin' weed and puffing their chests in defiance of people that advocate gun control . . . that they would not have discussed retribution or threatening attacks, ya know, against these citizens, either verbally, by letter, email or by actually physically harming them."

"I saw or heard nothing of that sort," repeated the detective. "My report details the gist of the conversations that we experienced, and I surely couldn't take copious notes . . . especially in front of these yee-ha focus groups. I was maintaining an undercover investigation but nothing was implied by their actions or speech that might *hint* of harming Stillwater."

Chief Randall defended his detective. "Good job, detective. Gentlemen, he has reported what they saw and heard. Except for drunkenness and the occasional slanderous comment about government in general, no one apparently threatened anyone of note at the rally, Attorney Stillwater or otherwise."

He hesitated as people nodded in agreement. "I read his full report and conclude that there was no one exhibiting threatening traits."

Another member of the group commended the officer for his work and report.

"Fine work, detective. Nice job. Compliments to your colleagues as well!"

After the PowerPoint presentation, it was generally agreed that the police were *back to square one* in the investigation. More intelligence was needed.

They had the direct evidence at the scene of the crime, a pistol with some fingerprints, a car that was stolen by one or two perpetrators, and the indication that someone may have fled into the woods ten miles outside of town. Other than that, they had little else to go on for hard evidence.

A police dog that had initially followed a scent from the stolen car quickly lost the trail of anyone who had fled into the woods. The wet weather and rain made the initial search difficult for both man and dog. Footprints were obliterated and the musty, earthy smell of the forest counteracted the dog's ability to locate anything or anyone of suspect for that matter.

Barnaby Stillwater was already six feet underground and the police were at a loss as to what really had occurred after the shooting. The murder case seemed stagnated and the police needed help from the public in pursuing new leads and information. The police needed massive media exposure.

Chief Randall appeared on local TV and requested information from the public on anyone of suspicion or subjects of interest who citizens might have noticed in the crime area or surrounding woods. The chief pleaded for any "tidbits" that might have been observed—perhaps something unusual that night, or a strange person or persons behaving oddly—someone looking for a ride. Initial observations at the railroad station pub were a beginning, but the trail ended there.

After the TV appearance, a number of locals called to report they had seen one or two people downtown who were vagrant, unfamiliar or appeared to be from "out of town." Each of those leads fell dead until the stolen car was located at the base of the mountain.

* * *

Two days after the plea on television, the chief heard from a trucker who called to say he had picked up a stranger on a major highway, someone thumbing who appeared to have been injured in the woods.

"The man came out of the woods near Mt. Hoosac—it was at night," the trucker offered, "and needed a ride. He was limping." He obliged since the man appeared injured and his clothes were stained bright red with blood. The police chief asked the trucker to come to the police station for an interview as soon as possible. It was critical to the investigation and the chief was ecstatic at the breakthrough.

The man agreed to the interrogation—he wanted to assist in the investigation if in fact the stranger was associated or implicated in a crime. No one knew if there was a direct relationship. Within an hour, the driver was at the police station.

"You say the man was injured. How so?" asked the chief impatiently. "Where was the injury? Was the person young or old?"

He apologized for his excitement. The driver understood his anxiety and desire for information. Ron Corvallis, the well-seasoned trucker, with decades of experience on the road, indicated that the man was in his 20's or perhaps early 30's and bleeding from the upper and lower torso as if he had injured his arms and thighs.

"The blood was speckled," he offered. "His shirt and pants had blood stains here and there," he added. "His pants were dirty as if he had fallen in mud, perhaps in the woods."

"Had he been shot, ya think?" the chief asked, stroking his forehead and perplexed. He paced back and forth, waiting for more descriptive information about the rider.

"Might he have been wounded from a gunshot? A hunter's accident perhaps?"

"Don't know, but there were pinpricks of blood like one might see from birdshot, shot that had spread out from a distance. Guess he could have been shot and was lying to me. He said he was hiking and had fallen in the woods injuring himself. He claimed it was from branches that broke and stabbed him in a couple of places. There were no *long* rips in his clothing or jeans—like one would see from a sharp stick. I asked if he wanted to go to the hospital or to see a doctor."

"What was his reply?" asked the chief, impatiently, pacing. He then stopped and leaned over the desk facing the driver.

"Did he say where he was headed . . . or have a name?"

"No. He said everything was fine and that he could wash up and get a Band Aid or two to keep the dirt out. It wasn't that bad," he said. "He mentioned that he was from out of town and merely wanted a ride into town where he could get cleaned up in a public restroom and get some disinfectant and bandages. I think he had an accent . . . like someone from down south."

"Band-Aid? That's odd, especially since you indicated that he was bleeding pretty good from multiple wounds. Did he seem dazed? Incoherent?"

"Dazed no, perhaps 'stoned' though . . . he smelled of marijuana. It's a pretty distinctive odor."

He hesitated. "I thought so as well, regarding the severity of his injuries . . . Band-Aids would do little good . . . he could have fainted in my cab I suppose, or stained my new truck seat, but he didn't seem to be in severe pain."

The chief cocked his head and smiled. "Southern accent like the Carolina's perhaps?"

"I assume so," said Ron Corvallis. "Not sure. They all sound the same."

"Hope he didn't faint."

"I was lucky. He didn't," added Ron. "He seemed to doze off a couple of times. He needed rest as if he was exhausted and cold or . . . on the run. He may have been travelin' a long time."

The trucker gave the police all the details that he could recall, indicating that he left the man near the local Dollar Store. He assumed he would get basic gauze and tape and hydrogen peroxide, or some antibiotic cream.

The driver offered to let him out at a gas station where he could clean up, but the man refused, indicating that he could do the same elsewhere.

"He seemed in no particular hurry, yet he claimed he had to be in southern New Hampshire that evening," stated Ron Corvallis.

"Really? One more thing," added the police chief. "Did he say where he was going in the southern part of the state—like a final destination?" He waited patiently for a reply.

"Come to think of it, the man said he was hopin' to reach southwestern New Hampshire by late evening. There was some 'patriot rally' there, a rock concert perhaps."

"Interesting. That's helpful, Mr. Corvallis. Thank you. There *was* a rock concert and rally down there this past weekend and it may still be going on. Perhaps that was his desired destination, the Keene area. A bunch of political extremists are gathering there for a Revolutionary War reenactment and festival."

The chief explained to Corvallis why the interview was critical, reiterating the fact that a local lawyer had been slain—a prominent lawyer, and that there were one or two suspects who might be on the run in the Lakes Region . . . obviously seeking somewhere to hide.

"The surrounding, dense woods are a great place to start . . . and hide out," offered the chief.

The senior officer thanked the driver for his input and asked him to remain in touch so they could corroborate other information, which might be related to the heinous Stillwater murder. They traded cell phone numbers and promised to stay in touch, as needed.

"I run this route often," said the driver. "I can be available anytime, chief. I usually pass this way at least once a week. Call me please if you need me."

"Excellent," said the chief, "thanks for your help and willingness to come forward. You've been of great assistance. We especially appreciate that you've provided us with a description of the unknown man in your truck. Knowing the age range, type of clothing and injuries which you described narrows down a potential suspect." He hesitated.

"He was Caucasian, correct?"

"Yes—he was the stereotype of a redneck. You know the kind."

"For sure. Thanks again for all your help."

"You're welcome. Glad to assist."

Ron Corvallis left the police station and maneuvered his diesel around the parking lot as if he were delivering goods on a normal route. He was a pro at driving rigs and turned left and out of the parking lot. The nearest highway would take him east—he still had more deliveries in Alton, and later in Newmarket near the seacoast.

It had already been a long day and he still had another two hours of work.

Chapter 19

The cold and damp weather seemed to permeate the bones of Festus Gravel. He could generally handle any adverse weather conditions and often worked outside in the worst of it. Today, however, he felt awful, as if a cold was coming on. He tried an herbal tea that he had brewed, but the congestion in his chest and pain in his joints was excruciating. If it was the flu, it had arrived early in the season, he thought.

The day was overcast and fog hung over the tops of the nearest mountain peaks. He managed to settle into his recliner and covered up with a worn, hand-crocheted blanket, one that he had found during one of his dump visits a year earlier. It smelled musty but he could care less. Come late "spring" he would soak it in the nearby stream and wash it with some leftover soap powder he had found at the landfill. An old tin wash bin leaned against the shed. He used that to soak clothes.

That was one of his post winter chores—to soak winter's clothing in a lukewarm stream, then air-dry the garments and blankets on a rope he had tied between two pines. During fall and winter he was less likely to clean or disinfect anything frequently.

He coughed once or twice as he moaned and groaned, basically pissed at the illness that had befallen him. Simple antihistamines or cold medications like pseudophedrine would have alleviated much of his misery but he had none; he relied mostly on homeopathic medications that he had tried and found to achieve similar results in curing ailments. It was clear to him that he had a fever for he felt hot with frequent sweats that saturated his clothing with moisture and made matters even worse. Intermittent chills indicated that the fever was "breaking."

THE DOG IN THE OUTHOUSE

Thunder lay near him knowing that his master was not his usual self. Dogs somehow know when their masters do not feel well. How they recognize the symptoms is beyond understanding to mortal man or even to a veterinarian. They sense malaise.

Few people know dog psychology if there is such a thing. Perhaps the routine of the day is altered in some fashion, so dogs and other companion animals adjust to the change by lying nearby their master until there is a sign or clue as to when there might be a return to normal daily activities.

"Good boy," Festus murmured, "ya know I feel like shit, don't ya?" Festus whispered. He coughed repeatedly until sputum came up. He spit into a rag that he kept nearby. It was not pleasant—the phlegm contained a tinge of blood. Festus knew that it meant that a vessel or capillaries in his throat had burst, or something worse from his windpipe or lungs, perhaps from his prior days of smoking—but something from deep within.

He had noticed a similar event before when he had the flu the year before. It didn't concern him for he always seemed to recover. His ears felt blocked so that when he spoke, they rang out with an echo—tinnitus-like. Whatever he had, was everywhere in his body it seemed. He felt miserable.

Living as he did, both solitary and desolate at times, made him aware of the fact that he had no medical doctor, hospital or health insurance for life-threatening maladies in the modern era. The "flu" and pneumonia were common occurrences in New England and morbidity was high in the elderly. He "weathered the storm" so to speak like English Jack had—solo and over time. Time always healed.

While he rested in the recliner, the dog's ears suddenly perked up. Thunder's head tilted to the right and the dog's eyes seemed to widen. There was the inkling that someone was on the property.

The dog didn't bark . . . but slowly stood and cautiously approached the door. He sniffed the crack by the door jam. Festus's eyes were closed. He thought that by relaxing, he could "will away" the illness. A shot of applejack a half hour earlier seemed to help.

Thunder stood silent for a moment, his tail stiffened, and he looked repeatedly at his master and then back again at the door. Festus was unaware of the unusual activity of Thunder. He was almost asleep.

The dog snarled low, almost inaudible to Festus's poor hearing. His tail remained stagnant as Thunder focused his eyes on the door. He hardly blinked and his rear legs stiffened in defense as if he was *pointing*. His snout was pressed against the door, his nostrils flaring as he inhaled and exhaled, repeatedly.

Suddenly the unsecured door burst open! It was lightening fast. Festus was shocked by the abrupt entry of a man. He threw off the blanket on his lap and attempted to get up when he received a sharp blow to the head by the intruder. The man held up a thick piece of deadwood about 3 feet in length. It was solid oak and old.

The man hit the dog beside the head, knocking Thunder out before he had a chance to attack, or even yelp. The dog was moaning on the floor, coma-like. His eyes were dilated and head was bleeding. His chest was heaving as he breathed. His rear legs twitched occasionally, but he was alive.

"What the fuck?" Festus coughed out, in pain. "What the . . . ?" he gasped for air, holding his head.

Festus tried to reach behind him for his shotgun as the door opened but his arm was bent back by the man who overpowered the sickly and seriously weakened man. There was a "crack" in the bone of his right arm, his strongest arm. He cried out in pain as the man stood directly in front of him with piercing eyes wide opened from rage. Adrenaline poured through his blood.

"Where's Ryan, my buddy?" he screamed at the old man. "You bastard! What did you do with my friend? Answer me!"

Festus said nothing . . . but stared straight ahead at the man. The old man lay crumpled in the chair, bleeding from the head and moaning from the agony of his injured arm and skull. The arm had a compound fracture with a portion of one bone, the radius, sticking through his skin and clothes. Blood saturated the fabric. His other hand was holding his damaged arm for support.

"*What* buddy . . . who is Ryan?" Festus responded, in distress, pleading ignorance. The man hit him on the side of the head with the butt end of a pistol. Festus shrieked out in pain once again.

"I don't know what you're talkin' 'bout . . . what buddy?" he murmured, lower lip now bleeding. His mouth quivered and cheek was now bloodied but he knew not to move. The younger man would surely kill him.

"*You* know what the fuck I mean, old man," screamed Bobby Cummings, with distain.

"You shot me and my friend the other day . . . he dropped out *there*, by the rock," he said, pointing to the property outside.

"Where the fuck is Ryan? Did ya kill him?" he said, standing over him, and close enough for Festus to see the veins in his forehead throbbing. He could smell chewing tobacco on his breath. The intruder spit on the floor and backed away from Festus's face.

"I don't know nobody by that name," said Festus, in a low voice. "I live here alone and have no visitors."

"You liar!" the man stammered, enraged. "You killed my buddy. Where is he?"

Festus looked away.

"You lyin' sack-o-shit," Bobby continued, taking Festus's broken arm and twisting it until Festus almost blacked out in agony. His face went white and he grimaced from the abuse. Bobby Cummings laughed, and repeated the question.

"Where is he?" he reiterated, with clenched teeth and a closed right fist, knuckles white. "I'll twist your goddamn arm off, like a chicken wing, old man."

Festus said nothing. Bobby could see that the man was in misery and suffering from an illness.

"You got a . . . little cold, mista? Huh? Poor baby. If so, that's the least of your miserable little problems."

Festus stayed silent, his eyes closed in fear.

"You know what I'm talkin' about," Cummings said, opening up his shirt and showing the old man the wounds from the pellets that had hit him.

"You killed him, I assume!" he screamed in the man's face. "Open your eyes, you fool! Look! See the buckshot I took."

Festus relented, blinking his eyes in fear. "I didn't kill no one."

"Liar!" Cummings was seething at this point.

"I didn't shoot you or nobody," Festus lied. "Why would I do that?"

"Short memory, old man," responded a now agitated Bobby Cummings. "Where'd ya bury my friend?"

Just as the man was about to slap the old man, the dog revived and lunged at Cummings, both front paws on his leg, nails extended. In an instant he bit the intruder's leg almost ripping off a chuck of thigh.

Startled, Bobby fell to the floor in agony. Before he could take his pistol and shoot the dog, Thunder ran out the door and into the nearby woods. Two shots rang out from the floor of the doorway . . . where the assailant lay gripping his leg in pain. The shots missed the dog who managed to hightail it around the back of the cabin and into the nearby brush. In a flash, he was out of sight.

"Fuckin' vicious dog ya got there, ol' Man. I don't take kindly to that. Look at my leg!" he demanded, hitting Festus across the knee with the oak stick. Festus cried out once more, his patella broken.

The fear and excitement released adrenaline that cleared up his throat and nasal passages—a "fight or flight" mechanism. He was beyond misery but unable to fend off the intruder. He was fading in and out of consciousness.

Bobby looked around the room, and knowing that Festus could not move, started throwing things around, in a vitriolic fit of terror. He finally found the wooden trunk that he "trashed" to open. The wallet appeared as Cummings cleared the shelves of books, looking for Ryan's other possessions.

In the trunk and a box was the license plate and backpack belonging to his friend. He turned slowly, squinting in rage, teeth grinding like an animal. He stared at Festus.

"You lyin' sack-o'-shit!" he bellowed, slowly and deliberately, holding up Ryan's I.D.

He then held the knapsack and wallet in front of Festus and the old man turned away gasping, then licking his lips in fear and anxiety.

"What's *this*?" screamed the man. "What the fuck is *this* . . . if it's not Ryan's stuff?"

Festus said nothing.

"You old coot . . . you're a damn hermit . . . did ya eat him? Probably did, you shit."

Festus again, said nothing.

Bobby approached the old man in the chair and placed the handgun near his temple.

"Are ya sure you don't know where he is?"

Festus didn't move. He turned his head away. The barrel of the pistol followed his temple.

"I'll find him you prick. I don't need you no more . . ." Bobby Cummings taunted.

Festus closed his eyes, in fear of the psycho's demeanor. He couldn't tolerate any more pain and knew anything he said would be met by more assaults. The intruder was on a mission from hell. Festus felt doomed and for the first time in his life . . . said a prayer to the heavens.

In his other hand, Bobby held his friend's knapsack, the license plate and the wallet. He found the baseball caps as well, one that he had worn and left behind in the fray and the other that Ryan had worn at his death. The intruder placed his hat back on his head, centering the lid. He then studied Ryan's cap . . . there was blood on it.

He approached the chair where Festus was slumped all bloodied and agonizing from the heinous abuse. Festus wanted to die at this point.

Bobby stood over him and stared at his crumpled body.

"You look like shit, old man," he uttered, unsympathetically. "I've been waitin' to return here to see who the hell shot at us. Turns out to be a *snake*, you deranged recluse!"

Festus mumbled something religious for the first time, and then stated clearly, "Long live John Stark's memory. He would not have been proud of you scum. You killed the lawyer, didn't ya? Read it in the paper!"

A confused Bobby Cummings leaned in, smiling and asked Festus to repeat what he had just said.

Festus didn't reply but kept his eyes shut. He was now quivering in the chair, fevered, broken and scared to death.

Cummings said no more since he could not understand the last words Festus had said.

"Did you say we killed someone . . . *that* what you said, you *snake*?"

Festus repeated the words, softly. "You *killed* the lawyer."

"Maybe so . . . you'll never know, old man . . . this one's for Ryan . . . you bastard," pointing the handgun toward the disabled man.

Without hesitation or warning, the cold-blooded murderer and political fanatic fired a shot into Festus's head blowing part of his brains onto the wall near the chair. It was a 9 mm weapon. He watched the man sink deeper into the recliner and his face turn gray. Festus's eyes were wide open and then his eyelids closed in mortal relaxation.

Cummings placed a second shot straight into his chest, mid-ventral, where the heart is located, and at close range. It didn't matter since Festus was already dead from the headshot. The bullet went right through him and into the recliner.

The brazen young man stood over his victim like he had shot a deer during hunting season. He smiled and seemed proud of his "kill,"—payback on behalf of his missing friend.

Cummings didn't know where his friend was, or whether he was dead or alive. He just assumed that he was dead and buried somewhere on the property.

He had no time to look for his buddy. He was unsure as to whether anyone had heard the two gunshots and he decided to leave the cabin and property, a property that Festus had personally cleared for planting gardens, and maintained for survival as a hermit. It was all for naught.

The dog didn't return while Cummings remained there. As Bobby departed, he spit on the old man and left the door partially ajar, purposefully, so animals could enter and devour the hermit, as if it mattered.

* * *

By nightfall, the fire in the fireplace waned and formed a bed of glimmering coals in the hearth. An orange hue filled the room. The nearby wood stove went cold. In the limited flickering light, the body of Festus Gravel slowly stiffened. The blood on the walls turned dark reddish brown. Pieces of tissue and hair were splattered on the wall.

The door to the cabin remained open, moving occasionally with the wind. Thunder returned, limping from his injuries and dazed from the head wound. He cautiously looked to see if the intruder was still there. He had hid in the woods and finally returned home only to find his master unresponsive but still in his chair. The dog whimpered and licked a blood spot on the arm of Festus, knowing that something was desperately wrong.

He put his paws in his master's lap and sniffed his cold dead face, or what remained of it after the gunshot. He stared at his now gray hand that draped over the arm of the chair. The dog knew death, what dried blood tasted like, and he lay beside the rocker and close to Festus's feet.

Dogs can sense death and Thunder put his head on the seed sack. He stared at the embers in the crackling fireplace. Occasionally an ember would pop and skim across the fireplace screen. The dog focused on the fire, blinking until his eyes gently closed. He whimpered in his sleep. His leg twitched as if in a dream.

He wouldn't leave his master's side. He was hungry and knew it was beyond feeding time. His natural instincts were to seek food, "scraps" that Festus kept dried in a nearby basket. He had salted and dried jerky all summer and fall.

Water, the dog could get from the stream and that was the only time he left his master's side, to drink. The dog was dehydrated and he infrequently needed to go outside to void. He would seek water in due time.

Well into the darkness of the cabin, the windows and room now lacked light. The moon was absent, the sky overcast. The embers cooled and the main room where Festus sat deceased was now completely dark. The dog slept and became a John Stark-like sentry, in an uncanny way. He stayed with his master and stared into the nothingness and solitude of the cabin. He could hear rodents scurrying outside in the leaves—nocturnal scavengers. He knew nighttime was their *daytime*, creatures that were waking up in darkness, but the dog never gave chase. The companion animal had no appetite and was protective of his master. No vermin would come near the body, at least while he was "on duty."

Chapter 20

Bobby Cummings exited the woods at virtually the same spot he had left during his last perilous visit to the cabin. He hid out near the dump area until darkness came. He only saw two other persons during the late afternoon hours. A man was teaching his young son how to separate glass refuse from the plastic and paper for recycling.

Bobby hid behind a boulder until the sun set. He spent his idle time looking though the wallet of his friend, sifting through the photos and credit cards stored in a center compartment. It depressed him to think that his buddy was dead in the nearby woods. It was unlikely he could find him easily, or could take the time to hang around while being pursued by the local authorities.

In darkness, he meandered out to the highway to hitch a ride.

He took a chance just coming back to the area since he knew the police would be fastidious in their search for Stillwater's killer or killers. He was a man on the run, once again, with *two* murders to his credit.

* * *

The impact of Festus Gravel on the world was nothing that would have impressed anyone in particular, save for the fact that he was an unknown patriot—albeit one who was in charge of an army of *one*. He was no John Stark in principles, but he did represent the right-wing element that thought that "liberty" was the sole objective of American history. He had studied the American Revolution in his youth and was quite aware of the role of military generals who led the charge against the British.

Festus had focused his casual reading time on the history of New England, mostly that of Boston in colonial days and the Vermont and New Hampshire military regiments that were part of the French and Indian Wars and the subsequent Revolutionary War and War of 1812. He knew of the New Hampshire regiments and the historic buildings that still remained from days of old. There were encampments from some Vermont battles still standing by the Connecticut River and also in central New Hampshire, especially near Lake Winnipesaukee.

Statues of celebrated generals and patriots adorned parks and civics buildings, and Festus, when younger, had visited many of the graves and memorials that attested to the various war heroes' fame. He had made a point of seeking them out and paying them his respect. They inspired him—false icons in a way since his quest for "freedom" and "liberty" was aimed at reducing government intervention in life, not opposing foreign intruders as General Stark had achieved.

Where Festus was noteworthy and a "legacy of his own" was in his *independence*, an independence that was instilled in him from his earliest days as a youngster. Yes, he was quirky and a loner, a hermit, but New Hampshire leaned that way in attracting that type of person, especially in the northern part of the state and in the remote White Mountains. It had the ability to foster and sustain nomadic life through Nature's provisions.

Survivalists from many parts of the United States were drawn by the state's motto (Live Free or Die) and the principles that "less government was more." Rebels that settled in the woods to the north were for less taxes, or no taxes at all, freedom of speech and the right to keep and bear arms, unrestricted.

The renegades that "immigrated" from other states cared nothing of *other* U. S. Constitutional amendments in the Bill of Rights; they merely focused on living free and unobstructed by laws and the authorities that were in place to maintain a civil society.

Festus Gravel, an advocate of the 233-year-old laws of the 1700's, was of the same school of thought, self taught by hand-picking selected books that leaned to the "right" in political thought. There was no balance to his ideology. It was his way, as an independent free thinker, or no way at all. He merely wanted to be left alone.

With his death, America had lost a pioneer of free thought, as radical as he was, and as lonely as he was. He knew he would eventually die in the woods and be left to Nature's ways, accepting that he would "dissolve and physically recycle" into the decaying natural environment of the world.

He was the salt of the earth and believed in reincarnation. He could care less about death, except that he never thought he would die by the hands of a murderer. Death by natural causes would have been his desire, yet his protection of his property in a way caused his premature tragedy—he, being a self-induced *target* for confrontation, should someone venture onto his land. Someone had to win, and this time he lost.

He fired his shotgun before thinking of the ramifications and it resulted in a direct rebuttal by a vindictive young man who sought him out and eliminated him from society by intentional and callous murder. Retribution! Villains beget villains.

The sad part of the scenario is that Festus was of the same mindset as the man that killed him, just not as radical in appearance or actions. Festus was not a "Type A" personality like Cummings.

Bobby Cummings knew nothing of Festus Gravel's beliefs in freedom. The difference in philosophies was ironic in that Festus protested constraints by the authorities but he did so *passively*. He acted independently and in concert with nature, in a way that, until recently, had never harmed people in his life. The killing of Ryan Cooper was a fluke—his mistake ironically with "freedoms he professed," that being to only confront another person, if challenged. In hindsight, he never should have shot *blindly* into the woods. The pistol in the mist elicited a protective response.

Bobby Cummings on the other hand was a cold-blooded murderer with a mission—the Stillwater mission. He wanted to move to New Hampshire along with others, settle in and impact a new way of thinking by New Hampshire residents, verbally advocating and eventually voting in future elections for candidates that placed "liberty" *above* governmental authority and independence. He was an anarchist by nature, almost a Fascist.

The U.S. Constitution was Bobby's bible but he was not a learned man in that regard. He hardly knew the document's contents but followed others of like-mind like sheep, the proponents of the Freestate movement—because *some* of their ideals, right, wrong or unorthodox, appealed to him. He and Ryan Cooper were "outliers," a "fringe element" of the basic premise and principles for which the Freestate movement stoically stood.

The FSP movement would not have condoned the killing of Barnaby Stillwater, or the murder of Festus Gravel. They would have used other means to protect their interpretation of the 2nd Amendment by amassing people into New Hampshire to join an ideology of their liking.

They offered no specific candidates and no specific agenda, except to broadly protect *themselves, liberty* and *freedom*. It remains today, a narrow-minded agenda. That seems to be their entire mission and they reinforce their agenda by quoting the exact words of Constitutional amendments.

It was now 2010, not 1776.

Anarchy has never worked in the United States. There are too many sane and rational common folk who view murder or insolence as unacceptable—New Hampshire residents that suppress *en masse* the feelings and unorthodox agendas of a select few radicals, especially from out-of-state.

"Majority still rules" and the Forefathers wanted change by *majority* consensus of an informed populous, not rebellion.

Festus Gravel was a man who showed his distain for the infringement of, or restriction of freedoms, by government—political parties or laws that impacted basic life and daily routines in general. Politicians were corrupt in his mind, in both major parties. He was odd, but not stupid. Many lawmakers had torrid pasts, accepted bribes and were devious. He called them slugs.

People tolerated the fact that he was his own "island" and left him to commune with Nature. Local residents, those that had actually heard of him, deemed Festus "a character." He was known for his unorthodox and solitary ways in the woods. Some equated him to the famed English Jack, but far more reclusive.

The odd man just wanted to live alone. Perhaps one that had a pet or wild animal as a companion, a living being that followed his every command like a soldier would, and one that was obedient without talking back. Animals didn't care what he *thought*. Festus needed food, water and shelter—the basics. Animals had the same needs.

Thunder met those needs. The dog's allegiance was to his new master, a master who didn't care from where the animal originated. Festus surely didn't know his origin but concluded that he was a lost, feral critter.

The dog was *a stray,* somewhat analogous to Festus Gravel who deviated from a complex world that was moving too fast for him, literally and figuratively. Both were creatures of habit and simplicity.

With Festus's passing, Thunder was now reliant on his own instincts, not co-dependence. Those instincts were primal, animalistic and inherent in his canine bloodline. The dog knew the way to the dump and understood the physical protection of the cabin in adverse weather—a shelter as needed.

The dog would remain there for a while, protecting his master even in silent, decaying and putrid conditions.

Chapter 21

Ron Corvallis drove his normal route from the seacoast to the central part of the Lakes Region of New Hampshire. This evening's trek was no different. Headlights and guardrails, and a white line or two guided him back and forth along a familiar highway. He knew it by heart. The white lines could be memorizing, paralyzing—white line, space, while line, space repeatedly.

On this route, he was familiar with every corner and intersection by heart, even the locations where the police might radar drivers for speeding infractions. The truck had the same sound, same drone, and a unique engine whine with brakes that squealed when the pedal was depressed. He could traverse the route blindfolded and often relied on the dashboard FM radio or CD player for entertainment and the alleviation of boredom. Talk show radio helped him pass the miles, but he hated the political banter on AM radio. The likes of Limbaugh on syndicated radio (seemingly every other station) irritated him but NHPR and NPR had substance and diverse programs and intelligent discussions.

Ron frequently drove in a sweatshirt, or a polo shirt and jeans. He delivered the goods to local stores and was not required to have a white-collar dress code. That pleased him, not being management. Some of the deliveries were heavy, dusty or dirty; therefore "dressing up" to impress clients was not mandatory. There was no one to impress anyway—he merely drove truck and dropped off boxes and crates.

The fifty-year-old driver sympathized with folks that were stranded in the night. He witnessed many. If a car were broken down, he would stop and try to help, or at least seek assistance on their behalf. His toolbox was at the ready and behind the driver's seat. He carried jumper cables and an extra pint or two of oil or gallon of gas, if needed. The gas can was strapped to the side of the running board on the driver's side. Most frequently, people ran out of regular gas. Ron ran diesel but carried the extra supply of regular fuel. He was thoughtful.

Ron rounded a familiar corner in the road when he noted the shadow of a man ahead in his lights; he sat on the right side of the road. Two cars, ahead of him, passed the isolated stranger in the night. It was a darkened portion of the highway, though a familiar stretch of highway for Ron. The man was sitting on the metal guardrail having stood for a long time attempting to hitch a ride. His thumb and arm were extended lazily now, as if he knew no one would stop that late in the evening. He was tired and chilled to the bone.

Ron Corvallis slowed down . . . and after repeatedly checking his rear view mirror he approached the pebbled apron of the road. The exhaust pipe reverberated a backpressure rumble as the truck decelerated to a crawl. He downshifted a gear or two to stop. The airbrakes hissed and popped on the edge of the road, a narrow apron that paralleled the guardrail and a stand of trees and dense, scraggly brush. The engine was that of a diesel, which idled loud with a predictable "knock"—the exhaust pipe reaching to the sky and spewing black carbon into the air like a fine mist.

The embankment on the opposite side of the guardrail was some thirty feet of incline with standing poplars and maples. A small creek was bubbling at the bottom of a ravine. It was swollen from the recent rains.

That part of the roadway was not well lit, with occasional passing headlights reflecting off iridescent red and yellow safety tape on the rails suggesting "caution—sharp turn."

Ron illuminated his warning flashers, the rear ones reflecting red intermittently off the hitchhiker's body. The periodic glow of the thankful figure approaching . . . was both ominous and surreal for Ron.

He checked the right rearview mirror on the passenger side. He could see the young man running toward the truck. He had twenty yards to get to his ride.

Uncaring, irritated passenger car drivers honked, then passed on the left side of the truck—they were traveling at a high rate of speed and quickly slowed once they spotted the truck on the side of the road. It was not a safe area to stop, or thumb for that matter. The road narrowed perilously at that juncture.

Bobby Cummings opened the passenger side door, hopped into the cab and swung himself into the right seat, backpack in hand. His jeans revealed a deep red stain on one side, the result of the dog bite at the cabin.

"Thanks . . . thanks for stopping."

The interior cab light shone directly on the face of the killer and Ron almost went white with fear. He recognized the man having given him a ride previously.

"Glad I could help."

He patronized the man by welcoming him warmly, even though he was apprehensive knowing that the police were after the suspected felon. Ron knew the face under the ball cap.

"Hey . . . I know you, don't I," he offered, with a cordial smile. "You're the guy I gave a lift to . . . a week or so ago. You were headin' south I thought."

"Right," offered Bobby, "I got off track for a while but I did manage to get to Jaffrey, thanks to you. This state is pretty big and most drivers don't want to stop for hitchhikers—must be a law against it."

Ron nodded . . . but was nervous. He maintained a cool head.

"You okay now? I remember you were injured in a fall in the woods. I see you're still bleedin' a bit, eh?"

"Nothin' much to it, thanks . . . I still have one cut that refuses to heal—it 'weeps' at times, but I'm okay. It opened up when I ran for your truck, I guess."

"Looks nasty," Ron said, grimacing. "Glad I was passing by."

"Yup, good timing mister . . . thanks."

"That's a lot of blood for one cut," offered Ron. "I have some bandages in the med kit behind your seat if you need some. I added them to my emergency supplies after seeing you the last time. 'Had no idea that I'd see ya again," he laughed. "Your good fortune, I guess."

Bobby thanked him for his kindness and reached for the medical kit behind the seat. Blood oozed from the wound as he turned to grab the kit.

Ron engaged the clutch and first gear and started back out on the highway. He turned on the interior overhead light so the stranger could see the wound and apply the bandage. He figured that the stranger would need some illumination.

"No need for that," offered Bobby, reaching up and clicking off the light, "I can see by the light of the moon," he smiled. "I've got great eyesight, just like a cat in the night."

Ron shuddered.

A cat in the night? For sure! More like a cat on the run.

He ripped open the area of his jeans where he had been bitten. As the truck crossed a well-lit intersection, flashes of light crossed the pant leg and Ron could see what appeared to be teeth marks from an animal. There was a brief, intermittent flash from the amber streetlights; it was clear that the wound was different and more recent than last time.

This guy was having a streak of bad luck, Ron thought. He was also lying!

The sight of the injury sickened Ron. Bobby poured some hydrogen peroxide from the medical kit onto the open laceration. The hydrogen peroxide bubbled as it mixed with the fresh blood, flushing the wound clean. The mixture dripped onto the floor and Ron was annoyed. He knew that he had an unpredictable, potentially violent villain in his cab. He said nothing but stared straight ahead through the windshield into the night. Knowing the man's prior history, he was in fear for his life.

Bobby wrapped the wound with sterile gauze, a lengthy roll of it; this stopped the oozing of blood and eventually hid the vicious damage from the dog. He applied sterile adhesive tape over the gauze, the well-known J&J brand.

Cummings sat back daydreaming, and deep in thought, as it crossed his mind for the first time that the damn dog might have had rabies. The wound was flaming red and erythematic at the edges, and then streaked along vessels on the skin's surface. Perhaps microbes had resulted in wide spread septicemia.

Cummings saw no collar or tags on the dog, just before it attacked him. For all he knew it was a feral dog in the woods that might have serious diseases from other animals, like raccoons, skunks or bats. Rabies was not uncommon in the Northeast. He was fearful of that as he closed the ripped flap on his Levi's.

The tattered denim material was encrusted with dried and fresh blood, varying from dark brown to light crimson in color.

Ron's face went from pale to flesh tone as he drove at increasing speed hoping to get the man to his destination, wherever that was. No cops were in sight.

The wound was no longer visible. Ron swallowed hard once or twice, nauseated from the injury he had witnessed on Cummings's leg. Saliva accumulated in his mouth, a precursor to vomiting. It soon subsided and his stomach settled down.

"You okay?" he asked, with concern, attempting to show compassion. "That wound looked nasty."

"Yup. I'm fine," Bobby lied. "Thanks for the medical stuff in the kit."

"Where ya goin' this time? Same area I dropped you off last time?"

"Yes, please."

Ron didn't want him in the cab any longer than he had to be, knowing full well that the man was "wanted."

The police had informed Ron that the suspect was probably armed and dangerous and thought to be one of the murderers of the prominent lawyer.

Ron had no clue what was in the knapsack. There might be a gun or other weapons concealed there. It was logical that the man was on the run, and a coincidence that the trucker would end up giving him a second ride . . . in less than a week. Ron was apprehensive but remained focused on the road ahead.

"You were in the middle of nowhere," suggested Ron, pleasantly. "Hard to get a ride in these parts. People don't stop at night."

"Yah, I was thumbing for a while, maybe an hour. Appreciate you stoppin' once again. I was gettin' lazy and thumbin' from a sittin' down position. The leg was aching. I didn't mean to appear lazy," he laughed. Ron laughed with him.

"You looked like you'd been there a while. I've picked up people in the past, ya know, especially in times of need," added Ron, who wanted to maintain small talk just to pass the time.

"I'll get you into town, then I have to head home myself."

"I was hopin' for a place to sleep at this late hour," Bobby Cummings added. "You don't have an extra bunk, do ya? It's late and I'll never get a room at this hour. You live local?"

"Sorry, I don't or I'd take ya in. I still have a long ride home and can't accommodate ya." Ron became nervous. No way did he want the rider to know where he lived or to stay there. Ron worried.

Ron thought that *a jail cell* would be a great place for the man to sleep! He tried to appear nonchalant but was scheming on how he could get the passenger into the hands of the police. Surely he couldn't call the chief of police on his cell, especially with the *wanted man* sitting right next to him.

He spent idle time thinking of how he could alert the authorities to the potentially perilous situation—a ride that Ron wanted to end.

One idea that he conjured up was novel. If he drove fast enough, some local cop might stop him for speeding. That wasn't working thus far, he thought.

His mind was thinking of other scenarios that might work as well. He could drive the guy straight to the police station and somehow escort him into the facility, forcibly. That would be chancy. He thought twice about that idea. The man was gnarly and might overpower him or even kill him, especially if a weapon was hidden in his backpack.

He thought of making a "fake" telephone call to home by cell phone; one in which he could actually call the police chief's number stored in memory, leaving the phone open-lined. That way the chief could hear the conversation and track the call on GPS. He would know of Ron's concerns just by the conversation that Ron was having in the cab of the truck.

Based on the conversation, the chief would know the nature of the issue and respond with adequate police forces, including S.W.A.T. members, if needed.

Bobby Cummings struck up a new conversation.

"I'll probably try and head south again," offered the passenger. "You can let me off anywhere where you think I can get another ride . . . the last place worked okay. I got a ride from there last weekend."

"Not a problem, buddy," responded Ron, occasionally checking his rearview mirror. "I can drop you off at the same place. It takes you to that highway that you need. I can head north after that. Glad to help," he offered, in an appeasing manner.

The trucker drove another seven miles continuing to make small talk—he was close to the same geographical area where there were small strip malls, residential homes and car dealerships. The area was fairly densely populated now and Ron felt more secure. He could stop at any red light and *bolt* if he had too.

"You know the area?" asked Ron. The killer shook his head.

"No," he responded. "Can't say that I do. Haven't been through here much," he offered. "Pretty country though. A lot different from North Carolina."

Ron now knew where he was from.

The trucker agreed. "Yup, love this state. It offers *freedom* to its residents. Small towns with lots of amenities, low taxes and lots of woods."

Bobby smiled in agreement. "That's exactly why I planned on moving here. Hope to anyway. They allow ya to do what ya want without rules and 'the fuzz' watchin' over ya."

Ron felt uncomfortable now. He knew the man probably didn't care for the law. Ron concurred with Bobby's perspective, just to appease him.

"Live free or die! That's what we say in these parts."

"Ditto," said the killer, "best phrase in the country. All states should be 'pro-liberty,' like this one. We need to return to the basic principles of the Constitution. Ya know?"

"Yup."

Ron began to sweat under his arms. He felt uncomfortable with the conversation. The man leaned "right" for sure. A southern renegade of sorts. Anything the kid said, Ron agreed with, to pacify him. He wanted no altercations.

Bobby reached for a pack of cigarettes, hidden in his shirt pocket. Camels. Ron hated when anyone smoked in the cab. He kept the truck pristine clean and was already concerned about the blood that dripped on the floor mat.

"Care if I smoke?" asked Bobby, cordially. "Want one?" he offered the driver, extending the pack toward him, one cigarette sticking out of the pack.

"No . . . no thanks. Feel free. I gave that stuff up years ago, sorry to say. I miss the pleasure. Tough to break the habit."

Bobby agreed and indicated that people should be able to smoke anywhere—bars, restaurants, public places, even on high school property.

"Damn straight, pal," he blurted out, "damn government tries to tell people what to do. They don't know the fuckin' Constitution, eh? We smokers have rights. Freedom of expression, free speech!"

"Agreed," Ron offered, smiling.

Ron stared out the windshield. He only had a few miles to go.

"'Government controls everyone," Ron baited him. "They try to take away our guns too. Bastards!"

Bobby nodded, "Yah . . . the shitheads need to be contained. Our 2nd Amendment rights are being violated. The bastards. I believe in guns, the protection of home, family, life and the 'right to conceal.' I pack heat all the time."

Ron reiterated his beliefs in the 2nd. "Yah, the 'right to keep and bear arms.' That's my motto." Ron was lying, but knew the passenger confirmed that he had weapons on him at all times—even now!

The match was struck and cigarette lit. He tossed the match out the window, took a drag and exhaled slowly tilting his head back against the seat. He was obviously in pain and tired from a long day of hiding in the woods and hanging out on a highway in the dark.

The driver coughed from the smoke in the cab—a blue mist in small quarters. He asked for the passenger to open the window, if he didn't mind.

"Sure 'nough. Be glad to," Cummings replied, blowing a smoke ring upward.

Ron thought he saw Bobby's eyes shut once or twice during the ride. Bobby Cummings never even took the time to fasten his own seat belt. It was too constraining. *Another government imposition, in his mind.* Most people of his ideology hated rules and constraints where *free will* was the desired order of the day. They hated being told what to do, what insurance to buy, and what rules to play by in life.

Seat beat laws and mandatory helmets on motorcycles were irritants to those who objected to the local or federal government controlling "free will," or day-to-day life's choices. Freedom of choice was paramount in their way of thinking and that was the mindset of Bobby Cummings and his close circle of friends. *Who the hell was the government to tell them what to do?*

New Hampshire seemed to have more freedoms than many other states. Adults in New Hampshire were not *required* to buckle up as yet.

Movement to the state by liberty advocates was attractive for that reason, in addition to the fact that is was "a beautiful place to live" with wide open spaces and no taxes—those taxes only encumbered those with little money to start.

Chapter 22

The evening shift was already in operation at the police station—the graveyard shift, skeleton-like at best. There had been two local events that evening that warranted the police chief being alerted. Domestic altercations were common in the town where Stillwater had been killed. Low income housing rentals on Strawberry lane generated frequent patrol missions late at night.

Barnaby had represented both male and female victims of those crimes in court in the past, especially when someone was battered, male or female—mostly female. Most issues were alcohol related and domestic violence. The unemployed lived on the edge of anxiety, usually money issues.

This one particular evening the chief was in his office reviewing a robbery case that needed his input. There was also a trial and other arraignments that week in the local courthouse. It was the County seat. A boating accident on the Big Lake," Lake "Winni," had precedence since a boater/ passenger had been killed during an evening excursion. Alcohol and speed was in question.

He sat as his desk while other officers booked a couple of drunks for assault and disorderly conduct. The men were in two holding cells and passed out. There had been an alleged fight at the local pub and the police were summoned to the business to remove the alcohol-infused rowdies from the popular establishment. It was not unusual for people to get into a fight after drinking all evening.

This one altercation was over a "third party," a girlfriend who could not decide on one beau or another.

A new suitor was "hot for the woman" and the previous boyfriend was not enamored by the blatant "hits" on his former girlfriend. She was apparently attracted to the new suitor. He was classier and appeared to have more money than her current "ex." She was known to be a gold digger and money was attractive to her, a priority. The new man had coin and a professional job.

As the chief jotted notes and reviewed charges for the next day's arraignment of a burglar, he was pleased to see that the night had been "relatively" quiet. Chief Randall had not been *disturbed* the entire evening and he had accomplished much in the way of reviewing the impending case in the morning. He would testify for the prosecution and the homeowner who had been robbed of cash and jewelry.

Only one officer that evening needed to check in with him and brief the chief on recent developments and activities. They chatted for ten minutes, shot the bull for another fifteen and the officer left for a routine patrol of neighborhoods where there had been recent break-ins or family discord. He patrolled a number of local streets shining a spotlight onto homes, doorways and yards that were darkened. He sought out wayward teens as well since they frequented a local skateboard park, even at night and after hours.

He continually focused the spotlight on driveways, parked cars and bushes where someone might hide during or after a crime, or an attempt to steal a vehicle. That's how the perpetrators of the Stillwater murder apparently acquired the stolen SUV.

Except for the recent Stillwater murder case, nothing quite as devious or tragic had ever occurred in the quaint town. The chief was pleased that it had been ten years since the last murder and that one occurrence was related to a motorcycle gang member who had attacked another rival club's member with a knife. The wound was fatal. Short of that, nothing quite that criminal had been noted in recent years.

The front door to the police station was locked at night and required a buzzer to access a patrolman on duty, and the premises. Visitors were required to stand in front of a surveillance camera and identify themselves as well as describe the concerns that they might have for police assistance. The double doors were glass and the lobby quite spacious and well lit. Video cameras were activated if someone entered the foyer.

There were cement barriers in place, mostly outside the front of the lobby, a carryover concept from the Homeland Security period when suspected terrorists would try and enter a government facility in a truck or vehicle—a car/truck bomb approach like in Oklahoma City or in the Mid East.

Small towns in New Hampshire installed the often "less than adequate" barriers as part of congressional "earmarks" or perks from Washington DC funds—those that gave local authorities added revenue for police station renovations or protection. Protection at all levels, even in small towns, was part of the billions of dollars that Federal funds were being allocated to many U.S. cities and states. Obscure municipalities, where terrorism might never occur, took the money anyway. It was free!

Remote towns wouldn't necessarily use the funds for "anti-terror" protection, but applied the added revenue to pay off other budget shortfalls that were deemed "security related" in one way or another. Fences or barriers were installed for impounded cars or other motor vehicles and boats following accidents or crimes. The monies met both needs, the shortfall debts and potential security issues.

State buildings were upgraded for the handicapped or ADA-related compliance, or monies were shuffled to other needs at the police and fire facilities. New locks and bulletproof windows, as well as bomb squad mechanical robots for explosives detection were purchased for the rare occasions when pipe bombs, biohazards and other threats had to be recovered or detonated safely.

Special Kevlar uniforms and vests for defusing bombs or dodging bullets were costly and the S.W.A.T. units had an arsenal of anti-terrorist countermeasures should the need for a riot squad be implemented.

It was unlikely that those events might occur other than the obscure copycat Columbine-like school shootings—tragic episodes that wreaked havoc in Colorado and other states.

Monies from the Feds were destined for local law enforcement, gobbled up and used for *anything* related to protecting citizens in towns and cities, large and small, nationwide.

The protective cement barriers in front of the lobby looked like multiple obelisks, a Washington monument-like series of icons but shorter in stature. They were redesigned to please the town hall councilmen who thought bulky protective barriers were contrary to the style of the Victorian architectural history of the town. They wanted them to be protective from assaults, but much smaller in nature to augment the aesthetics, history and local ambiance of New England structures and character. The police chief had voted for something with more bulk and substance, not something designed to be aesthetically pleasing to the public eye.

Politics, being what it is in a small New England town with a mix of old money and artistic preservationists, favored the balance of beauty with adequate protection. The boondoggle appropriations looked as if the police station was being protected by "cute" cement piers—i.e. heavy, linked, nautical chains between the barriers that might be typical of a Mystic Seaport berthing area for tall ships in Connecticut. They took the same approach with the outside décor of the courthouse and city hall.

In the end, the "aesthetic squad" won and the police agreed not to inflame the situation by demanding more protection at the expense of an ugly design. The city council was constantly "middle of the road" conservative anyway, rarely ruffling the feathers of anyone. They merely accepted the money from the Feds and distributed it, generally after much debate, subcommittee reviews and delays in distribution. Dysfunctional was the order of the day.

Residents in New Hampshire hated taxes but the state was right in line to receive someone else's money from afar, especially when it came from the District of Columbia. They hated spending "local funds" for the *same* protection of their government buildings. Property taxes would have to be elevated to do that and the controlling conservative base was predominant in the recent city council elections.

Chapter 23

Ron Corvallis had been driving diesel rigs for years. He knew the capabilities of the truck and could maneuver it on a dime. He realized that his passenger was fading in and out of consciousness, probably due to the pain of his injuries. Ron was convinced that the teeth marks were from an animal. He guessed that the recent wound was fresh since his old wounds would have healed by now.

This rider had bad luck two weeks in a row and Ron knew from the police interrogation and description of the suspects provided, that this young man was one of two perpetrators of a violent, murderous crime. He had obviously been on the run for a weekend or more and somehow had ended back up in the Lakes Region of New Hampshire. If he had in fact killed the lawyer, *why would he return to the area?*

The police had said that there might be more than one person involved in the killing of Attorney Stillwater. *Did this guy return to hook up with his accomplice or was he merely trying to lead the police astray?*

As the passenger dozed in and out, Ron gently tested the brakes of the cab. Each time he did, he watched the young man move forward from the momentum. The rider would then lean back against the seat, eyes flickering in fatigue and head bobbing right to left and back. There was no seat belt to hold him secure. Bobby hated seat belts and any laws that mandated their use. *Big* government interference with personal choice.

The rider didn't know where they were geographically since he had only traveled that road once or twice in the past. At night each small town looked the same. Streetlights were infrequent and dim, generally located at major intersections or crossroads—then it was dark again.

"Where are we?" he asked, awakening and dazed.

"Not far from where I left you off last time . . . a few more miles I would guess."

"Great," said the passenger, exasperated. "It all looks the same to me. Woods and roads, woods and roads."

He leaned against the right side window of the cab and his injured leg twitched from time to time. The pain in his leg was obviously getting to him. His attempts to clean, hide or cover the wound may have been too late. Bacteria had most likely already contaminated the site and multiplied in the open wound, traveling throughout the blood system systemically.

"Let me know when we're close, okay buddy? I need to rest a bit," he commented, feeling warm. "Is it hot in here? Feels really hot."

"Not really. Ya better get that leg looked at, son. You may have a fever," said Ron, for the sake of conversation.

The rider didn't seem to hear him. Ron thought he might be delirious from the obvious blood loss. He *really* hoped the man had rabies. In his mind, Ron felt he *deserved* it.

In town, Ron slowly turned right instead of left toward the Dollar Store and the rider didn't notice. Bobby was basically out of it at this point, his eyes closed more often than not. Ron didn't want him to escape again. He wanted to make sure the police apprehended the suspect if he could help them.

He had less than a mile to go to the police station on Depot street. He remembered the route that he had taken to meet with the police chief for the interview. He was on track. Every few seconds, he cautiously looked over at the injured man. The rider remained still, head cocked back at an angle, mouth open.

He thought of how he could accomplish the task of getting the police directly involved at this point. No one had stopped him on the darkened highway even though he had exceeded the speed limit by 35 MPH. That initial plan, although imaginative, had failed.

He didn't have much time and Ron didn't want the suspect to wake up and see the lighted sign in front of the police station. Cummings surely would react in some manner, probably adversely, by perhaps attacking the driver. *Maybe he would go ballistic and grab the wheel*, Ron thought, *or jump from the cab in an attempt to escape.*

He didn't even know the guy's name and didn't care to at this point. Ron focused on the task ahead. He was on a mission, a potentially dangerous one.

As the big rig approached the police station from the east, Ron Corvallis saw no one near the front entrance of the station. The hour was late. He became more nervous but desired for the trip to end. His knuckles were "white" as he firmly gripped the steering wheel—he felt his pulse race and his forehead sweat. He could see his passenger stir and then look immediately at the well-lit sign that read in block letters, "Police Station."

Bobby reacted as any man might on the run. He sat forward, blinking his eyes repeatedly. His vision was fuzzy, and then began to clear.

Adrenaline flowed immediately. It was a response of "fight or flight" . . . a release of epinephrine from his adrenals straight into the bloodstream. He looked at Ron with intense eyes. They widened in anger, as the sign appeared larger and inherently more visible.

"What the fuck is this? Why are we here?" he reacted, violently.

Ron said nothing and turned *abruptly* left and directly toward the front yard of the police building. The passenger's head slammed sideways against the right side window—he tried to brace himself on the dash.

"Ouch! Crap!" Cummings screamed, in agony. More pain. "You bastard!"

There was no one in the direct line of Ron's vision or ahead of him in the lobby. He accelerated the big rig from forty feet out and hit the cement barriers at a high rate of speed knowing that his passenger had no restraint. The cab almost separated from the trailer portion of the rig, due in part to the sharp angle that Ron negotiated in an unorthodox approach to the facility. There was no driveway in front of him, merely grass and bushes and the Homeland Security cement barriers. That was Ron's intended target.

The heavy chains on the aesthetic cement posts were no match for the bumper. Cement shattered into missiles. The metal links snapped and the cab abruptly plowed into the doors of the front foyer, shards of glass flying in all directions from the two glass-paneled doors.

Ron intentionally jumped on the airbrakes and the deceleration of the vehicle and the continued momentum of the men in the cab sent Bobby flying forward.

Ron's seatbelt strained, but held. He was kept securely in his seat. He felt a bruise in his chest almost knocking the wind out of him.

The entryway was decimated by the impact of the front of the rig's cab, and Bobby Cummings, without seatbelt, lunged forward from the impact, slamming headfirst into the passenger side windshield.

He screamed momentarily as he was launched *in toto* and headfirst through the glass, then rolled slowly off the hood and onto the lobby floor with a loud thud. The sound made Ron sick.

Alarms in the lobby and overall facility sounded loudly. All staff in the police station immediately responded to the intrusion, fearing the worst—a bomb. *Had they been attacked?*

Ron unbuckled his seat belt, grabbed his chest and blew his air horn loudly and unnecessarily to alert the cops, then jumped out and stumbled around to the front of the cab. The young man lay on the floor as the police chief and two other officers came running into the shattered foyer, guns drawn. They saw the injured man, bleeding profusely from the head and immobile. He looked like a bloodied rag doll.

Bobby Cummings was alive, but his head and shoulders were bruised, cut and bleeding.

The chief immediately ran to the driver thinking he might be having a heart attack.

"What the hell?" the chief screamed. "You okay? What are you doin', Ron?" he yelled again, assessing the destruction and human carnage in front of him. There were cement chunks and shards of glass everywhere—some pieces were impaled in the lobby wallboard, like knives or daggers. Crystal-like glass pieces from the windshield covered the floor.

The front of the cab was demolished from the impact and steam rose from the damaged radiator. Green coolant poured from the front end of the rig and onto the floor. The radiator had been punctured by the impact, and the Mountain Dew-colored hot water mixed with the blood surrounding Bobby Cummings's broken torso.

He was alive, but barely. He moaned out loud but was near the physiologic state of coma—blood pressure dropping every second. There were obvious broken bones in his arms and legs.

"Help me," he whispered, eyes closed. "I'm . . . ." he mumbled, never finishing the sentence.

The police chief assured him that help was on the way.

"I brought you the Stillwater suspect," Ron offered, wincing from the crash and grabbing his chest. "It's your killer, the one that you wanted . . . one of the lawyer's killers," he stated, proudly.

The chief stood over Bobby Cummings and looked at the surrounding mess in the police station. He looked at Ron, then back at the victim. He shook his head in amazement and confusion.

"Jesus, Ron, did ya have to get him here this way?" asked the chief, whose heart rate was just settling down. "Holy shit."

Another officer tried to handcuff the immobilized but traumatized suspect and the rescue squad was summoned from the local fire station. A dispatcher seated behind the side window in the lobby called in all "on site" medical responders.

"Don't bother cuffing him," said the chief, "his arm is broken."

One policeman, trained as an EMT, attended to Cummings even though he really didn't know if the man would live or die. He had an emergency kit near the lobby—fully equipped for rapid response. A portable defibrillator was mounted on the wall if needed.

It was his obligation to stabilize the victim, but the officer couldn't help but think of how Stillwater was callously murdered. He knew that the injured man might be a Stillwater killer . . . but that was for a court to decide. He managed to stop some of the profuse bleeding from the head wounds, applying pressure but unsure if glass fragments were present in the head wounds.

The blood supply to the head is intense with numerous superficial blood vessels—one can easily go into shock from a simple wound. This, however, was not a simple cut but a series of lacerations from the glass windshield that now looked like a spider's web of radiant crystals reflecting off the bright ceiling fixtures in the foyer.

A chilling wind added to the confusion. The front entrance became as cold as the outside autumn air. The EMT-trained policeman requested a blanket for the victim. He didn't want to move Cummings, further jeopardizing the patient's medical condition. No one knew if there had been cervical injuries or other spinal fractures from the accident. It was best to wait for the ambulance and staff, experts that had proper immobilizing boards and gurneys for safe transport to the hospital. The trauma center could airlift him to Dartmouth Medical Center in Hanover, if needed.

Another officer confiscated and began inspecting the backpack from the cab. It had been thrown under the dash. Wedged in a corner of the floor was the missing AMEND2 license plate. He knew it had been absconded as a souvenir during the Stillwater crime. The aluminum plate was bent at a right angle from the intensity of the crash. The license plate was hard evidence implicating the wounded suspect in the heinous murder of the attorney.

"Guess this says a lot," he said, holding it high in the air for all to see. He then located a pistol; a 9 mm weapon on the floor of the truck and fully loaded. It was thrown out of the backpack by the impact of the rig.

The officer used a ballpoint pen to remove the handgun. He placed the pen in the trigger loop and carried it upside down in search of a waiting officer who transferred it to an evidence bag in the facility. Ballistics would later confirm if it was the murder weapon used on Stillwater.

The scene in the lobby was surreal to all involved and it took minutes for the chief and the officers to fully grasp and assess the dire situation.

In the distance could be heard the sound of sirens, the EMS's response to the dispatcher's request. An ambulance and a fire truck were *en route*. The fire station was less than a mile from the police station.

A local newspaper reporter, who kept a police scanner in his home, rushed to the scene, knowing from the dialogue on the home monitor that the situation was extraordinary. He grabbed a camera bag from his desk and rushed out the door, notepad and pen in hand. This would be a front-page photo and breaking news story for the early edition. His deadline was imminent.

Ron Corvallis was escorted into the chief's office once an EMT examined his injured chest and shoulder. He seemed dazed, but coherent, as his mind finally realized what he had done. The night would be long, very long.

He called home to tell his wife he would be late—later than normal, but that he was okay. He didn't share the details of the scenario at hand. She merely assumed that he had a late delivery. It was not the first time that he had been delayed in transit.

Chapter 24

The debriefing of Ron Corvallis by the chief at the police station went well into the night. Someone ran to Dunkin' Donuts for a "Box 'O Joe" and two-dozen donuts. Ron felt coherent enough to describe the ride and the gist of the conversation with the suspect.

The police had many questions concerning the location where he had picked up Bobby Cummings, the interaction and dialogue that had ensued, and the contents of the backpack Cummings had in his possession.

Meanwhile, Cummings was stabilized with an IV by the EMT's and rushed to the local hospital and trauma facility, lights flashing and sirens screaming. He was to have an armed policeman outside his hospital room door from that point on.

After surgical repair of his face and torso, he was assigned to intensive care with an IV in each arm and a heart monitor. A number of surgeons attended to his multiple wounds and bone breaks, including the animal bite. Casts were applied to one arm and one leg. To say that he was "all broken up," would be an understatement.

The police wanted desperately to interview him as soon as he was conscious—that is if he made it back from his brush with death. He was sedated to alleviate the intense and excruciating pain. It would be a few days before the police could talk to him.

In the meantime, they had a host of evidence to work with, the AMEND2 license plate, personal identification cards and other evidence, including credit cards and receipts that might offer a trace of the places that he had visited and spent money in New Hampshire.

They noted his jewelry as well. The KKK ring was of serious interest.

There were now *two wallets* with a host of intelligence for the police; one was Bobby's and the other was Ryan Cooper's—the missing accomplice. Cummings had retrieved the wallet of his friend from Festus's cabin.

They now had suspected murderer Cummings in custody, albeit under guard in the hospital, thanks to the unorthodox presentation and delivery of the suspect by Ron Corvallis.

But where was the person named Cooper? The police were mystified by the new lead with the apprehension of Cummings.

* * *

Man's best friend remained near his dead master. Thunder only wandered outside to relieve himself near the door or to chase some pesky feral animal that was scrounging for food. Festus sometimes fed local animals in winter, when food was difficult to find in snow. Other times he would bait them with apples and acorns in fall, to kill and eat the wildlife later. Squirrels were prevalent and he often caught them, those that were seeking seeds and nuts in preparation for winter.

The door to the cabin remained partially open. It was stuck at a 30-degree angle; basically because of the piece of oak that Bobby Cummings had left behind on the floor, which jammed the door in an open position.

The recent death of Festus caused the cabin to have a pungent, putrid odor of decay. He was decomposing rapidly, even though the weather had been cool. There was no way for anyone to know that he had been killed, or that he was deceased for that matter. The dog chased off a fox or two at night since the predators, given the chance, would eat the remains.

As the odor permeated the surrounding area, the chance of more scavengers appearing increased. Death was an attractant to feral animals and predator birds. Thunder was protective of his master.

Two days after Festus was killed, a stray hunter was drawn to the sound of the moaning of a dog in the distance. He knew the sound of pain—an unknown animal in distress perhaps. At first, the wild turkey hunter thought that a dog or other animal had been "trapped," or poached, perhaps by an illegal hunter seeking pelts i.e. muskrat or beaver. The sound was distinctly more of a "canine in peril," but not that of a wolf. Wolfs were rare in the mountainous area, driven away by the encroaching human population.

The hunter followed the sound, which became louder. He curiously sought out its origin in the distant woods. He wanted to be of assistance but caution prevailed. *Was it an animal gone mad?* He surely didn't want to encounter one.

Joseph McNulty had been a hunter all his life. He was middle-aged and a respected woodsman, obeying the laws of the woods and the sport of hunting. He sought out turkeys, bear, deer and other game each year. He was in the New Hampshire lottery each year to hunt moose as well. Every year, the New Hampshire Fish and Game Department allowed hunters to enter a lottery to cull excessive numbers of wildlife. Often deer or moose were the animals that needed to be reduced.

Competition for food in the New Hampshire woods was often fierce. Starvation was prevalent late in the season. They fed off of the cornfields in fall. Animals lived off the local orchards in winter where they might find apples or pears that had fallen to the ground. In some cases they could reach the remaining fruit of autumn, attached directly to the lower branches of the tree. They feasted on the Macintosh and Cortland apples, those left behind unpicked in September and October. Orchards were prevalent in the Lakes Region and fruit trees abundant.

Joe was dressed from head to toe in hunter's camo, but he also wore the appropriate iridescent orange accents that helped him avoid becoming a target for some other careless sportsman. He displayed his hunting permit on his chest pocket flap and carried his gun across the front of his vest. The shotgun was open and maintained at a safe angle, preventing premature firing if he were to stumble or fall. He took safety seriously.

He could hear the cries clearly now and followed the sound, which increased in volume. He was close. It was difficult to pinpoint at first, since the sound reverberated off the nearby hills and cliffs confusing Joe. At one point he got turned around and was headed in the wrong direction until he followed a stream, the same brook that led to the cabin. He wanted desperately to find the suffering animal and was ready, if need be, to put it out of its misery with his shotgun.

Once he was on track with the cries for help, he moved slowly and cautiously. Just because it sounded like a dog, didn't mean it was one—he decided to take no chances. His gun was loaded and at the ready should the animal be something other than what he had anticipated.

Joe followed the sound, leaves and sticks beneath his feet crunching with each cautious step. Small dead branches snapped from his foot travel. There was no way to sneak up quietly.

The cry seemed more hoarse now and he knew that he was nearing the place where he could get a look at the source, a view from a safe distance. He had binoculars and removed them from a fanny-pack. He could easily see anything of note from a few hundred yards away.

The trees thinned. He approached an unexpected clearing, which was unknown to him but part of the Festus Gravel property. It was two o'clock in the afternoon and Joe had been in the woods since 6 A.M. He noted the small cabin and then the presence of a dog in the doorway. Thunder was peering out of the door, howling as if in pain. His head was elevated and his mouth was positioned like a wolf baying at the moon. Joe raised his binoculars again and scanned the cabin and surrounding area for human activity. There appeared to be no one around but the dog. He thought that odd.

He noted a fiberboard sign on a tree at the perimeter that read: POSTED—NO TRESPASSING. He thought twice of traversing the open area. *Was it private property? On state land?* Nothing made sense. *Was someone living there? Permanently?* He would be a perfect target if someone were home and serious about the signs posted on trees. They were tacked up every fifty feet.

A second sign read: BEWARE OF OWNER. It showed the illustration of the barrel of a pistol facing the reader of the sign. Joe was concerned and was not one to trespass, but felt something was drastically wrong with the dog. It barked at his presence.

"Hello," he called out, with a resounding echo off the hills. "Anyone home?" There was no response. The dog stood silent, looking his way, then howled and barked repeatedly.

He decided to repeat the call, "hello," but to no avail. He noted that for a chilly day, no smoke was coming from the chimney. *Why was there no fire burning?* He knew that cabins leaked like sieves and there should be a fire going on a cold wet day, especially if someone lived there year-round.

He knew it was not a hiker's hut. It had too many amenities and pieces of trash around the building to be an Appalachian Mountain Club (AMC) trail hut for overnight hikers. It was uncomely, but probably someone's home.

Thunder spotted Joe and began to whimper and howl continuously. Joe saw that the dog was not chained or restricted in any way.

Something else was wrong, he thought. The dog did not approach him.

The dog ventured a few feet out of the doorway. Joe owned hunting dogs. He knew that they often conveyed messages by crying out as if they were injured, even when they were not.

"Hello . . . anyone there? I'm friendly," he shouted. Again, there was no response from any inhabitants in the cabin.

"Here, boy," he yelled from a distance. "Come, boy," he commanded. The dog cowered and yelped even louder. He kept looking back into the cabin. Joe became fearful, even apprehensive. *Why in the hell was the dog behaving oddly?*

Sensing that there was no one at home, Joe slowly approached the front of the building, cautiously and one step at a time. He held his gun at the ready. He was some 30-40 feet away when the dog came toward him wagging his tail furiously, but cowering. He was slouched like a Shepherd might stand, his rear low to the ground. He sensed that Joe was friendly and did not attack the man.

"Come, boy!" said Joe, firmly. He was down on one knee and beckoned the dog closer with his hand. The dog came forward and then stopped, his tail slowly wagging side to side.

"Come, boy . . . I won't hurt you. Come here," he said, softly. He was able to coax Thunder closer.

"Where's your Master, your owner?" Joe said, looking from side to side and then behind himself. He did not want to be jumped by an irate owner. The last thing he needed was someone who might accuse him of trespassing, or stealing his or her dog.

Joe was nervous but stood and asked the dog to come. Thunder responded and stood at his feet, whimpering. He looked back at the cabin and then at Joe. The hunter was confident that the dog was not vicious.

He knew that something was afoul. As he stepped closer to the building, there was a stench that permeated the air . . . the smell of death. Even the dog's fur smelled horrible. Joe patted the dog's head and then placed the palm of his hand next to his nose.

He gagged.

Whatever was on the dog's fur was now on his palm. It was putrid. Joe became nauseated by the odor. He continued forward sensing that something awful had happened in the cabin. He had been in the military service and he knew *death*.

"What the hell's that smell?" he said to himself. "Smells like something died *big time*."

Joe called out loudly once more, and with no reply peered into the darkened cabin. He saw the man in the chair and at first thought that he was asleep. Joe kept a handkerchief over his face as he entered. The hunter was mortified at the scene, odor and carnage.

The interior of the cabin was disheveled as if someone had been searching for something. He turned left and faced the dead man straight on. The scene was ghastly and he ran outside to vomit. Joe wretched his guts out—vomiting what lunch he had consumed earlier. The odor was overpowering and the sight of Festus Gravel cold, gray and dead was appalling and overwhelming. Blood and tissue parts covered the wall, next to the body.

"Jesus Christ," he said, running outside again. "What happened?" wishing the dog could talk.

Joe sat on a wooden bench fashioned from logs, ten yards from the cabin and some distance from the death scene. He grabbed his cell phone from his vest pocket. With shaking hands and an upset stomach, he dialed 9-1-1.

* * *

Bobby Cummings lay in the ICU with catheters inserted and IV's running. Oxygen flowed to an endotracheal tube. He was seriously injured and required wide spectrum antibiotics and supportive Ringers lactate solution to survive. The physicians had repaired the orthopedic breaks, cleaned out the glass chards in his tissues and sutured his superficial wounds. They had noted and repaired the "animal bite" on his thigh.

The patient was tested for rabies, but the doctors had no information where he might have encountered an animal. Both the police and the doctors felt that he had been hiding in the woods for a period of time. He could have been bitten by anything and one trauma doctor surmised that the wound was canine in origin—dog, wolf or coyote.

They were aware that Ron Corvallis had picked him up hitchhiking by the side of the road, some fifteen miles from the hospital. The location was near the recycling center and dump, and on a major east-west highway.

Coincidently, the 9-1-1 call from the hunter initiated an "all out" search by the New Hampshire Fish and Game, the State Police, a coroner and local police units from two local towns. The word was out that the hermit, Festus Gravel, had died by a gunshot wound to the head. Murder was suspected, not suicide. The Fish and Game division was to retrieve the body for an autopsy. The police had found the 9 mm weapon in the belongings of Bobby Cummings. It didn't take them long to assume that Bobby and Festus may have met either intentionally or by serendipity. The scenario was coming together, piecemeal.

Joe McNulty, the hunter, was interviewed by the first of the authorities to arrive at the scene. He was shocked and distressed by the ghastly experience. He kept the dog tethered by his side.

The first to arrive at the cabin was the State Police Special Unit who immediately descended by rope from the helicopter; they were able to access the open field near the cabin without actually landing. They did not have to traverse the woods this time.

The officers met Joe and were astonished by the murder scene and the macabre death of the hermit. Having been there previously, they never anticipated returning to what was another mysterious murder scene in the general geographical area of the Lakes Region.

After the initial photography of the crime scene and inspection in and outside the premises, the State Police were met by Fish and Game personnel and a coroner, experienced men who were there to examine and remove the deceased victim from his reclusive home. They had arrived by four wheel ATVs and had ample supplies to assist injured hikers or transport the dead, as needed. They used all terrain vehicles for other rescues year round. Sometimes their job was merely to transport an injured hiker or skier to a waiting ambulance.

This time their role was to assist, by physically transporting Festus Gravel to a waiting hearse at the bottom of the mountain.

Following the coroner's exam of the remains, two men in dark-green Fish and Game uniforms carried the black bag with Festus's body out of the cabin. They donned white surgical masks, similar to those worn by painters and medical personnel. The mask did little to squelch the stench of death, but was a protective barrier against microbes.

The dog watched from afar as the body of his master was removed from the scene. He whimpered in mourning. Joe tried to calm him down, but Thunder stood and faced the bag stoically, tail stiffened. He was protective of his master, dead or alive. Somehow he knew Festus was in the mortuary bag.

Joe walked him over to the enclosed remains—the dog licked the bag and turned away. The police looked confused by the unorthodox procedure.

"He was his master," Joe explained. "The dog was his best pal, I think."

The Fish and Game personnel were sympathetic of the dog's reaction. They patted his head reassuring the animal that all was okay.

"It's okay, boy . . . it's okay," one man said, remorsefully. Joe stepped back a few feet from the ATV and body. The coroner was making notes before they departed. He returned to the cabin to inspect other pathological specimens from the gunshots.

The local police were the last to arrive at the scene. They quickly viewed the body of Festus Gravel. These were detectives that Chief Randall's had sent to the scene for continuity in the investigation. The Fish and Game ATV then slowly left the scene.

The detectives combed the premises for more evidence. Some of the first items found in the cabin were the unique gold ring; the one that was Festus owned—a antique KKK ring that his father had left him along with a shotgun. They took both. They had already located Ryan's wallet and the AMEND2 license plate in the belongings that Bobby Cummings carried in the truck cab.

"Look at this ring!" one policeman said, mortified by the insignia. "It's KKK. Looks similar to one that the suspects had."

"Amazing," added another officer. "Who would have thought we had remnants of traditional KKK members in the area? The old man and the killers may have been members of a Klan? I can't believe that Festus was. He didn't hang with that crowd. He was a loner, a hermit."

The police surveyed the property and noted what appeared to be the recent move of the outhouse. It was a casual observation and considered inconsequential. They assumed that Festus had recently accomplished the task. They had spotted a Come-A-Long tool and rope inside the shed. There were eyehooks on the side of the commode. The recent scratches on the side of the outhouse and rough marks on a nearby tree suggested that someone had dragged the unit to the right. Underneath some leaves were skid marks that were not completely obliterated by the recent rain.

A curious policeman investigating the site scraped away some of the leaves to the left of the outhouse and noted fresh dirt that implied the old "pit" had been filled in. That was nothing unusual. Outhouses were often moved annually.

As he observed the older site more closely, leveling some dirt with his black boot, the dog began to bark wildly—he was facing the policeman who was examining the general area near the outhouse.

The dog was temporarily tied to a tree while Joe patted his head gently. Thunder stared at the officer and would not respond to Joe's command to quiet down, and sit. There was little tail wagging.

"Hush," commanded Joe. The dog paid him no mind.

With a sudden lurch of his body, the massive dog broke free of the rope and sniffed his way to the old pit, his nose pressed to the ground. The hunter and the policeman stopped and watched his behavior, intrigued by his determination to join the officer.

"What is it, boy?" one of the policemen said, watching the dog circle the area of fresh dirt. "He's *on* ta somethin'."

He was curious to know why the dog was obsessed with that one spot on the ground.

"Somethin' there, boy?"

"Jesus, guys," another officer commented in disgust. "It's the old shit hole. That's all." He laughed at the persistence of the dog.

The dog continued pacing. He entered the outhouse since the door was ajar and then went back to the site of the old pit. He continued the routine back and forth, and the police became even more suspicious. He whimpered as if there was something important at the site. He continued the routine, back and forth, circling and sniffing the area. Joe McNulty stood by him.

"Is this the animal that may have bitten the suspect in the hospital?" asked one astute officer. "He's a bit crazy, it seems."

"Not 'crazy,' but crazy like a fox!" offered Joe. "This dog was injured by someone . . . maybe one of the villains. "The dog has a good nose—he's a hunter for sure."

"The damn dog may have witnessed the crime," added another officer. "We can only surmise that the suspect, Cummings, killed Festus Gravel. The ballistics team in the cabin noted the bullet in the wall to the left of where the old man's head was leaning in the chair. That's where some of his brains were splattered."

A second officer qualified the fact that they would match the bullet from the gun with the crime, the same gun Bobby Cummings had in his backpack before the crash into the lobby. If the ballistics test matched or mimicked the profile of the 9-mm pistol, they "had" (in their minds) the murderer of Festus and, most likely, Attorney Stillwater.

The oak stick on the cabin floor was also evidentiary. It contained blood and hair, albeit suspected black hair from the injured dog or canine blood. Perhaps human blood as well. The forensic investigators would know the subtle difference between biological samples of man or dog. There were definitive differences in cell types and histopathology.

The dog continued the persistent pattern and finally stopped directly over the old pit. He stood there with his tail wagging repeatedly. The police were awestruck and knew that something was amiss.

The officials were unaware that the dog had followed the blanket and body of Ryan Cooper when Festus had dragged the dead man from the shallow streambed to the old outhouse pit. The dog knew the scent of Cooper and was luckily drawn to Cooper's final resting place.

One officer demanded that they dig up the area of the older pit. There could be evidence in the hole. Most of the other police staff thought he was nuts, and that the effort would be a waste of time. No one wanted the task of digging into the abyss.

"You want to dig up a shit hole?" one man cried out in disgust. "You crazy?"

"Why not?" the officer said, "we know there were two accomplices in the Stillwater crime. We only have *one* in custody and . . . my guess is, the other is either on the run or on this property. This dog knows something we don't know."

The hunter sided with the first officer.

"I think the dog's onta somethin'. I say dig!" added McNulty.

"Good. You dig up that crap, literally! You investigate a shit hole that was probably used for a year by the old man," a patrolman laughed. "I ain't doin' it."

The hunter spoke up. "I'm Joe. I'll help. I knew Attorney Stillwater quite well and I would be glad to be of assistance. Dogs are intuitive and have good memories. Got a shovel?"

On the side of the cabin were two spade shovels, lying propped against the wall. The wooden handles were weathered and the metal on one rusted except for the edge, which was gleaming silver from the apparent recent use.

The one that looked like it had been used recently was caked with mud. The officer and Joe grabbed the tools and began the grim process. The other officers thought they were nuts. The dog continued to bark.

It wasn't long before some white powder appeared; it was interspersed with the soil, which was not compacted. There was the smell of lye—a pungent odor that permeated the air.

"I smell a chemical," said the officer with a mission. The other officers laughed and said, "That's probably poop."

"No . . . it's not that . . . it's a chemical smell . . . I think it's lye. I've used it before to clean things."

One other officer peered into the hole and saw the white powder.

"That's the stuff they use to decompose excrement . . . ya know, shit! It's a common procedure with outhouses."

It was no more than two minutes, when Joe McNulty turned and became ill. He was overcome by the smell of human remains. An arm appeared and the hand was black. He had already thrown up from the sight and smell of Festus, and now he was overcome with the same feelings—there was nothing left in his stomach. He gagged and coughed. He had the dry-heaves. The officer with the second shovel backed off as well. Other policemen and a NH Fish and Game officer ran to help them.

"What's the matter?"

"Jesus! There's a man's body in the hole. The fuckin' dog was right. He was onto somethin'. Holy crap . . . this is disgusting."

"It's a recent death. You can tell by the condition of the torso. How many friggin' bodies are there on this property?" a policeman asked.

One of the forensic investigators donned a "two-canister" mask that absorbed odors, especially after death. It had a double charcoal filter and purified the air he was breathing. He wore vinyl gloves and gently exposed more of the torso, which was bent over and covered with a mixture of dirt and lye.

Chief Randall arrived a bit late and surmised that the gentleman in the pit was the suspect, Ryan Cooper, the second perpetrator in the murder of Stillwater.

Had the authorities not observed the repetitive and persistent actions of the dog, they might not have known of the impromptu shallow grave.

"Damn . . . this is disgusting," said the chief.

The dog ceased barking as the body was removed. It was clear that the man had been riddled with buckshot, no doubt the cause of his demise.

The tail of the dog was held steady between his legs, and he cowered from the sight. He whimpered as if he remembered something bad that had happened to him. He may have remembered that one of the men had beaten him with the stick of oak. The real villain was Bobby Cummings, not Cooper.

The coroner was contacted and asked to return to the scene. The state medical examiner would have *two* autopsies to perform now in Concord.

It was uncanny. Had the officer and Joe McNulty not followed their own premonition and the behavior of the dog, it is unlikely anyone would have found the corpse of Ryan Cooper, at least that day. The I.D. of the man was not yet confirmed, but the chief was sure that this was "the" Ryan Cooper, one of the same men that had killed Stillwater. This confirmed that the men had in fact met up with Festus Gravel.

What happened at the cabin was not known but the pieces of the crime were slowly coming together. The relationship between Festus Gravel and the two men in question was baffling and the investigation into any events at Festus's cabin was just beginning.

Joe McNulty sat on a log and watched the investigative process. He asked if he could take the dog home and bring him to a vet for a physical exam. The dog had injuries that needed attention. He limped and appeared to favor one leg. It was clear that he had been abused or injured by one of the perpetrators. No doubt he was defending his master when he was abused.

The police agreed with the plan since the dog had prior wounds. Although healing, they needed the attention of animal hospital staff. X-rays might be needed as well.

The police felt that the initial custody of the animal would be turned over to the Humane Society. That was normal procedure with strays or orphan animals. There was a facility ten miles from the scene. They were hoping Joe McNulty could adopt the animal.

Although Thunder had no collar or tags to I.D. him, or to locate an owner, he may have had a subdermal implant I.D. with the name of an owner other than Festus Gravel. Nothing was known of the dog other than the fact that he alerted the hunter and authorities to the death of his master and a suspected killer. The dog was effectively the hero of the day and dedicated to his master, even after death. That, in and of itself, was noteworthy and remarkable.

Chapter 25

An emergency page, one that came over the intercom above his head, alerted the officer who was guarding Bobby Cummings outside the door to the ICU. The message was "Code Blue," a call for the Code team at the hospital. The team was comprised of three nurses with emergency pagers clipped to their scrubs. Highly trained, they were the first to respond to any emergency call in the hospital.

"Code" nurses received the page directly and there was a simultaneous announcement over the hospital intercom as well. The elevators automatically went to the lowest floor to await any doctors that might need quick access to a critical case on the upper levels.

Any doctors near the "emergency," rushed to the scene assisting in any way that they could.

The responsibilities varied for each nurse.

The first nurse maintained the records.

The second nurse (usually the most experienced) ran the "crash cart." He or she applied the defibrillator pads, worked the monitor, obtained supplies, and defibrillated/ cardio-converted the patient, or handled the meds. This person *ran* the team.

The third nurse was assigned to the set up of the IVs or perfusions, and "pushed the meds," if required.

The Code cart contained medications, endotracheal tubes and heart instruments. Each drawer was colored coded like a rainbow. Each tray had specific instruments—all of them priorities for any emergency.

In that regard, the patient was being attended to by the best of the emergency responders.

The three nurses arrived *rapidly*, virtually pushing aside the police officer at the door. The unit doors opened violently. There was a critical issue with a patient and the patient was none other than the infamous, Bobby Cummings!

Cummings, almost comatose, was not conscious of their exemplary efforts. Electronically, he displayed ventricular fibrillation and life threatening cardiac arrhythmias. The monitor showed an abnormal sinus rhythm. On reality TV, they would have called it "flat-lining," an over-dramatic term for *asystole*—a term often used *incorrectly* in the real world of TV medical dramas. His heartbeat was rapid, exhibiting extreme tachycardia.

Essentially, the heart was not pumping blood; the muscular beats too rapid to be effective as a pump. There was no pulse. There were no synchronous beats for the heart to fill and evacuate blood, or operate rhythmically. The cardiac muscles were fatigued, demanding oxygen. Oxygen was not being provided by the coronaries or to the chambers of the heart.

The most experienced nurse responded by taking command. Cummings was in dire straights as she hovered over him. Conveniently, she was on the same floor as the ICU, attending to another patient in the respiratory ward.

"We have to zap him, stat!" the Code leader demanded. The "tech nurse" looked at the monitor and then ripped open the Johnny on Cummings's chest. She grabbed the paddles for the defibrillator.

She then applied gel to specific areas of the chest, for better conductivity. First near the right clavicle, then lower on the chest by the left pectoral muscle below the heart (the anterior-apex scheme).

Observing the cardiac monitor, she placed the paddles (pads) on the gelled, skin area and said, "Clear!"—the same term that is utilized to this day by pilots before they start a prop engine of an airplane. The warning helped prevent others from being shocked by the electrical charge to the chest.

The discharge from the defibrillator causes the patient to move a bit in response to the external stimulus. Unlike medical TV shows and other dramatic moments for entertainment, the man did not convulse or elevate off the bed—akin to Hollywood melodramatics.

For a moment, Bobby's heart regained a sinus rhythm, but it was not sustainable. He was in severe cardiac distress. His blood pressure was nil and the heart became non-responsive to the lifesaving measure. He was dying!

A doctor arrived on the scene quickly and tried to "defib" the patient a second time. There was no response and the man was obviously morbidly in peril. He had been intubated to maintain respiration and saturate him with oxygen, but his blood was not circulating.

The doctor called for epinephrine "stat," a heart stimulant. He used a 6" long needle to administer the therapeutic dose directly between the ribs, through the chest, and into the heart muscle. The cardiac muscle responded briefly and the normal innervation and *natural* pacemakers of the heart attempted to reset the heartbeat; it maintained a normal rhythm with a few immediate contractions.

An over-stimulated vagus nerve, which normally slows the heart rate, was overriding the process, shutting the heart down. No one knew why Cummings was unresponsive to a sustained rhythm.

The doctor ordered the patient brought directly into a nearby operating room, a room where they would attempt to massage the heart manually, by open chest. A critical cardiac team, an anesthesiologist and assistants had already assembled in Suite One.

The extreme efforts were to no avail, even after twenty minutes of desperate heroics and emergency response.

Cummings was now officially medically *flat-lined* and his brainwaves ceased on the EEG monitor. The brainstem pulses disappeared.

The surgical suite went silent . . . Bobby Cummings had succumbed.

* * *

Chief Randall, currently on site at the Festus Gravel cabin, was notified by cell phone of the death of Cummings, at first by the officer who was standing guard near the ICU, and then by the cardiac doctor who would confirm the death in a more formal manner. Formal paperwork would follow the verbal communication.

An autopsy would follow at the State Medical Examiner's office in Concord, the same M.E. that handled the bodies of Ryan Cooper and Festus Gravel.

The *post mortem* body investigation was designed to access all major organs and would determine any congenital, anatomical or pathological reasons for Cummings's demise. *Were there underlying pre-conditions that caused the heart to fail in a man that young?* The prior buckshot to the chest, dog wound, and the orthopedic and dermal trauma from the truck crash, although severe, was not deemed life threatening by the trauma team. Internal organs were basically functional but a clot could have dislodged—a fatal thrombus.

* * *

At autopsy, the medical examiner noted (grossly) that the heart had been *scarred* by prior drug abuse, mainly from cocaine, a natural anesthetic to heart muscle. Histopathology would confirm the observation microscopically.

A bioanalysis by GC-MS and toxicological review of Cummings's blood and low levels in tissue (by LC-MS/MS technique) confirmed recent use of illegal drugs, metabolites that could permanently damage the heart. The man had been an addict for years it was determined. The weakened heart could not sustain his life after trauma.

The unexpected death of Cummings, as well as the discovery of Ryan Cooper's remains in the outhouse pit, further complicated the investigation with respect to the Stillwater murder. All relevant suspects and participants, in *two* separate but related crimes, were dead before they could add real time information to the investigation and eventual murder trials.

Chapter 26

The police chief contacted Attorney Tom Moore, Stillwater's colleague, once the names of the suspects, now victims, had been confirmed. Moore was shocked and knew little of Ryan Cooper's participation in the death of Barnaby Stillwater. He was unaware of the death of Festus Gravel or a suspected relationship to his colleague's death.

There were no current cases involving either of the two decreased young men in the New Hampshire court system. Stillwater's office records showed *no* prior interaction with either man, or Festus Gravel, for that matter.

Three men were now dead and there was no motive in the investigation of either case.

If the Stillwater murder was a random act, and Barnaby an innocent victim, then why was the AMEND2 license plate stolen? The weapon at the Stillwater death scene, at Festus Gravel's home, as well as the one in the backpack of Bobby Cummings, were clearly linked to all three deaths. Forensic ballistic tests confirmed the evidence. The mystery at this point was an enigma.

* * *

Weekly discussions on the conservative AM radio show (WCON) alerted some of the Jaffrey FSP rally attendees of the now dead men involved in a series of bizarre crimes. Word spread throughout the Freestater Web site and by cell from member to member. It was suspected that two men who may have attended the annual rally were cohorts in killing a prominent lawyer and a recluse in the Lakes Region of New Hampshire.

The negative impacts of the allegations regarding the "Free State" movement were obvious, and their "liberty" agenda and image appeared compromised. More and more residents of New Hampshire were looking into their Web site for motives and their extreme political agenda. Locals were aghast at the trend *to upset* the state legislature's civil operation. The FSP went on the defensive, on line and vocally and on sympathetic conservative talk shows.

The local radio station personalities, who supported the agenda of the radical group espousing "freedom and liberty above all" and no gun "restrictions," were in a tizzy over the recent deaths. They cited the death of Bobby Cummings, in particular, as *murder* by an insane and deranged truck driver.

The FSP became more outspoken.

"The driver *charged* the police station with his rig, knowingly causing the man's eventual death," WCON radio show host, T.J. offered. "What's your opinion?" he asked of the listening audience.

"Tell us what *you* think. We think it's a travesty," he emphasized. "Call in."

Tom Taggert, the co-host agreed. "Sounds premeditated."

Incoming calls rang off the hook the morning of the broadcast. Members of the Freestate Project telephoned the radio station indicating that they may have witnessed Cummings at the rally, but knew nothing of his hidden agenda to harm or kill a lawyer.

One caller indicated that they had observed Ryan Cooper in Jaffrey prior to the Stillwater death. He had been drinking pretty heavily and blabbing about gun rights.

Both men may have been "jacked up" by the rally agenda, another caller suggested.

"No matter what he professed, if in fact it was him," offered T.J., "this man was killed because the truck driver intentionally ran into the building with a unknown passenger, one who he *knew* had no seatbelt buckled—that is, *no* protection from an abrupt stop! It was *intentional, premeditated* harm in my mind—evil intent to severely harm or kill the passenger, a human being. Murder!"

Most conservative listeners wanted to see the truck driver prosecuted for the preconceived, *intentional* death of the hitchhiker—i.e. vigilante justice in their minds. The driver *knew* the passenger might die!

Obviously, the truck driver never intended for the death of Cummings, merely the apprehension of a known suspect in a murder. Ron Corvallis assumed Cummings would be knocked out when he hit the windshield.

He didn't anticipate that the man would go through the windshield and land on the floor of the police station lobby, hemorrhaging and mortally wounded.

The discussion on the radio show continued for three hours, from nine to noon in the morning. The conservative hosts bantered on and on about the "rights" of the victim, caring little about the "rights" or fate of Stillwater or Festus Gravel for that matter.

"He never had a trial... Cummings died before they could try him for murder. Who says he killed Stillwater? It's a damn hoax. A sham against the constitutional liberties of individuals, defaming the FSP. They are scapegoats here! The kid was set up," offered T.J., in defiance.

Many callers agreed and voiced that here should be more respect for the "rights" of *all* people, including those accused of crimes or those who have no prior police record.

Listeners with opposing views were *culled* from the dialogue.

* * *

The now deceased Festus Gravel had no living relatives. There would be no formal funeral. To save money, the state of New Hampshire decided to have him cremated post autopsy. The autopsy showed that he was killed at close range with the weapon that the police had found in the possession of Cummings.

A single shot to the head was the cause of death. The second shot to the heart was insignificant, the medical examiner had determined. The temporal/cranial wound was instantaneous... and the shot to the heart *after* the fact.

A concerned and sympathetic Lakes Region resident (with money), volunteered to be responsible for Festus's remains and dispose of his ashes properly on the land he had claimed as his own. The man volunteered to pay for the urn if necessary. That was a decision for the state of New Hampshire. Since no one objected to the idea, the state saved on expenses for the burial of Festus Gravel, the Mt. Hoosac hermit.

* * *

Joe McNulty was allowed to take Thunder from the Humane Society to his own veterinarian to have the dog examined.

The physical exam showed minor bruises to the head and a fractured rib from the oak stick. There was a shadow on the X-ray, but a hairline fracture of the cranium was deemed minor. The doctor indicated that the dog would recover over time.

He scanned the dog's body for an identification chip, which might have been placed subcutaneously at the request of a previous owner. There was none. Nothing was found to indicate that the dog belonged to anyone aside from Festus Gravel.

The veterinarian suggested that Joe adopt the dog since he had passionate concern and experience for the animal's well being. He would back Joe's request as a personal reference, if needed. The dog would have a good home, the vet thought, since McNulty had two other hunting beagles that could keep the injured dog company.

Because of the circumstances related to the dog and the death of Festus, the vet waved all charges, *pro bono*. Joe and the Humane Society thought that kind of him but offered to pay anyway. The vet refused any remuneration. The public noted his kindness and complimented him on the gesture. His veterinary business increased that month, basically from thankful and concerned residents.

"Thanks Doc, nice of you," Joe said, with gratitude. "Appreciate the help."

"No problem, Joe. You're doing a good deed. I'll 'make up for it next time' you bring the beagles in for shots," he laughed.

Joe chuckled since he had given the vet plenty of money in the past. His other dogs had allergies and other issues—costly monthly expenses year round.

"I give you a lot each year," he chided the vet. "You're drainin' me."

"Yah, pays the bills," the doctor teased.

"I'll have to *name* the dog since we don't know his original name." The hunter tried to think of something novel—for a dark brown dog with glossy black highlights.

"'Blackie,'" one of the veterinary assistants, Susan, suggested, "how about Blackie?"

"Sounds good," added the veterinarian, thinking it was appropriate.

Joe agreed.

"Make me up a name tag will ya, or order one of those metal ones with his name and my address on it."

Susan agreed to order a special tag.

Joe agreed to register the dog at the local town hall.

"We'll call you when the tag comes in. Hopefully, the dog will never wander on ya. He's all set for heartworm testing, rabies shots and other vaccine boosters. We took care of that. Let us know if he has worms—keep a stool sample if you see any evidence of parasites. Okay?"

"Okay . . . thanks, doc . . . see ya soon."

Joe and Thunder (now named, "Blackie") left the veterinary clinic. The dog loved his new master. He and Joe were soon to appear all the newspapers—"headlines" of the hunter who saved an orphaned dog. The dog became the local hero, a human-interest story of dog and man.

A publicity photo was taken at the police station, complete with the police chief, Joe McNulty and the dog. It soon appeared on the front page of all local papers and on the Internet.

Blackie was now the "Wonder Dog," to children and the *darling* of the community, especially in the eyes of dog-lovers and pet advocates in the Lakes Region. People offered to open a Facebook page for the animal.

Chapter 27

The daily papers featuring the hunter and dog had been out a day when a man by the name of Charles Breckenridge informed the police that his dog, "Lucky" had been missing for a couple of weeks. Breckenridge had read of the heroics of Joe McNulty and an orphan dog. He called the police and indicated to the officer on duty that he had lost his pet and had placed an ad in the paper. The family had searched for Lucky for a solid week.

He emphasized how distressed his children were over the missing family companion. Breckenridge spoke confidently of the possibility that the dog in the paper was theirs.

"Looks like 'Blackie' may be my dog named 'Lucky,'" he offered. "'Saw the famed dog in the papers. 'Sure looks similar to ours."

"Really?" the attending officer at the front desk replied, "that might be your animal? Are you sure?"

"Yes . . . I'm sure that's our dog. We live near the area and the woods where the dog was found. Can we at least look at it? 'Sure looks like ours." He was hopefully optimistic.

He seemed knowledgeable about the lost animal and described to a tee the coloration and features of the missing animal. The details described the dog, now known as "Blackie."

"The dog had no collar or tags," offered the policeman on duty. "Did your dog have an I.D. or tags?"

"He had a collar at one point, but we noticed that the day he disappeared, he had broken free of the collar—it was attached to his chain in the backyard. We leave him out during the day."

The police officer was sympathetic and concerned. He wanted the dog to be returned to the rightful owner, if in fact that was the case. The officer was reticent to immediately inform the new caregiver, Joe McNulty, of the inquiry. Joe was a man who had basically *adopted* the dog after the Festus Gravel incident. The paperwork was not final. The officer wanted to be sure of the new information and informed Chief Randall of the phone call.

"Why not come down to the station," the officer recommended, "I'll ask the chief to get the dog into the police station. A local hunter, the one you noted in the paper, has been caring for the dog. If it's your dog, we need to return it to you, but please bring the old 'tags' and his broken collar as well as a personal I.D. or your driver's license. Obviously, we thought this was the hermit's dog when we first found it, but no one was sure."

The owner appreciated the efforts of the police. "Yes, we would be grateful to have the opportunity to see the dog. In the news, it certainly looks like our 'Lucky.' I saw the white spot under his chin and I'm sure it's our family dog."

"Lucky? We've been callin' him 'Blackie' since we didn't know his real name," the officer on duty laughed.

"It would be nice to see the dog returned to its rightful owner," continued the officer. "I'll call you when we have the dog at the station. A local vet examined him, as you might have read in the papers. He was injured or abused in the last week or so. The dog is strong and is doing very well now."

"Thanks officer for the update and your concern," added Breckenridge.

"Please let us know when we can see the dog. The kids are in school today and will want to be there of course. They are thirteen and eleven and will be ecstatic to see their friend. As you can imagine, many tears have been shed in the last couple of weeks. It would be a nice surprise for them if the dog were, in fact, ours. We all feared the worst!"

"Agreed," offered the officer, sympathetically, "the loss of a family pet can be devastating to kids. We want them to have their dog back. If the dog responds to the name you gave him, I'm sure that will be proof to everyone involved."

"Yes, try 'Lucky!'"

"Okay. We'll be in touch, Mr. Breckenridge," added the officer, with assurance. "Hope this is your 'lucky' day—no pun intended," said the policeman. Breckenridge chuckled at the pun. "We hope so too, officer."

Breckenridge was pleased by the officer's input, his help and concerns on the phone. He was sure from the photos in the newspaper that "Blackie, the Wonder Dog" was their pet, Lucky. He was anxious to tell the rest of the family of the news and hopeful that the police would get back to him that day.

Charles Breckenridge was also appreciative that the unknown hunter had been willing to care for and even adopt the dog. Festus Gravel had been tragically murdered and the dog showed dedication to protecting his newfound master, even in death.

The stories in the local newspaper were heartwarming. Lucky had always been an even-tempered and considerate pet, graceful with children and friendly to all neighbors.

The thought that he had been abused, if in fact this was the Breckenridge's dog, was distressful to the actual owner. The dog might need more medical care and attention from their own local veterinarian. The dog was a part of the family, a critical member and eight-years-old.

The Breckenridge family had acquired the dog from a humane shelter in southern New Hampshire. Breckenridge was confident that the family and the dog would be reunited.

He phoned his wife at work and told her the positive news—at least the fact that the police were willing to let them see the animal. She cried at the hopeful thought that the "family" might be reunited. Like the kids, she had been in tears since the dog ran away.

Chapter 28

Ron Corvallis, who had slammed his truck into the entrance of the police station, was being accosted by "letters to the editor" in local newspapers. Many mini-editorials from "right-wing gun rights and liberty proponents" were published—writers who thought that the city should sue Corvallis for intentional destruction of public property and premeditated murder. Even the ACLU got involved in a potential wrongful death suit, citing the right for Cummings "to carry." He was presumed innocent until proven guilty, and obviously could never be brought to trial.

Who was going to pay for the repairs to the city building? they wondered. *Who was going to charge the driver with homicide, negligent homicide, vehicular homicide or wrongful death?*

Freestaters were irate and their ire was elevated when, unexpectedly, Attorney Tom Moore decided to defend the truck driver and represent him against any and all allegations. He offered to help *pro bono*, since his friend and colleague, Barnaby Stillwater had been gunned down by Cummings and his pal, Ryan Cooper—two thugs, in Moore's mind, who had strong principles and ideology in the "freedom and liberty movement." They were suspected of killing a prominent professional man and legal expert for no reason, other than for an *opposing* opinion on gun regulations.

The suspected motive was the opposition to a U.S. Constitutional amendment that Stillwater said was antiquated and often misinterpreted to this day, at least in many peoples' minds, and Barnaby's. He was not alone in his thinking.

Ron Corvallis was pleased to have Tom Moore represent him, or to be an ambassador against the insinuations and allegations from the "right" and even the NRA. He knew in his heart that he had intended on "knocking the man out" by the abrupt stop of the truck.

The intent was to facilitate the police department's apprehension of the suspect. He was aware that the man was not restrained but *that* was *his own* choice.

Ron had no intention of causing life-threatening injuries to anyone, injuries that ultimately enhanced the probability of the young man's death. It was not premeditated by any stretch of the imagination and Tom Moore felt that the *loss of life* was not intentional or desired by his client, Ron Corvallis. That was the key defense in any suit.

At most, manslaughter charges might be brought against the truck driver and Moore felt that he could defend the right of the driver to *defend* himself (in the cab) knowing full well that the passenger was a wanted suspect, and was known to have a weapon. He was also wanted by the police . . . for murder.

The general public, other than the extreme right-wing advocates, were sympathetic to the driver's intensions. Some thought the suspect deserved the punishment! They concurred that Ron was in possible danger since a weapon had been confirmed in the cab of the truck immediately after the collision. That weapon had been used in the Festus Gravel murder—a point blank shot to the head—killing a defenseless recluse who wanted nothing other than to be left alone in the woods.

"I think that if anyone charges you with reckless endangerment, vehicular homicide or any other crime relative to the Cummings death, you will be vindicated. It's almost like you were exercising a "citizen's arrest." You surely didn't mean for the man to die," offered Moore in consolation. "You were aiding in his apprehension."

Ron agreed, but was scared.

"I think these letters in the newspapers will foster hatred that could threaten my life or the lives of my family members. There are other radicals out there that may be close friends of Cummings. Now that he's dead, they could seek *retribution*, if you know what I mean."

"True," cited Moore, "the police are on your side, however. You solved part of the crime—two crimes, in fact. The damage to the building, or to the truck, was reckless and costly in normal circumstances and could have been interpreted as threatening a public building or the general public, I suppose. But that was not your intent," he said, emphatically. "The manner you chose was not an orthodox procedure, but in a crisis you did what you thought was self-protection and would help apprehend the killer . . . or 'what you had to do!' You were emotionally charged and even distressed by his threatening presence, especially when he saw the police station sign!"

"That's what I was trying to do," offered Ron, nodding in agreement. "I didn't want the man to get away a second time . . . I had picked him up once before. What is the chance of running into him twice, anyway?"

"Probably zero to none," said Moore, in total concurrence.

"What will happen next?" asked Ron, with concern and trepidation. "Will I be forced to hide out? Run?"

"No, but not sure," said Moore, stroking his chin. "People are jacked up. Let's see if the city, city council or others decide to sue to reclaim repairs for the building . . . or if anyone from the killer's family wants to go after us with any formal wrongful death accusations. I don't know if Cummings had relatives."

Moore continued.

"These things take time as more and more people take issue with the unusual situation. You will have supporters that we can play off of. It's not *all* negative. Many sympathizers are on your side."

"Agreed," mentioned Ron, "I'm sure someone from the Jaffrey FSP rally will take issue with the loss of one of their supporters. The newspaper has already shown us that extremists are writing letters of protest, citing the abuse of 'liberty.' They've already said that there was little proof of the murders to date and that Bobby Cummings had the right to carry a pistol. They're wrong! It's already clear from the forensic evidence that he was involved. The gun and bullets in the crimes match! These advocates are pro-gun nut-jobs and will be in my face."

"Yah, the pistol that killed Festus Gravel had already been linked forensically to his death, but the FSP doesn't know that yet," offered Moore. "We can prove that the man was a cold-blooded murderer, since the shot to Festus Gravel's head was at *point blank* range. There was black powder on his temple. We may not know all the details of the crime, but Cummings surely killed Festus Gravel and probably would have gotten *life in the clink* anyway. This state has a death penalty but rarely uses it. Hanging is still on the books!"

"They'll want to hang me!"

Ron was sick to his stomach. He didn't know how to deal with the forthcoming adverse notoriety and his shipping company had already received anonymous death threats directed at him and at the management.

Ron had yet to face his own superiors and the company VP's or fellow co-workers. After all the publicity, he would probably be losing his job. He knew that, and that realization added more pressure and angst in his life.

Chapter 29

The history of the independence movement in New England fostered and nourished many mavericks and patriots who impacted our modern day freedoms. General John Stark was significant since New Hampshire's militia played a key role in the American Revolution. He stood out in history like Daniel Webster and Franklin Pierce as well as other prominent figures from the Granite State who followed in their footsteps. Together, they refined the principles of a modern society that started in New England and more predominantly in the surrounding Boston area. New Hampshire played a role however, and its statesmen were hailed as the forbearers of our principles we hold in esteem today.

So much so were their roles in an early America that they are immortalized to this day with statues or tributes in front of, and on the grounds and in buildings of the New Hampshire State House in Concord.

Stark (1728-1822) was not the only patriot to be recognized. Daniel Webster (1782-1852) was notable, as well as Commodore George Hamilton Perkins (1835-1899), President Franklin Pierce (1804-1869) and John Parker Hale (1806-1873).

Each of the men was a forbearer of the liberties and freedoms that New Hampshire residents hold close to the vest and in high regard.

Many of the statues that surround the "replica" of the Liberty Bell are located on the front lawn of the New Hampshire State House. Each state has a facsimile of the original bell. The cast metal replica is the national symbol and a reminder for all who reside in New Hampshire that some people sometimes take the freedoms espoused by the patriots to the *extreme*.

Of late, New Hampshire had drawn some newer residents who are the *antithesis* of what the early statesmen stood for by their presence and their principles. They did not believe in tyranny and anarchy to achieve change. Civil discourse predominates as well as majority rule, not screaming "liberty" from the legislative chamber gallery.

Commodore Perkins attended the U.S. Naval Academy in 1851. In the Civil War, he was notable—he was also part of the military and an officer near Fort Jackson and Fort St. Philip. In 1862, Perkins was involved in the capture of New Orleans. In 1864, he commanded the monitor, *Chickasaw*—at the battle of Mobile Bay, Alabama. He became a Captain in 1882, sixty years after Stark's death, and then became Commodore in 1896. He was a native of Hopkinton, New Hampshire, a small town near Concord, and not far from Stark's residence in Dunbarton.

By far, the most notable person held in high regard besides Stark in New Hampshire's philosophies and history was Daniel Webster. Born in Franklin, New Hampshire, he lived during Stark's life and Webster was deemed one of the *greatest orators* of all time. A shrewd lawyer, he attended Dartmouth College in Hanover. He was a Federalist and took pride in defending the shipping interests for New England.

A member of the U.S. House of Representatives, he was an acclaimed speaker and later became a senator. Unlike some radical movements and "marauders" who forget history and human suffering even to this day, *Webster considered slavery evil.*

He and Stark were, in fact, similar in that regard. They were the antithesis of the racists and bigots of a modern 21st century but still fostered the preservation of "liberty."

John Parker Hale was also involved in the antislavery movement and his statue stands in front of the New Hampshire State Capitol as well (since 1892). A lawyer and politician, he mimicked and endorsed the philosophies of the patriots before him. Again, civility was paramount and he followed Stark's mantra.

Concurrent with his ideology was the life of Franklin Pierce, New Hampshire's only president of the United States. His life and presidency were met with consternation and resistance, and less respect for him, especially during his reign in the White House.

First, a proponent of antislavery, he was later said to vacillate on the issue, resulting in rebellion by the populous. Pierce was a strong nationalist and the 14th president of the United States. After much criticism and a lackluster term during his political stint, he died in virtual obscurity in 1869. Few biographies will attest to his life while president, but he remained New Hampshire's own nonetheless. He died from cirrhosis of the liver in Concord at age 64. Alcohol was deemed the culprit in his morbidity. He was later buried in the capital city.

Festus Gravel had visited the statue of John Stark well before his nomadic life in the woods. His admiration for the man was insurmountable, but he failed to understand that Stark was a father, husband and a farmer *first*, and who also loved to lead a militia when needed.

Gravel had few of Stark's qualities, if any at all. He realized that the statue in front of the State House was historic. He seemed to gaze at it for inspiration and guidance, but his life was not of the same ideology as Stark's—a far cry from it. Stark was a brilliant strategist in life, and in battle. Stark was neighborly, Festus Gravel was not.

The General Stark statue was first conceived and considered for creation in 1855. A descendent of Stark, General George Stark was charged with the feasibility of seeking a sculptor to honor John Stark.

Nothing happened until 1889 when a local minister reminded the state of New Hampshire that *nothing* had been done to commemorate Stark's impact on New Hampshire and the Nation.

That spurred the New Hampshire Sons of the American Revolution to take up the task. Shortly thereafter in 1889, the house, senate and governor approved a resolution for the likeness of Stark to grace the front lawn of the Capitol.

By 1890, Carl Conrads, a sculptor and a veteran of the Union Army, *won* the bid and prototype "model" development for a statue. Conrads had worked for a granite company in Connecticut. He was uniquely qualified and experienced.

In the end, the final mold of the statue was cast in bronze in Chicopee, Massachusetts. Conrads's winning bid also *included* the granite pedestal to support the statue. He collaborated with a man named Fox. John A. Fox of Boston aided Conrads and fashioned a design for a pedestal that Festus Gravel sometimes stood before in his younger adult life.

In October 1890, the statue of General Stark was dedicated for all of posterity.

Festus tried to embody Stark's brilliance and drive, idolizing the cast metal accolade and rock-steady granite base. He was idolizing a false god. He resigned himself to being a recluse, a hermit with limited human interaction and intelligence. He was a misguided loner who Stark would have regarded as a marauder.

In the end, the late Festus Gravel was a mere *rebel*, but "one without a cause." Most of his life, he lived in the past and alone, impacting no one or the world, in general.

Chapter 30

The first reaction to, and protests concerning Ron Corvallis's evil deed, was covered in the local news and on the Internet. The remnants of the "liberty in our lifetime" group from the Jaffrey rally of Freestaters championed the effort. They congregated in front of the State Capitol and, in particular, in front of Stark's statuesque bronze icon.

They were inspired by Stark's physical size and impact, looming over those who looked up to him in adoration from the grassy lawn.

The local Concord newspaper covered and photographed the mini-rally, which was primarily composed of those stragglers and remnants that remained after the rally week and weekend.

The AP newswire picked up the local photographer's photo of the impromptu congregation—the word quickly spread nationally, then internationally by way of the Internet. Political blogs captured the "threads" and soon the momentum of the protest agenda grew.

Before long, Attorney Thomas Moore and the truck driver were aware of the *impact* the story might have worldwide—the accompanying photos and signs told the story and agenda of the protest!

What the attorney for Ron didn't need, was that hundreds of "freedom advocates" and supporters were blowing the details of the death of their rally compatriot (Cummings) out of proportion. TV coverage only *enabled* the revelers.

Eventually, Moore's phone was ringing off the hook daily. He was verbally chastised by the sympathetic masses for defending or representing the driver of the truck, a trucker who no one had heard of before. They jammed Moore's Web site and email address with hundreds of written accusations almost shutting down the site with spam and viruses.

The 1890's statue of Stark and his motto, took on a new battle cry, especially for the small crowd of right-wing extremists who equated their Ron Corvallis protest agenda to Stark's ideology of liberty and freedom. The context of the famed quote was once again, off base.

The premise that the cold-blooded killers of two people were to be defended by right-wing members posthumously was mind-boggling—all because of the now deceased men's "right to keep and bear arms" without restrictions. They cared little that the vile men were implicated in *murder*. Their civil rights had been breached, especially those of Bobby Cummings.

Ron Corvallis now feared for his life. The recent event had taken on a life of it's own and the Web contained a bastion of critics with erroneous or embellished negative information to incite the emotions of extreme Libertarian proponents.

"Tea Party" advocates that followed the radical agenda of Charles Alan Dyer and the Oath Keepers in Oklahoma reacted adversely as well. They were out for blood, Corvallis's blood.

Even the local NRA regional membership and national headquarters were "tuned in" to the *fiasco*, as they called it—a fiasco in which the "corrupt police" may have intentionally targeted the wrong person(s), at least in their minds.

The serenity of a Lakes Region New Hampshire town was about to become national news and a truck driver, well intentioned and with a desire for justice, was potentially *life threatened* now. He was now into a full defensive legal mode, targeted by mass verbal protests in all media venues. The stress was overwhelming for Ron Corvallis.

* * *

The Charles Breckenridge family piled into their Volvo station wagon and the children fastened their seatbelts. Susan, the oldest of the Breckenridge kids, had just turned 13-years-old. Sam, her younger brother, was eleven.

In the state of New Hampshire, it was mandatory for children at that age to be secured in a moving vehicle. Adults were immune to the law, but most responsible people buckled up.

The New Hampshire legislature had voted the *adult* seatbelt bill down, another measure by modern day "freedom, liberty and Republican rights advocates" expressing their God-given and constitutional right—to a freedom of choice. Less government intervention was better than being oppressed by legislators who might favor or enforce the protective seatbelt as a mandate. It was common sense in the public eye, but the Republican legislators were stalwart.

Many states in the Union had enacted the seatbelt law for good reason—medically it was wise for everyone, actually reducing deaths, and healthcare and medical costs. It was prudent to "buckle up."

Additionally, there were statistics to show that it saved lives and helped reduce auto insurance rates annually. New Hampshire's Republican legislators thought otherwise and touted it as an infringement of one's freedom of choice. Government had too much say, they professed.

The recent fatal injuries of Bobby Cummings had shown just the opposite. A man was now dead and his personal freedoms and *elective choice* had ended his life!

The children's mother made sure that the kids were secure in the backseat. "Overly protective" was not an optional word for the family. She considered her children her obligation, for safe measure, twenty-four-hours a day.

The parents smiled at one another. The family was excited to visit the dog, mindful of the fact that it might not be theirs. *Hopeful* was the attitude of the family of four.

The parents had been through hell with the children, knowing that the loss of the dog had profound psychological effects on everyone. Stress levels were high and voices often elevated out of fear that the dog had run away and was dead.

It was a short ride to the police station, maybe fifteen miles or so, where Chief Randall had asked Joe McNulty to bring the dog in for the Breckenridge family to see. Joe had pretty much accepted that it was the Breckenridge's dog. That made for a bittersweet moment for him. He had become quite attached to "Blackie." From an experienced hunter's point of view, it was a good bird dog, but he surely wished the animal to be returned to its rightful owner. That was only fair.

"It's probably theirs," said Chief Randall, with some satisfaction. "If it was my dog and missing, I'd want it back. They become part of the family."

"I know," added McNulty, "the kids need their pet back."

At the police station, the dog and Joe sat quietly in an adjoining conference room off the lobby. He patted his head and stroked his back assuring the dog that all was okay. The dog licked his hand with affection.

The police chief approached the dog and leaned over to pet the animal. His waistline was a bit broad and his shirt and stomach hug over his belt. He was not in the best of shape but the blue uniform was not unattractive on him.

"I want to try something," he offered, looking first at McNulty . . . and then looking directly at the dog.

"What's your name?" he said to the dog. The dog was basically unresponsive to the question. The dog stared at him and cocked his head in confusion. Joe was confused by the chief's question. *Did the cop expect the dog to answer?*

"Is it 'Blackie'?" voiced the policeman. The dog didn't respond. "How about 'Pal?'"

"I just say, 'here boy,'" McNulty added, perplexed.

"Watch this," the police chief said, with confidence.

"Is it Lucky? Is your name, *Lucky*?"

The dog wagged his tail like a metronome, back and forth. His head rocked as he stood on all fours.

"*Lucky?*" he repeated, more loudly and forcefully. The dog's tail became more active and animated, flipping back and forth with increasing speed. Lucky's head was cocked and his ears elevated in response to the familiar name.

Joe smiled. "So . . . *that's* your name, eh boy? . . . *Lucky?*" The dog reacted again, staring at him directly, his face almost smiling, the upper lip elevated in pleasure.

"How did ya know, chief? I assume the family shared their lost pet's name."

"Yes, earlier today . . . they asked us to try the name, 'Lucky.'"

The dog faced his temporary master. His eyes brightened and he looked at the chief . . . and then back toward Joe McNulty. It was obvious that he knew his name.

"It's pretty clear to me that the dog's responsive to his *real* name. I think the Breckenridge's will be happy that you found their pet," offered Chief Randall. "They should be here in a few minutes."

As they awaited the family's arrival, a fellow female officer brought the dog a bowl of fresh water and a dog treat. She had a bag of Purina dog biscuits for the K-9 dog, a trained Shepherd who was part of the overall team. The police used the canine in the S.W.A.T. team exercises and illegal drug searches in airports, homes, schools and automobiles.

* * *

The Breckenridge's Volvo pulled into the police parking lot. Peering out of the rear side windows were two kids with wide eyes and excitement. They were out of the car before the parents opened their doors, heading impromptu to the front of the police station. They were beyond anxious.

"Wait kids," the mother commanded. "Wait for us, please."

A dispatcher buzzed them in. The two children were inside the building before the parents reached the lobby. There was still damage to the foyer, but a high priority construction crew was there to repair the damage from the truck. The damaged truck was secured in the back lot and behind a chain-linked fence, impounded by the police.

The chief greeted the kids and shook hands with each one, towering over the kids with an austere presence. He was smiling.

"Hi kids. I'm Chief Randall. You must be Sam and you . . . must be Susan I would guess," he stated, shaking their hands, individually.

"Are you the Breckenridge kids? Why are you here?" he teased. "Do we have something that's yours?" The children's eyes brightened and Sam was nodding his head, "yes," in anticipation of seeing the family pet.

"You have our dog, right?" Susan said, almost in tears. "Lucky?"

"I think so, young lady," the chief offered, "he answers to that name. Come on in."

She smiled at her brother, eyebrows raised and her lips pursed with excitement.

The parents caught up and shook the hand of the officer, apologizing for the children's rambunctious behavior . . . then introduced themselves more formally. They were beaming.

The children followed the chief into another room where Joe McNulty and the dog were waiting.

"Lucky!" screamed Sam. "*My* Lucky! Where have you been, doggie?"

Seeing the children, the dog leaped, straining Joe's arm and leash and then ran to each child individually, repeatedly licking their faces, one and then the other.

Joe smiled at the reunion. How could he not?

The dog was ecstatic to see them, wagging his tail repeatedly. His rear end was moving in a rhythm that was unstoppable. Lucky greeted the parents as well, first sniffing them and then the kids. He whimpered joyously as he greeted each of the family members.

Joe McNulty stood and shook hands with the parents . . . and then with the children. He could see their pleasure, the faces of a family who were ecstatic over the reunion of a family member.

"Thank you so much, Mr. McNulty, for all you have done. You are a lifesaver."

The mother welled up with tears. She hugged and thanked the man who had found the dog in the woods. Joe knew that reuniting the dog with the proper owners was the right thing to do. He wiped his eyes with the back of his hand. As a dog owner himself, he knew the inseparable bond of "Man" and dog.

"Thank you," offered Charles Breckenridge to the man who had been so caring of Lucky. "I can't thank you enough," he repeated.

Charles was emotional. "The kids have been quite distressed since their family friend wandered off."

"My pleasure. I can only imagine," Joe said, with a smile. "I'm pleased that Lucky is back with his rightful owners. He's been through a lot."

Joe relayed to the father each of the medical issues that the veterinarian had found with the dog. He reaffirmed that Lucky had been injured but none of the abuses had been life threatening or disabling. The dog had a slight limp but it wasn't noticeable during the reunion. A contusion near the dog's head was healing as was the dog's injured ribs.

Sam knelt on one knee and hugged the dog tightly.

"Don't choke him, honey," the mother said. "Let him breathe, honey," she added, concerned. "His ribs may still hurt."

The child didn't relent, and instead was joined by his sister who was equally as excited to place her arms around the dog's midriff. The dog didn't mind the restraint and seemed to enjoy the love and affection, even with sore ribs.

"Where have you been, you crazy dog?" asked Sam. "You ran away," he scolded.

The father held up a broken collar with nametags and a rabies vaccine certification and tag from two years back. The dog smelled the collar, a familiar smell and then returned to the children.

"This is a joyous day," the chief whispered to the mother. "It's always best when we reunite a family. The dog is a 'hero' as well."

"He sure is. Thank you so much," the mother offered to each of the men in the police station.

"Our next stop will be the pet shop at the mall. We need a stronger collar, I guess," she voiced, raising an eyebrow in embarrassment.

"Yah, we can't have him wanderin' again," Sam said, eyes widened. "You were missed, doggie."

The mother spoke up. "Kids . . . thank the nice man for finding your dog, and for taking care of him."

Joe was flattered by the compliments from the children—they hugged him.

"No problem, ma'am. Glad to be of help. I have dogs too, and know what they mean to a family."

The police chief asked for Charles Breckenridge's photo I.D. for formality and then shook hands with everyone. He escorted them outside to their respective cars. He was beaming at the thought that something pleasant came out of multiple situations, those being the death of Festus, the demise of the men, Cummings and Cooper and the abuse of the dog. It had a *positive* outcome—the reunion and quick healing from his injuries.

"I'll make the newspapers aware of the reunion," offered Chief Randall. "They'll surely want to do a follow up story. I'm sorry that I didn't think to have them here today," he whispered to Charles Breckenridge. "I was concerned for the kids, should the dog *not* have been yours—a photo op and story at your home might be more relevant now."

Charles nodded in agreement.

"Thanks chief, the human interest story sounds nice. It would have been awful if it was not Lucky . . . thanks for all your help. You and Mr. McNulty have saved the day."

Joe McNulty smiled and winked. He patted the dog one more time. "Bye Lucky—come visit me."

Mr. Breckenridge shook his hand firmly. "Thanks. We'll be glad to visit ya. Your dogs and Lucky can have a play date."

"Glad to be a part of the happy ending," Joe added. "Here's my address and number. Please call anytime."

Chapter 31

Ron Corvallis was depressed by the attention and notoriety that he had gained from the death of the hitchhiker. The pieces of the two crimes were coming together, almost daily. Bobby Cummings and Ryan Cooper were villains in the eyes of the general public, especially to those friends and acquaintances of Barnaby Stillwater.

Tom Moore was on a mission to protect the legacy of his former associate. They had disagreed on many aspects of the Bill of Rights and its implications in the modern world, but that was *academic* in nature. They were close friends. Moore was still in favor of Barnaby's "voice" under the 1st Amendment—the right to want to see the 2nd Amendment revised in some respects, perhaps defining more readily what a modern day militia was, and controlling the possession of unnecessary automatic weapons, especially in the wrong hands. Moore knew Stillwater's passion.

Moore had mellowed in opinion regarding "gun rights" and the abolition or constraints on the ownership of assault rifles and automatic handguns. He was becoming more moderate in his views, especially after the death of Stillwater. Owning a gun may have been the right of citizens under the law, but slowly he was seeing loopholes in laws that did not regulate gun shows or the acquisition of assault weapons on the Internet. He knew that gun shows were less regulated for consumers with respect to background checks of individuals who wanted to secure unusual weapons. Those weapons had in the past been used for mass killings in schools or other public places. The weapons could fire voluminous rounds, literally, in seconds.

People at gun shows were not only acquiring antiques for personal collections, but functional and unusual gun brands and models from overseas manufacturers. Russian, Israeli or Eastern European-made weapons were popular and unnecessary, he felt. In the wrong hands, the guns were a challenge for local law enforcement to counteract with commonly issued police weapons, especially in severe crime situations and confrontations involving the authorities.

The firepower was so incredible that police needed S.W.A.T. military weapons to fire back and defend themselves.

Moore knew the dangers and agreed somewhat with his deceased friend's philosophical point of view.

Thomas Moore's general surface mail (and emails to his Web site for his legal office) was inundated and jammed with trash by gun rights advocates and people who had attended the Jaffrey, New Hampshire rally of the FSP.

The *absolute freedom* supporters were infuriated by the truck driver's deadly actions.

The ongoing police investigation had already discerned that Bobby Cummings had in his possession a few ounces of marijuana. That was not deemed relevant to the death of, or actions of, Bobby Cummings although the demise of Barnaby Stillwater may have in fact been accomplished or stimulated by the influence of alcohol or other mind-altering drugs. There was no way to know the actual illegal drug levels, pending the toxicological bioanalysis of his bodily fluids.

The autopsy of Cummings by the medical examiner included blood samples for further toxicological evaluations at an independent lab. Bioanalytical assays would reveal if there were any remnants or metabolites of illegal drugs in his body. The lasting effects of marijuana residues could be present as much as 30 days after smoking "weed," although the direct CNS effects were long gone. Cocaine would explain his damaged heart muscles seen grossly.

The "FreeState" advocates were proponents of the complete freedom to legalize marijuana possession and use. They surely used the excuse and relevance of its medical application as an ant-nausea and anti-emetic therapeutic. After all, if someone had cancer in their coalition and was suffering from chemo or radiation therapy, it seemed right and just to the freedom advocates to have their member gain access to marijuana therapy to abate the chemo side effects.

They were savvy enough to have researched the fact that most drugs in modern medicine had their origins in plants and botanicals throughout the world. To them, there was no difference in marijuana use from that of similar holistic extracts of plants for arthritis, pain or nutritional immune system boosting.

The anonymous caustic notes to Attorney Moore were accusatory and disrespectful of Barnaby Stillwater, implying that he was against guns in general, all guns, and the holistic therapeutic rights of citizens. To them, they were choices and God-given rights mandated by way of the Forefathers of the new nation.

The extrapolation of "freedoms" to gun regulations or marijuana use, and the current New Hampshire state laws was irrelevant to the thinking of Stillwater. At no time had he expressed a negative opinion regarding marijuana restriction, or its legalization and use for medical treatment.

The Freestaters had used the gun platform to their own advantage. It was supposition and innuendo that led the extreme coalition to conclude that Barnaby Stillwater had an opinion of current marijuana laws and restrictions. Falsehoods and rumors begat more falsehoods, labeling him pro-restriction of *all* civil rights. The advocates were delusional.

* * *

In the immediate weeks to come, Ron would lose his job with the shipping company—the trucking company had a reputation to protect and the recent distraction by Ron and the ultimate death of Cummings had tainted the company's image in general. *Had they hired a maniac driver?* They verbally divorced themselves from Ron's dilemma just to get the protestors off their backs.

They also had to contend with the trucking company's insurance purveyor who, after hearing of the incident, was unwilling to reimburse them for the repairs to the truck or the police building, both of which had been severely damaged.

The insurance carrier for the fleet of twenty-five trucks felt that Ron had intentionally destroyed the vehicle and that was preventable in *normal* driving operations. They questioned Ron's psyche and ability to drive for the trucking company in a safe and respectful manner, especially in the future. He could have killed anyone in the lobby, even if he was being a Good Samaritan for the police. They felt that there was no reason to trash the truck. Other measures to "present" the suspect to the police could have been used.

The trucking company was tired of the press coverage as well. The whole episode seemed unnecessary especially to the top management of the company.

Attorney Moore was to enter into discussions with Ron's company and the insurance carrier at some point. He was flabbergasted that the company had fired Ron. He would sue to get Ron's job back, but more urgent issues were a priority—fending off the attackers. He first had to defend Ron from the mass of protesters and the supporters of "liberty in our lifetime."

* * *

The constant reminder of recent events took its toll on Ron Corvallis. Even his family was distressed by the death threats and accusations by unknown people who desired to burn down their home, harass their children or even *kill* Ron. His wife, Maryann became distraught at the implications and rhetoric in the newspapers. She was scared naturally for the family unit. They were "targeted" and Ron was also jobless. Since his wife didn't work, he was the sole provider and breadwinner. The marriage, which was already rocky from his constant travel and occasional separation from the family, was strained even more now that Ron was viewed negatively in the public eye.

He was "noted" in their immediate community, as well as a celebrity across the nation. It was not a celebrity status that was *positive*, but the opposite—a *negative* tragedy of emmense proportions.

Once the AP newswire caught wind of the bizarre accident, everyone had heard of the *infamous* Ron Corvallis. He begged for privacy but it was never possible in a high visibility case. Fame begat exposure, worldwide.

Chapter 32

The Jaffrey rally of the Civil Libertarians and "liberty" advocates had always inspired the attendees to defend to the death all freedoms that the Forefathers penned in the 1700's.

They often used annual celebrations and reenactments (pompous revelry) from the Revolutionary War, to be inspired. One or two of the events included the firing of cannons and powder kegs, military reenactments of battles past, much to the chagrin of local New Hampshire residents who wondered what the purpose of the rally was, and why it was necessary to have a reenactment at all in *their* particular town.

The influx of Freestaters to the southwest portion of the state once a year was somewhat *intimidating* to residents who wondered why Jaffrey was selected for the annual week and weekend of frivolity and pseudo-patriotism. It was a disruption to a small town but an economy booster for the locals—it was, however, becoming a *guy thing,* even though some women attended.

Keynote speakers at rally weekend discussed subjects like the "Citizens' Rights to Bear Arms," especially by a well known Libertarian speaker, and related female topics i.e. "Woman's Gun Rights" with a noted female speaker from the group known as the "Second Amendment Sisters."

It was well known by Tom Moore, Barnaby's colleague, that Stillwater sought out the planned agenda of the annual FSP rally for his own personal intelligence, since he opposed *most, if not all* of the objectives that the speakers professed at the gathering.

Perhaps he was targeted or killed for his opposition to this year's specific agenda. That had crossed Moore's mind. Moore and the police detectives were investigating all motives in Barnaby's fate.

The "firing off" of cannons was in some ways a tribute to the American Revolution, but at the same time, a testimonial to John Stark's (and wife, Molly's) memory and his purported patriotic accolades that they espoused in a modern society. They relished his achievements.

Correlating with those celebratory events were mock battle reenactments by FSP members and the "After Dark Cannon Volleys To Mt. Monadnock," a tribute to the nearby popular mountain range. The adoration of the mountain was an *enigma* to most residents in the quiet, southwest New Hampshire town.

Perhaps they had Molly Stark in mind, not John Stark.

John Stark's wife had a cannon named after her—the "Molly Stark" cannon, nicknamed, "Old Molly."

During the War of 1812, (known as the 2nd Revolutionary War), the cannon opposed the British siege in Michigan, particularly in Detroit. The British captured the cannon only to have the Americans *reclaim* "Old Molly" at the battle of Fort George in New York State. In 1822, Old Molly was removed from an arsenal in Old Watervliet (Watervaliet) New York. At that time, the town was known as "Arsenal City." The arsenal, perhaps the oldest known, remains today.

The New Boston Artillery Company (9th Regiment in New Hampshire), not far from Jaffrey, received the prestigious "Molly" cannon from Stark, soon after it was retired from active duty.

It was John Stark's *gift* in recognition of New Boston's contribution of men at the Battle of Bennington (in concert with the defeat of the British).

In 1852, the artillery division of the New Hampshire militia was disbanded. Everything that belonged to the militia was returned to the State of New Hampshire, except for "Old Molly." Historically, the cannon had relevance in many battles.

The "Molly" cannon of note was originally cast in Paris, France in 1743. It once served under the French flag, the British flag twice, and the American flag twice. The cannon was "protected" by the astute residents of the town of New Boston, especially after a failed plan by others to move her permanently to Manchester, New Hampshire. Toward that end, and to protect their treasure, the town of New Boston *reorganized* and *revived* the old Artillery Company in June 1938. By August of that year, they retained custody of "Old Molly."

Some critics and historians feel to this day that the current cannon is not the *original* one. They claimed that the "specs" of the weapon had been questioned by some historians, citing inaccuracies in the dimensions of the barrel of the gun.

The Civil Libertarians, some of whom were savvy in the history of the Stark battles, have reenacted the famed legacy of firing a cannon; one similar to the one General Stark so generously gave to the small town in southern New Hampshire.

In that regard, the motto, "Live Free or Die" was being perpetuated, but *out of the context* with the original written footnote (quotation) by Stark.

In a way, the Freestaters were, and remain, in rebellion against their own government's laws and restrictions that have been lawfully legislated.

Stark feared the British even *after* all the battles were won. *Would they return to dissolve the union?* he wondered. It is unlikely that he would have approved of a modern day movement like the FSP.

The liberty advocates in Jaffrey, most of who do not know of Stark's legacy as a farmer, husband and father, or his life in total, emulate him only for their own purposes. To them, the part-time military man enabled "their advocacy" of a renewed nation for "all of America's liberties penned in the 1700s." They assume he was, and is, a "symbol" or "figurehead" in their attempts to foster radical change—that is to directly impact many states with less than 1.5-million residents by encouraging thousands of their own kind to infiltrate and retrofit those 21st-century communities back to the "original freedoms" of a nation defined centuries ago.

New Hampshire was their *first State* of choice. They favored presidential candidate, Ron Paul, thinking erroneously that he is/was a reincarnation of Stark or one of the original Forefathers. In 2008, he met their requirements for a return to *basic* constitutional rhetoric by preserving, to the *exact* words, that which they espoused. Their plan in a nutshell: start with the small states like New Hampshire . . . then grow the movement to be the total agenda of the FSP *nationwide*.

Barnaby Stillwater was opposed to their agenda—seeing a small portion of the Constitution and Bill of Rights out of touch without *minor* revision, at least statewide.

Contrary to the FSP and to his credit, Barnaby merely wanted to make the nation more civil, more judicial and protect the citizens from the "abuses and misinterpretation of the '2nd.'"

Cannons were no longer a part of protectionism and the changing gun manufacturing industry (highly technical weaponry) had advanced, in his mind, to insane levels of un-needed modernization for the common citizen's needs.

To Barnaby, it was a far cry from muzzle-loaded rifles and bayonets.

Stark probably would have agreed with him, had he in fact been born in the 20th or 21st centuries.

Chapter 33

The despondency of Ron Corvallis was growing more evident. He withdrew from his family and often sat in solemn silence. His wife and children noticed the change in his demeanor. He didn't know what to do for a job. Odd jobs might be a temporary alternative but his way of life, training and occupation was really "driving truck," both daily and weekly. He was unsure of an alternative income source. Ron was desperate, having been let-go by his employer.

Other local trucking companies wouldn't touch him. He loved the occupation, before the recent debacle. His life to date had been on the road.

Ron had called a few friends to see if he could help them, but most were not hiring new help, primarily due to a faltering economy. Jobs were scarce across the nation and driving truck had been affected by cutbacks and high maintenance costs for vehicles. Gas and diesel prices were elevated and trucking companies were laying-off drivers nationwide to cut costs.

Shipments of goods were down, especially produce and other perishables from the west coast to the east. Deliveries to restaurants were slashed since many restaurants were seeing a falling-off in clientele. No one was spending money frivolously.

The eating establishments that remained open were barely getting by. Their own wait-staff were either out of work or reduced in scope and hours of work. Regular customers were hanging on to their cash and visiting McDonalds, not boutique restaurants and cafes with quality food and ambiance. Belts were being tightened and some families were staying home to eat. It was less expensive.

There was other trucking needs, however, even in a slowed economy. It was limited. Construction materials needed distribution other than by rail or ship. Attempts to break into those "driving" needs were met with resistance. Those drivers were out of work as well due to a decline in construction, both residential and commercial.

Ron was caught in a quandary and with no real alternative for an income. He had no other blue-collar related job training. Truck driving was all he knew and he was good at it. Now he was in peril, financially.

One promising interview with HR at a regional truck company fifty miles away had caught wind that he was the guy who had smashed his truck into the local police station. He was about to be hired but some union driver ratted on him. The company and its insurance purveyor wanted nothing to do with him. His actions behind the wheel the day that Bobby Cummings had been fatally injured had tainted his stellar record forever.

He was now a "marked" man in the trucking world. Personal references and referrals "disappeared" before he had a chance to defend himself or to tout his twenty-year, impeccable safety record behind the wheel.

Students at school unfairly razzed his children, well-mannered Corvallis kids who were young and impressionable. Attacks by peers were hurtful. The children fended off harassment and even defended their father's actions, saying that he was not a *bad* man, but by his actions, was quite the opposite—a brave and *good* man. He was a hero in their eyes. He was defended by their love and admiration for he had been a good father and hard worker, dedicated to putting in long hours on the road, away from home. He had missed many of their ballgames or concerts and plays, but was personally there for them—always.

Ron Corvallis was a veteran of the Vietnam War. He played down his role in the U.S. Army infantry since many Americans were still opposed to the war and its legacy. He knew death firsthand; he had killed some members of the Vietcong in the 1960's. That was their job back then, to kill the enemy. The Vietcong were flushed out by napalm and helicopter gun ships—the enemy on the run automatically became targets in the scope of U.S. Army rifles. He was an expert marksman fighting a sometimes unjust war. None of his accolades, medals or ribbons, which he was awarded for his service, was a source of pride for him. He hated war, a constant reminder of death and tragedy, decades later.

Psychologically, war and death had taken its toll on him. He had nightmares to this day and was often distraught over the memory of watching his friends and comrades lose limbs or succumb to enemy fire.

He refused to visit VFW's or American Legion halls and commiserate with his fellow veterans from decades earlier. He wanted nothing to do with their banter, boasting, or fraternal camaraderie embellished with cheap liquor and low prices. He was not attracted to their fundraising evenings of bingo or other community gatherings.

He had left the Army behind, a memory, and he was not a drinker anyway. Revisiting battles and war tales was not his bag. It was painful at best.

Ron Corvallis was merely a dedicated workingman who wanted to provide for his family. Trucking was his grandfather's and his father's occupation as well, and he was proud to perform the duties necessary to achieve a stable household unencumbered by debt. Now he was faced with no job and mounting, insurmountable bills for the basic necessities of life.

Insurance payments were due, both for home and medical premiums. They fell behind. His groceries bills were more costly. His wife was juggling the bills but they kept appearing in the mail.

He received threatening letters of policy termination for insurance coverage, and a lien was about to be placed on his home—the mortgage payment was behind. The mortgage company had no sympathy for his personal plight. He was one of hundreds in the state of New Hampshire in the same dire economic situation.

His car had been paid off, but the vehicle was in poor shape, often breaking down. He could fix most of the problems when it was a muffler, spark plugs, brakes or other essentials required for yearly inspection at the local gas station, but buying the parts became a problem. He didn't have the income to buy the hundreds of dollars worth of replacement parts. He was distraught. It felt like he had a load of bricks on his shoulders.

Ron Corvallis's life became "a rock in a hard place." There was little he could do to help himself. There were no relatives from whom he could borrow money.

The depression was further complicated by calls from Attorney Thomas Moore who knew that the Civil Libertarian advocates were a constant thorn in Ron's side and threatening to sue him. They wanted him arrested for murder, or at the very least, for manslaughter. Letters flooded the attorney's office.

"They keep callin' the office," Moore told Ron one morning. "The bastards will not let up and I have many other cases that need my attention. They can surely gang up on ya."

"I know the feeling," Ron concurred, "they have been calling here as well. I changed my phone number and they still found it. The harassment is daily. My family is fed up with the notoriety, both good and bad. My wife has threatened to leave me. She is stressed by my job loss. The constant newspaper articles and personal harassment regarding my crash is overpowering. She found a part time job but it doesn't cover the bills."

Moore was concerned. "Ya have to hang in there since they have no case to seek charges against you. To be honest, they are merely making noise to attract new recruits into the state. People nationwide are reading of the murders and the police activities with respect to the deaths in this town. It's gore and *sensationalism* that attracts readers so newspapers and tabloids will sell, especially in an economy that is depressed for that *newsprint* industry. The Internet is kicking their ass. It's not really news—its crap and gossip like the shows on TV at 7 P.M. nightly."

"I know. I've stopped getting home delivery of the paper. I can't afford it from a financial or psychological point of view. I'm in the damn paper *daily*," Ron offered, his voice falling off in volume. "Reporters hound me for interviews."

Moore was sympathetic. "I get the same mail you do. They want to know why I continue to represent you. Stay away from the reporters. They are like leaches."

Ron rebutted, "Not sure why you are doing that either . . . that is, representing me."

"We have to stick together, Ron. I find myself taking the side of Barnaby Stillwater more and more each day. He may have been right in his actions and philosophy. I look at the AMEND2 plate that he had on his car. I see it perpetually in my mind. The police let me hold on to the one from the front of his car—the one that the killers never got off the bumper on that fateful evening. He was my friend and that plate has opened my eyes. It sits on my bookshelf in plain view and across from my desk—the *license plate,* a constant positive reminder of my colleague every time I lift up my head from my desk."

Ron was quiet. He knew that the loss of Stillwater was painful for the attorney who worked with him almost daily. "I'm sorry for you as well."

"I have to go to court this morning," offered Moore with reticence. "I have a divorce case to present and the judge is fanatical about lawyers being on time."

"Mine might be next," Ron whispered, quietly but audible to Moore's ear.

"Hope not, Ron," Attorney Moore replied, "really hope not."

The men agreed to talk later in the day after the court case or *ad hoc*, as needed. Ron was to try and get a job interview at a local grocery store. He knew the owner personally since he had shopped there for decades giving his wages to a local purveyor. He avoided big-box chain stores with 100,000 items on the shelf. Ron supported the local businesses knowing they were struggling to survive against the giants and monopolies. Now he could use *their* help—a job.

With the local stores, he could shop in a matter of minutes, and close by. What little income they had now, they still spent with their friend's businesses. They had to survive too. Ron tended to always think of the other person, the little guy. He was now the *little guy*.

Chapter 34

It was mid-afternoon and the day was slow—Ron Corvallis was feeling down. The grocery store manager had not called back. He poured himself a shot of Canadian Club into a small glass. He grabbed a cold Budweiser from the refrigerator and went outside on to the back veranda. A Cape Cod like chair was there . . . Adirondack-style. It was chilly, but tolerable. He stared at the nearby woods, which were barren from the recent loss of leaves. The pines of green now dominated, interspersed with a white birch or two, the "State" tree. He squinted and studied the familiar landscape. That enabled him to see a good distance into the now denuded forest. His nearest neighbors were a quarter-of-a-mile away on both sides of his home.

The semi-private road to his home was dirt, too long to economically pave to his home. The expense for the town was prohibitive to maintain since the Corvallis home was one of two houses at the distal portion of the road. No way would the town bother to lay down asphalt for a single house or two. The most that they maintained was to smooth ruts from the winter frost and traffic, scraping the surface of the street with a special Ford tractor and leveling blade.

In the old days, the town would often oil the road to abate any dust storms from passing cars. They would also spread a road salt mixture in July and August, which attracted humidity from the air and kept the surface moist, thereby cutting down the dust plumes from passing vehicles. It was a natural desiccant but the town had cut back on the procedure and costly materials.

The newest environmental regulations by the EPA and ordinances by local officials in conservation groups or on the city council prevented the surrounding towns from using oil or salt any longer. Construction companies had used the salt mixture for years in heavily traveled traffic areas where heavy equipment was being used and kicking up dust.

It was early afternoon and the kids were still in school. His wife was working and would be home at 5:30 P.M. Ron sat alone staring into space—the "back forty" so to speak. It was tranquil.

Ron drank a shot of whiskey and chased it with a beer. He leaned back in the slanted Adirondack chair, one he had fashioned himself from a kit and then painted white. They were popular chairs on New England porches and decks. The back of the chair was comfortable as he perused the back yard, the tool shed and forest in his direct line of vision. He blinked repeatedly, the effects of the liquor surpassing rational thought over time. He began to think deeply—alcohol having stimulatory effects initially, and then depressive effects.

The tool shed was showing some wear, he thought, the result of the roof caving in slightly in the middle from severe winters and heavy wet snows of the past. He had no extra money to repair the roof or to even re-shingle it before the coming snows of December.

A thirty-degree wooden ramp led to the front double doors of the 10' by 10' foot structure of pine. It housed his lawn mower, a rake or two and a snow blower. There was hardly room to move about the space in autumn—all the garden tools and children's summer toys were packed in there, except for the center access. Bikes and soccer nets and various sports equipment were stacked for winter storage. The pesky wasps in the rafters were gone, avoiding the cold.

The roof was pitched and graded to 10 feet at the apex. He often hung lawn chairs and garden items like hoses or the kid's rafts and tubes from the rafters. He had used old timbers from a local barn to support much of the frame. The rafters were of strong hardwood, but the sub-roofing of plywood was water stained and old, soaked by spring and summer rains. He had built the shed with inexpensive materials years earlier.

The door was ajar since the latch had been broken and hinges were loose. The occasional skunk or gopher wandered into the shed at night, mostly in search of stored garden bulbs (a savory treat) for the next season's planting. He had shot more than one critter that desired to devour his annual seeds and other perennials in the storage bins.

Raccoons were smart and could open covered garbage cans and plastic storage bins easily. They would pop off the covers and steal anything grain-like, grass seed, onion and garlic sets or dried vegetables.

Pumpkin and squash seeds disappeared like magic with only the seed coats remaining.

Ron poured another shot of whiskey and reached in the frig for the remainder of a six-pack of beer. He was feeling no pain at this point—after the second and third rounds. It was a stimulating "high" at first and the natural but naked beauty of the woods before him looked serene. There was little noise except for the light wind that carried a lone dried leaf here and there. A brook in the distance could be heard babbling and an occasional bird chirped drawing his eyes to the treetops. Sparrows were prevalent.

Part of a small stream ran through his back lot. The kids played in the brook in summer especially when the heat was oppressive. The water was not deep on his property and they could cool off in the wider areas of the stream without their parents worrying about the danger. They often caught crayfish and salamanders or the occasional fry from some pan fish breeding area. The state of New Hampshire did not stock the brook. It was too shallow and warm for trout.

After a few minutes he staggered over to the shed, beer can in hand. He almost tripped and fell from the inebriation of the whiskey and beer combination. He was not a heavy drinker, but today his psyche had gotten the best of him. The more he drank, the more the depression set in. Alcohol by nature was first a stimulant making one "high." It quickly plays games with the brain however, and in time fostered an increased CNS depressive state, a "downer" effect.

Ron had crossed the tipping point. He no longer felt euphoria and giddiness. He grabbed a folded beach chair from the rafters and settled into it near the door of the shed. He was looking back at the house and saw that it needed painting, and a new gutter system. A window or two needed repair—broken by one of the kids. He became overwhelmed by the vision of home issues and tasks (a to-do list) to be fixed or refurbished. The woods in the other direction had looked pleasingly serene earlier—a view from his house. Now, from a new vantage point, everything looked foreboding and at times, even evil. His eyes blurred.

Ron couldn't see his way out of the list of things that were now his albatross, a burden to the mind if he was to correct all the things that needed repair or were neglected. His lack of an income made matters all the worse.

He thought of the repairs required and the mounting bills stacked on the kitchen counter. He originally had a plan to do one *priority* task at a time over the winter, and then . . . into next spring—a new year.

The demons of life were setting in as the alcohol permeated his brain. He was overwhelmed with guilt and a "false sense of timing"—all these issues had to be dealt with, seemingly at once. That wasn't really the case, but to him, it felt that way.

He staggered to the house and kitchen, pitching a beer bottle into the woods behind him. He wrote a note to his wife, a tender recollection of their life in the good ol' days. He wrote a cryptic, but loving note to his kids, to each one separately. He told them that he loved them and to be good for their mother. He mentioned seeing them again down the road. Tears welled up in both eyes, one or two followed down onto the notes. He stared at a family picture and individual school photographs.

He could hear the phone ringing in the other room. He didn't bother to answer it as he blinked repeatedly from the inebriation and struggled to read the caller I.D. display. It was no more than a haze to him, confounded by an opaque fluid of proteins produced from his distressed eyes. He thought it might be Attorney Moore or just another heckler harassing him over the Cummings incident.

He systematically climbed the stairs and visited the bedrooms on the second floor, one by one. He kissed the pillows in each room and began to cry profusely. His tears formed tracks and followed the crevices on his cheeks—a route for the natural saline to follow. He could taste the salt as well, eventually licking his top lip with his tongue. He knelt before a crucifix in the master bedroom and begged for forgiveness from the Lord above. He was blaming no one but himself especially for the misery in the last few weeks—the misery he felt was insurmountable and unjustified, but self-inflicted. The alcohol did not alleviate the pain.

Ron Corvallis headed back to the shed, beer in hand, the last one of a six-pack. The whiskey bottle sat opened on the kitchen counter. Somewhere in the last hour or so he had consumed six beers and six shots, never even knowing the total. The "dead soldiers" in the backyard told the tale.

A handwritten note by the whiskey bottle reiterated his love for his family. He closed the shed doors from the inside. Except for a ray of light peering through the front windowpane above a window box, the interior was almost dark and quiet. A light wind was the only sound, piercing the spaces in the shed walls.

A strong piece of marine-grade rope was tethered to a coat hook on a sidewall of the shed. He normally used it for the anchor in his 18-foot bow-rider, a boat he often took the kids fishing in, in freshwater lakes all over the surrounding towns and region.

He removed the coiled rope from the hook and almost tripped over a weed-whacker that had fallen at an obtuse angle in front of him. It hit one knee head-on as he felt the acute pain through his jeans. His white T-shirt was dirty from the chafe of the rope, pieces of the braid that were dry to the touch and covering his chest like Spanish moss. He tossed the strong hemp over the antiquated barn center beam. It took him three tries to center it, and even longer to fashion a noose. He knew from a pictorial history of lynching, that it would be a fast goodbye. He desired that.

Chapter 35

The phone call to Chief Randall that Ron Corvallis had taken his own life was a shock beyond compare. A local sheriff had contacted the officer from a neighboring town. He was a first-responder to the scene at the shed after Ron's wife had discovered her deceased husband. She had noticed the beer bottles and a shot glass in the back lawn. The shed door was slightly ajar from the wind. The sheriff attempted to console the distraught spouse.

The sound of a fire truck and an ambulance could be heard in the distance. They were headed for Pine Hollow Road, the site of the residence of Ron and his family. EMT's rode in both vehicles; it was a normal response effort to reports of this nature. Blue and red lights lit up the driveway, reflecting off the home of white clapboards.

The local police had already arrived and had summoned the county coroner. The medical examiner in Concord had been alerted as well. In any violent or unexpected death, an autopsy would need to be performed on the deceased victim.

A policewoman comforted the children while the sheriff assisted Ron's wife, Maryann. The Corvallis's had been married fifteen years, and although they were experiencing hard times and frequent arguments over finances and the stress of the Cummings death, she loved him dearly. She sat in a state of disbelief and catatonia.

The notes that he left told the story of his love for them, but also his fears for the future.

Thomas Moore had just left the courthouse and a divorce proceeding and headed for the Corvallis residence. Moore was dumbfounded by the news—overwrought with pain. He had previously met with the family numerous times during the recent events regarding the Stillwater and Cummings deaths. He thought he might be able to comfort the family.

The children were in shock from the unanticipated event, and loss of their father. They were secluded in their rooms, sobbing as Moore arrived at the house. He hugged Ron's wife, consoling her and later went straight to the kid's rooms to help them with their grief. Moore was in tears as he hugged them all. Words were of little consolation.

"Those bastards drove him to this," she whispered. "They are sick individuals," she said, referring to the extremists. "I guess they're happy now!"

Tom Moore looked down and then directly at Ron's wife. "We could have beaten them, I'm sure. This is awful and a tragedy. They drove him into the ground."

Ron Corvallis had always been there for the family if not in person, he was in spirit. He attended baseball games and dance recitals, when he could—school chorus functions and band concerts when home. He coached Little League for a number of years and even basketball in the winter months when trucking was slow. His son, Chad was a rising star locally. Brittany was a ballet dancer and wanted to go to New York when she grew up. Her fantasy was to perform at Radio City Music Hall.

Out the window of the home, they watched the coroner and staff in blue uniforms remove a large black bag from the shed. They placed Ron on a gurney and rolled it to a waiting black SUV. The side of the vehicle read, CORONER.

They knew their father was leaving their home for the last time, a home they had grown up in from infancy.

Attorney Moore and Ron's wife sat at the kitchen table during Ron's departure. He held her as she cried out in pain. She couldn't bear to see her husband leave the property, even if he was deceased.

The rope in the shed was coiled on the floor. The police removed it as evidence. A tall, galvanized trashcan lay on its side, a reminder that the expression "kicked the bucket" came from the technique of actually standing on and then kicking a can or bucket away as a solo act of desperation and despair, resulting in the body falling quickly and stopping inches from the floor. The noose tightened severing the spinal cord. It was purported to be a quick way to go, and painless, but who would know other than the victim of the depression. *What state of mind would drive someone to end his or her life prematurely?* Moore thought.

A neck snap and subsequent suffocation was obviously irreversible.

THE DOG IN THE OUTHOUSE

Ron had been suspended in the shed for a while, perhaps two hours, so there was nothing any EMT could do upon arrival. He was cold to the touch, eyes widened and pupils fixed. There was no pulse or heartbeat.

A couple of beer bottles remained scattered on the lawn, remnants of his drunken debauchery that early afternoon. A policeman photographed the scene and then removed the bottles from the grass. An autopsy and forensic evaluation of his blood would confirm his level of inebriation prior to the deed, and his presumed clinical state of mind at that point. The tender notes left behind would aid the police in confirming his despondency, and the reasons for his suicide. Murder never crossed their minds.

"He didn't even like to drink," said his distraught wife. "He hated alcohol having seen many car crashes and deaths in his days on the road."

"I know," said Moore. "He had told me that recently. He felt that alcohol was the root of most evil. I told him it was *money*, not alcohol," he said reluctantly.

"Why did he do this . . . to himself and to our family?" she cried out in pain. "Was it the lack of money . . . or guilt?"

"I wish I knew," offered Moore, disillusioned by the tragedy and untimely ending.

Just then, two neighbors arrived from down the road. They greeted and embraced Ron's wife, and like Attorney Moore, one quickly headed up to the children's bedrooms to visit the kids. Moore was pleased that people were focused on the children's needs.

The neighbors had children of their own, children who the Corvallis kids played with, and went to school with daily.

Moore was concerned for Maryann. He offered to be of assistance in any way he could. He was distraught over the entire scenario in the last few weeks. All he had seen was murder, death and the destruction of families generated from unnecessary misery.

It all started with the murder of Barnaby Stillwater, and then the subsequent deaths of Festus Gravel, two killers and now Ron Corvallis, an innocent bystander and unintentional, but willing public servant. Even the dog, Lucky, was a victim for a while, first lost, then beaten and finally the only product of a *happy* ending . . . the one positive ending with a family *reunited*.

* * *

It was clear in Attorney Moore's mind, that he needed to help finalize and perpetuate Barnaby Stillwater's wishes, not in total, but in part, due to differing philosophical principals. Moore could impact the state of New Hampshire vocally and in literary form, but stopped short of advocating a revision of the 2nd Amendment in Washington. In time perhaps, he might be able to call to the attention of the legislators in D.C. the abuses of the 2nd Amendment that facilitated the placement and acquisition of weapons in the hands of the wrong people. It wasn't the hunters and target shooters that were to blame, it was the villains of the world that used powerful weapons to commit crimes in which people were callously killed for no reason, with demented individuals using unnecessary assault hardware.

In the case of Barnaby Stillwater's murder, it was his forthright opinions that resulted in his demise most probably, a "right" guaranteed under the 1st Amendment—the same Amendment that the Freestaters wanted to protect as part of their agenda and without modification at any time in the future.

Epilogue

In the evolution of Libertarianism in the Granite State, as well as extremist advocates of *liberty* at all costs, members from around the country (some 10,000 in force) had the objective of encouraging 20,000 advocates to move to New Hampshire. There are presently about 700 committed to the agenda, far shy of what they desired since the planned *invasion* was only conceived a few years back.

The New Hampshire headquarters remains in Keene, much to the chagrin of local residents.

Originally, they had scared the hell out of the residents of Grafton New Hampshire to the north. Grafton was one of their "first choices" and the townspeople were afraid that the movement was going to control their town, its operation and even change the local government by some resurrection, or insurrection.

With every group that is politically influential, there are always outliers and extremists, people who take the principles to an unanticipated level of intensity thereby achieving their goals by potential anarchy and sheer numbers, intimidation, or by violence. Bobby Cummings and Ryan Cooper were of that mold. They chose violence, vigilante style.

The "early movers" as they are referred to, the first to become residents of New Hampshire from other geographical sources and states, entered the Granite State with an agenda. Their motto, "Liberty in Our Lifetime" began in September 2001 and continues to this day.

Although the Free State Project (FSP) does not formally "offer up" candidates for office in elections (to accomplish legislative change), a number of their followers have now been surreptitiously elected to the New Hampshire State House.

It all started with Joel Winters in 2006. Later in 2008, six members won seats in the New Hampshire House. Mr. Winters ran as a "Democrat," but Libertarians are usually not associated with the Democratic agenda or philosophy. Their sympathizers are generally in concert with the Republican side of thinking, or from some "lone wolf" Independent subgroup, with active registered Independents about one-third of the voters in the Granite State.

Often the "Fiscal Conservative" movement plays to their hand, the Republican hands. The New Hampshire Liberty Alliance also follows their lead since they are a powerful body that can lean *left* or *right*. They can be an enigma but favor the *right*.

Democrats won handily in the 2006 and 2008 elections, however. It made sense for FSP candidates to usurp the popular Democratic Party platform to their advantage to achieve seats in the state legislative chambers, perhaps under false pretenses and with grassroots campaigns of suspicious origin. They knew they would benefit from straight ticket party voters who were Democratically aligned. The FSP candidates would then vote, as they liked once elected, and not necessarily Democratic.

It is well known that the Free State Project supports free markets and constitutional federalism. The pro-liberty organization's objective continues to be: "to exert a practical effort toward the creation of a society in which the maximum role of government is the protection of life, liberty and property."

Cummings and Cooper knew that and endorsed it. A number of Internet sites attest to those objectives of the FSP. Attorney Moore studied the movement and concluded that the "Project" would attempt to reduce taxes and regulations in general, so that individual rights could eventually be expanded. Gun and marijuana laws would be reduced or abated allowing for rampant use at their leisure. From the incubator groups, a restoration of Federalism would then spread across the country in accordance with their mantra. The FSP was somewhat akin to the New Hampshire Republican Liberty Alliance and the Republican Liberty Political Action Committee. Add to that the disgruntled "Tea Party" advocates that oppose taxes and the size of government.

Attorney Moore was witnessing an event few lay people knew about, or cared to study. He knew that the FSP ideology and methods could change the state in more ways than Barnaby Stillwater's envisioned before he died. *Did Barnaby sense this before his death? Was that the reason for his defiance against guns, unless laws were increased and enacted?*

Moore was beginning to piece together Barnaby's insight and intuition. AMEND2 had a deeper meaning than originally thought. *Why in the hell would the Republican right and conservatives want to see the government change so drastically in modern times? It was no longer 1776,* Moore wondered. *Did people really know their future if the 'Project' succeeded?* Probably not, or at least, not yet.

Moore was a student of Tort law. He was experienced in some U.S. Constitutional law. As a student, he had studied in Boston, at one of the best institutions in that field of study. He knew the basics of the U. S. Constitution and even Federalism as a form of government. In his own state of New Hampshire, he was seeing subtle rebellion, clouds of discontent before an active tornado of an extreme political movement in the making. He was aghast at what might happen in the chaos of a statewide effort to change the laws and government of New Hampshire or in the United States in general.

He became inspired. It was after the tragedy of the last few weeks that Thomas Moore decided to run for office in the state of New Hampshire. He ran for governor, the top spot. It was the apparent ghost of Barnaby Stillwater who permeated his brain in words and deed, even philosophy. Moore maintained his legal office until he was elected in 2010.

The campaign that he ran touted both the Democratic and Republican principles of government and the positive, civil way of life displayed during the American Revolution. He won on those principles, and an opposition to tyranny and anarchy at all levels.

He was inspired by New Hampshire's history, the history of law and the inspiration of Daniel Webster and General John Stark.

During his term, Governor Moore was able to curb the influence of radical movements in New Hampshire. They were suppressed by the election of new blood to the chambers of the State House—young blood that was home grown, not imports with radical ideas from afar. New Hampshire's citizens took pride in his personal campaign and the grass roots effort acquired the Independent voters of the state that resulted in an election of enormous proportions for Moore—perpetuated by a call to action by ordinary citizens that desired to maintain the "serenity" of the state.

They wanted laws changed gradually, laws that represented *them* and their children directly, not instigated by an obtuse national movement of advocates desiring a virtual secession from the union, akin to Governor Perry and Texas, but one of established national principles in a modern changing world.

Moore was able to support and endorse "changes in the right to bear arms" for the protection of one's family and home. The bills submitted to the legislature under the name of the "Stillwater Papers," eventually supported citizens with their rights to keep and bear arms, but with constraints "for safety" build in. It was a series of amendments at the state level that were more protective of the New Hampshire population and children. Other New England states kept abreast of the transition in New Hampshire and followed suit, eventually initiating changes as well.

From the grave, Barnaby Stillwater impacted some of the state's representatives by way of one former colleague, a small town attorney and now Governor Thomas Moore. The AMEND2 license plate graced the desk of the governor and reminded everyone who visited his executive office that *one person*, with intelligence and common sense, could impact a town, a state or . . . the nation.

* * *

General John Stark's legacy has inspired many individuals in New Hampshire. Some inspirations were or are for the better and others are not as principled as his life's teachings. "Live Free or Die" is a motto often taken out of context and not dissimilar to the abuse of the United States Bill of Rights, in particular, the 1st and 2nd Amendments.

The patriots who wrote their ideology for a new nation never knew how the nation would evolve, regarding its people, massive population or its government in the 21st century.

Stark and the Forefathers of the nation would most likely have been at odds with some of the radical movements that threaten our democracy today—people that demand change based on 200-year-old words that often have limited relevance to modern day culture and liberty. Barnaby Stillwater and Thomas Moore, well versed and educated in Constitutional law, inspired a thought process for change that would eventually impact the nation.

The quest to amend irrelevant and outdated prose from the earliest formation of the Union will always be initiated, first by the people, then by the state and then by the national government. With intelligent discussion, change will manifest itself in a timely and deliberate way. In the end, all peoples of these Unite States still desire liberty and freedom, and civil rights.

As Governor Moore experienced, change can occur from time to time to protect the *majority* of the population. The process is slow sometimes, but with forethought and discussion by intelligent individuals, positive actions usually follow. Only then will systemic change occur for the benefit of the nation *en masse*, in a progressive manner.

As Attorney Moore found out, "Live Free or Die" may not be the greatest of evils, but "Life" isn't either. In "Life," which is dynamic, change is sometimes needed through civil discussion and progress, an amalgamation of independent thoughts.

In the end, the citizenry of the country must be safe from harm and from obsolete laws rendered outdated by two centuries of dynamics and a modern society. Festus Gravel, Bobby Cummings and Ryan Cooper never understood those principles, but General John Stark did.

Acknowledgements

Special thanks are extended to my loving wife, Brenda for reviewing the manuscript and offering suggestions, and for using her "eagle eyes" for errors in text and composition. Her support of my writing, and that of my children, is endless encouragement.

Cover photo credit:

The cover photo used is a reprint/ reproduction of a 1912 photo from the booklet by Daniel P. Connor titled, "Our House of Jack" by Concobar, Manchester NH
LOC # 0-013-984-792-1
The photo is of "English Jack's" hermit cabin. He was a noted recluse in the Crawford Notch area of the White Mountains of New Hampshire.

Author photo credit:

Photo cropping by daughter, Stephanie Lynn Polidoro, age 14
Location: January at Gunstock Ski Area, Gilford NH,

© 2010 J. P. Polidoro, Longtail Publishing, Laconia NH
All Rights Reserved

Books/ Novels* by J. P. Polidoro

Rapid Descent—Disaster in Boston Harbor
Project Samuel—The Quest for the Centennial Nobel Prize
Return to Raby
Sniff—A Novel
Lavatory 101—A Bathroom Book of Knowledge
Tattoo—Incident at the Weirs
The Christmas Chiave—A Boston Novella
The Dog in the Outhouse—The John Stark Marauders
Six Feet From Grace (An "essay" on Grace Metalious, author of Peyton Place)

---

*See Amazon.com and Longtailpublishing.com for details

Made in the USA
Lexington, KY
12 September 2013